What I'd Say To

AGATHA CHRISTIE

If I Met Her

AT THE KNITTING CIRCLE

Frank Talaber

What I'd Say To Agatha Christie, If I Met Her At The Knitting Circle?

Short Story Anthology Book:, Volume 3

Frank Talaber

Published by Frank Talaber, 2025.

Print ISBN: 978-1-998052-03-5

Epub ISBN: 978-1-998052-04-2

Audio ISBN: 978-1-998052-05-9

Copyright 2025 by Frank Talaber

Cover art by: Miblart

WHAT I'D SAY TO AGATHA CHRISTIE, IF I MET HER AT THE KNITTING CIRCLE?

First edition. August 12, 2025.

ISBN: 978-1998052035

Written by Frank Talaber.

Creative Non-Fiction

Novel Teasers

Foreword

I have often been asked how I weave such bizarre ideas and unexpected twists into my writing. To be honest, many of my best plot lines have arisen from what I like doing best, talking to people, and I have found that indeed truth *is* stranger than fiction. After listening to these strange tales my imagination takes over and I weave and embellish the tale I've just heard by asking "what if?". Like the curious tale gleaned from the concierge at Victoria's Empress Hotel. Some guests had checked out only one day into their stay. Apparently, when unpacking after exploring the hotel, the wife found all of her husband's clothes gone and what she described as "ghost clothes" in their place. Upon hearing this, the "what if" took over, and Francis Rattenbury made an entrance into The Mystery of Ms Teak, the "what if" prompting the thought that perhaps the ghost had materialised into our time and needed to change out of his conspicuous garb. Of course, like most writers, many of my storylines have also been based on my own life and experiences. I believe you will find many examples of both that and "what if" within these pages.

For those of you who may be interested, I have written a few short lines on how each of these stories found life.

Night Muses Stalking was written in tribute to my son Rory after he passed away. My way of saying I'll meet him in Valhalla one day and we'll shoot the shit around a campfire.

By Life's Seaside. This came about from attending several self-discovery courses run by a group called Context. If they are still around perhaps check them out. You will unravel your truths and beliefs and begin making realizations on how to improve and change your life. It did wonders for me and many others I knew.

Wes' Echo Harp was written a long time ago during these courses, about meeting a fellow and wondering why he kept such odd trinkets and why they meant so much to him.

Were-Lovers of the Ethereal was a rather off-beat tale about meeting a wolf, only it turns out not to be merely a wolf, but so much more. This garnered second place in The Spooky Tales Contest: New Canadian Magazine.

The Eyes Don't Lie. As a teenager my two buddies and I would hang out in a twenty-four hour truck stop, sipping free coffee, read books, and just hang out until the wee hours of the morning. The waitresses didn't mind as it kept them company and feeling safe, especially with some of the strange men that came in.

Don't Cry Jack, Daddy Will Save You was based on some studies of multiple personalities. For those interested read When Rabbit Howls. It is amazing what the human mind can do and perform when needed to protect itself. Why send several people to Mars if you can send only one who had the minds of several?

The Doctor to the Rescue! My dentist, who I knew very well and who loved my writings, once asked me how come dentists are never featured in any books or television shows. I told him that's because you're all dweebs! He agreed and said give me a story. So that afternoon I thought what if? and wove a story about a strange patient that shows up in his office. The original is called **The Myzsterious Mr. Jones** and is in Volume Two, **What I'd Say To Einstein If I Met Him On The Dance Floor** (a teaser for you, now you'll have to buy that novel as well!). I later wove this into a contest regarding putting myself into a certain popular television series.

Havens of the Heart. I don't normally attempt poetic pieces but wrote this after attending a place called The Haven by the Sea. A course on improving your life and getting what you want out of it inspired me to write this piece and I left a framed print of it hanging on their wall.

Windsong's Calling was pulled from my novel **Raven's Lament** (the first in the Stillwaters Runs Deep series) for a novella contest and contains incredible scenes which many readers have told me is reminiscent of a being's next step of evolution and travelling through the earth via trees.

A Scratch in Time Saves Nine was written for a contest involving furry creatures.

A-Hunting We Will Go was pulled from my science fiction/ spiritual series, **Seeds Of Ascension** for another contest.

Sylvia's Sun-Catchers. Voted number one by the readers in an anthology of over three hundred entries. Most don't guess the ending. It is set in the Sylvia beach hotel in Oregon with each room dedicated to an author and decorated in such a style. There was even a knitting bag in the Agatha Christie room and I'm sure Miss Marple would have been amused by the many visitors who added a row or two. Unfortunately the original, beautiful, bewitching hotel is no more, and I can no longer relax on the plush sofa in the softly lit upstairs lounge drinking mulled wine whilst staring at the tumbling ocean and letting my muse take over. New owners have removed the heart and soul of this wonderful oasis of calm and serenity. The themed rooms are no more; all the same minimalist modern furniture and dull "greige" décor. They have kept the rooms names, but all that is left of each author is a generic sign on the door. Sometimes evolution is not a good thing.

I have also tried my hand at creative non-fiction in a series of articles that were published in RV World Magazine, plus a short story entitled **Trust Me, I Didn't Make This S**t Up** which is the basis for my first upcoming non-fiction novel.

And if I left you hanging and still wondering "What Would I'd say to Agatha Christie If I Met Her At the Knitting Circle" I'd ask her if she really didn't remember what happened when she disappeared...

(The story below as it appeared on Facebook and in other journals)

In 1926, Britain was shaken by a mystery straight out of a detective novel: a car was found abandoned on a country road—with a woman's fur coat left behind. The car belonged to none other than the world's most famous crime writer, Agatha Christie.

And she was missing.

Scotland Yard launched a nationwide search. Suspicions quickly turned to her husband, Archibald Christie, who had recently asked for a divorce and was spending that very night with his lover in the countryside. The public was furious. Newspapers called for his arrest. His mistress vanished. He was publicly shamed and disgraced.

Even Sir Arthur Conan Doyle got involved, allegedly consulting a medium in an attempt to find her.

Then, eleven days later... the case took a wild turn.

Agatha was found staying under a false name—Theresa Neele—at the luxurious Swan Hydropathic Hotel. Which by the way was the name of his lover. She had been relaxing, dancing, enjoying spa treatments, playing piano, and drinking fine wine.

When questioned, she claimed amnesia brought on by grief. But psychologists weren't convinced. Her behavior seemed far too composed for a woman in mental distress.

Many believe it wasn't a breakdown.

It was a masterfully executed act of revenge.

She humiliated her cheating husband, derailed his plans to remarry, and gave his mistress a front-row seat to scandal and disgrace. And instead of poison (which any mystery writer could've used), she served cold, calculated silence.

Later, Agatha would divorce Archibald and marry a charming archaeologist—15 years her junior. When asked about the age gap, she replied:

"It's so lovely to be married to an archaeologist. The older you get, the more he values you."

Agatha Christie didn't just write mysteries.

She lived one.

The post link below for credits.

https://www.facebook.com/WeeSurvived/posts/
pfbid02cptzMmVx3TbRQtAtorwhBWTmLtxto9KGsEr6r6syFvBG7LNW

Night Muses Stalking

Downtown streets of Victoria come alive in the dark where muses stalk the concrete and, in the absence of light, darkness reigns. Only not all darkness is bad, nor is all light good. Drug dealers cruise dressed nonchalantly recognizably in expensive leather shoes looking for those who need a fix, and artists of all genders and afflictions seeking inspiration or other carnal rewards of a shoddy ilk seek the inspiration to set their own brushstrokes to murals in their minds. Or them, the unknown, the muses that avoid sunlight like a plague swelling in the darkness, waiting for another meal.

If muses walk the night, do birds sing at midnight? Rory thought as he breathed deeply, once again inhaling the heady hypnotic fumes purchased from the dealers of the suede shoes sundering him from his realm and joined her, his mused affliction, in hers, and got into his gaming avatar's head, Xephos.

She would lead him again into the blood-crazed domain of a warrior born with the other members of his most famous guild. Where he was hers and he hated that, yet something compelling made her irresistible. Maligning good with bad, hungering on the taste of nectar's sweet blood licked from her own fingers. How he never tired of that craving, to suck from those hands.

Armor clinks into place. Faces tensioned for the battle. Knowing theirs might be one of the ones called to the halls of Valhalla. Each stare at their souls and at each other. Eyes reflect the terror about to come and the knowing that they would give their life for the others.

Xephos stared at his companions. This battle, as many others, challenged soul, mind, heart, stamina and courage. But above all else, courage. None of these were questioned, he and his battle-hardened companions were meld of the same hardened steel stamina. Still, a trickle of fear, of knowing. Instinctively does a warrior know when

Death's scythe, stilled for so long, whistled, calling from its razor's edge.

The hunger of the muse would dominate. Her calling, her needs, paramount. He knew her vengeful price must be met one day.

His eyes glared at the others. She knew his hunger all too well and fed it. Time and again.

"Xephos?" the others questioned their leader.

He gritted his teeth. There was only one way to go down. As a warrior born. Fighting.

He clapped them on the back. "We will win! Victory will be ours!"

A tear streamed down his face. They stared in utter shock. "The cost will be high, as it always is."

He planted his sword in the ground before him. "I will not waver!"

"I will not surrender!" The others thumped their chests in response.

Xephos cried to himself, *to this demon inside.* Sweat poured from his body as he mounted his stallion.

Against insurmountable odds. The guild of the famous strode into the forefront of the assembled horde. Skrillex and Funker lost in their own haze of blood, and lust led the others as they charged into the battleground behind their leader.

Xephos, somewhere ahead, they lost in a haze of battle drums pounding, horses screaming, and men raging in fearlessness before he was gone, swept by a wave of incoming warriors.

The two, blood streaking their bodies, stood at the hilltop looking for him as the vanquished before them ran away in defeat. Life below sang to the call of the scythe as it cut life like wheat before it.

The rest of the guild raged after them, taking down the weak, the chaff.

The two looked around expecting to hear the familiar laughter of Xephos and his kind voice. Only they stared in shock, for before them on the hill his horse nudged a still body. "NO!"

The one they would have named King.

Skrillex leaped from his horse as he thundered down the hill. Funker did the same. "He died alone."

Around him, a dozen he'd slain lay in a dismembered heap in homage to his berserker's stifled rage.

They lifted his body limp, already going cold, eyes closed. Overhead the wind gurgled like a muse beside herself with amusement, with a new one to entertain her for eternity. "We should have been beside you. The Guild always stick together," Skrillex said as he clapped his hand to his chest in homage, as did Funker.

The two knew now the fear he had cringed earlier was his own. They screamed their panic and heartbreak to the unhearing heavens as Ohealno came riding up. She fell out of her horse, tears streaking her armor. Knowing she'd never feel his heat against her, nor hear that soft laugh or witness his sly smile when the two were alone together ever again.

Xephos opens his eyes as a breath wafts its cooling warmth into the darkness.

I turn to answer the call from inside.

A cry rents stillness. It is not possible.

The pad of feet issues no reassurance that I shall leave here alive.

If, in only one piece.

If not all.

Coming here, not wise.

Chill surges upward, mists snake through the trees like a river of calling.

Asking for those that will speak to it.

Denying touch, sound, and taste.

Numbness remains its only way of being.

Leaves tremble, falling.
Moistness, dew drips. I take another step.
The calling begins.
To her, as she has done my whole life.
The curse, the thrill, the temptation that paled everything else into disbelief.
This muse that would always stalk my soul.

Xephos smiles as she caresses him. His knife springs free. Blood splatters them both as he slashes her lovely throat. "I'm yours, but I don't go down without a fight. Never have, never will."

Somewhere in Valhalla angels sing and the devil snorts back a fat rolled one as she splutters her last words. "You, silly boy."

The muse gasped on her final breath, knowing she would be back and wherever he went, she'd find him once again.

By Life's Seaside

Air repugnant with the salty decay wafted in as the waves lapped at the water's edge as the old man picks away at broken bits of seashell. Only his form and shadows of overhead seagulls grace the sands of this beach. Turning over shards, trying to visualize images of what was once alive and whole, like he is.

Alone now, after his recent marriage crashed away and visions of what encompasses his life now remained and the emptiness and loneliness beckon.

The irritating crunch of sand grating enters his memories as the ponderings of what once was and what is now disturbs his reverie.

A vision of radiant fluttering golden tresses enter his vision and a woman enters into focus.

Averting his gaze, he can only peer at the once was.

She approaches, stopping a few feet beside him, staring at each lapping wave as seagulls squawk and the breath of the ocean exhausts itself on the glittering sands.

Two seeking answers as a slight breeze stirs causing noses to wrinkle against the offending seaweed decomposing in the salty humidity.

Seeking an end to silence she clears her throat. "The waves aren't very strong today."

Silent he studies the limp wash of the water's edge knowing she is justifiably correct but remains silent.

Bored as is her life she speaks again wanting to lure a response, mere words, a conversation, something. "It is said when the ocean is calm it is at peace with itself."

Eliciting a response from deep within he speaks freely. "The ocean is full of life, always roiling with energy. It will never know calm nor tranquility always trying to tear against the barriers of solitude seeking answers to its restlessness."

The words spoken play back across his mind sensing this was the right thing to say but ponders where this inner voice came from.

"Is this the best we can do? Sit and watch the ocean wreak havoc on the shores of our serenity?" she replies, allowing her own inner consciousness to speak freely. "Watching it spit out broken remains of my tumultuous life?" Bitterness tinges her heart as the past rubs itself like salt water in her face treating her with the same insecurities of her life: a distant husband, failed marriage, abusive parents.

Studying the water as it washes before them an answer comes from him. "All enter the seas of life, some are crushed, others find happiness in the waves washing all around them. Others merely watch it lap ever closer to their feet, feeling the sand sinking away, knowing time weighs heavier with each passing wave and they either can't swim, nor want to." Sensing her puzzlement on the frowns etching her face he knows the answer he came here to seek is upon him.

Realizations like fog lifting off a mountainside brings the dawn to her after all of these years understanding she was one of the latter. Too afraid to enter her life's waters. "But time only has meaning to some. It means nothing to the ocean."

Only seeing it now, he smirks, it is so obvious he has given himself his own answer, like the chained man rattles his shackles as they fall away, he answers her. "Not so, for even the ocean dwells in a different reality growing desperate knowing that its time is drawing to a close and only tears down that which it seeks for itself and if this shore doesn't be gate that it seeks it will pound itself into the next and the next."

He stares at bits of sand clinging to his fingers, each grain weighing him down like a part of his past hanging on, pulling at him. Rising he brushes himself clean, too much of his past has been devoted to his life. It is over, the realization hits as shackles crumble away sliding from his body tumbling to his feet before him.

He smiles to the ocean admiring a new brilliance sheening off the horizon.

She sees he is not as old as she first thought but says nothing as she is lost in his words playing themselves across her mind.

With only the crash of surf to accompany him and his discarded chains he walks away without a word of thanks, satisfied. Kicking aside the broken shard of shell and the past littering the beach with a focus now only on the horizon and what awaits for him today and tomorrow.

Brisk breeze stirs the air torn from a darkening sky. Wrapping her arms around herself huddling in the sudden coolness, she stares at the broken pieces of shell the man picked at but finds no desire to touch the once was. Instead she glances at the now, hammering in desperation as the breeze stirs the currents. Nearby waves crash louder in desperation on solid rock.

She knows she is afraid to enter what is her life now. The comfort of a shell like those below is what she truly wants as the thunderous crash of surf makes her feel the pain endured by the rock face.

The energy stirred in the liveliness of each wave, hammering over and over. Surrendering itself to the granite wall, wholly and entirely, unafraid to try again and dash itself over and over like her. Still it returns as strong as ever, that tingly sensation of life, of being on the edge and living it unafraid. Can she enter her own life?

Approaching footsteps crunching disturbs her. Turning she spies a younger man striding towards her. He appears to be in his early twenties, walking with a casual strength, strong and defiant against the wind. Windswept hair reveals the rugged tanned features of his chiselled face. Eyes of deep blue that revel in the intensity of life he strides closer, confident yet very aware of her there, like a cougar on the prowl. Keeping a respectful distance he strides past her catching the crash of ocean against rock near them watching the ocean preparing to cast new merciless waves to smash in vain.

"It looks rather ominous out there, do you think there's a storm brewing?" His heavy voice cracks the silence. "I'd say by tomorrow we're in for bad weather."

She stares out across the water to gaze as far as she can. Feeling not so radiant and somewhat intimidated by the man's questions she bows her head.

"Tomorrow," she ponders the thought when her own future is uncertain. "Why worry about tomorrow?"

He steps closer to the waters edge is if daring it to wash him away. Each time the height of the wave begins to recede only inches from his feet.

"Tomorrow," he begins, "tomorrow is the future and the future is what holds all of our dreams and hopes." He turns to look up at her.

She sees his face so full of youthful exuberance, unmarred by the passage of time. "We attract from within that which we truly believe to be the truth and in so doing change our future in subtle and distinct ways."

She is puzzled.

He adds, "by holding our thoughts in our minds, we picture that which is the truth to ourselves. So, by our beliefs transpired in the past, we alter our present to form the future paths of our reality."

"So, we have only one future?" She reacts, stunned by what he just said sensing that it held a great deal of truth.

"Yes, for you have already formed your futures based on actions and opinions set in the past."

A limp breeze stirs the damp salty air. She huddles in the sudden chill while he stretches enjoying the goose dimpling effect of wind on exposed flesh.

She stammers out, as reality and her past smacks her across the face, "So I really have no future options."

"Not unless you decide to consciously change your beliefs, your perceptions of yourself and of the way you view life." He sighs.

Shivering she rose from the cooling sand. The facts no matter how she tried to juggle them, kept smacking her in the face. He was right. Unable to listen anymore she brushed away sand clinging to her and with a quiet thanks, walks away as the brutal reality sank in. The stirring and germination of new thoughts and attitudes blooms, knowing that her future for once remained open to all possibilities.

He studies the indentations made on the sand by her feet and knowing as with all things done, that come morning all trace of him and her will be gone to the memories of the past set only in their minds.

The sun has already begun its descent and as he stands lost in the nature of being surrounded by just himself in the wild as no one comes to answer his questions. Silently he slips away into the cool of the early night beginning. No one comes for this one.

Air, stillborn in the breath of the night, begins to stir as the first rays of sun penetrate the quiet orchestrating a symphony of colors as it begins its journey across the sky. Colors melding as the sun gains strength touching all with its warmth.

The beach is empty, still its serenity glistens with life even though there are none to ask questions, seek fulfillment or ponder life. A quiet exists, born of the gentlest peace. Only the sunlight has a voice as it dances over thin clouds across the mirrored surface of calm waters.

A small figure parts the yellow grasses and weeds lining the edge of the sands beach.

Warily a coyote tramps across the sands, its paws sinking into the dryness until it approaches the waters edge and sniffs the salty aroma, resisting the temptation to lick and merely sits down. He rests, letting his front paws rest in the waters cool enjoying the caress of the beach against his legs. His canine face allows him to grimace as much as possible in the simple pleasure of sheer relaxation.

For it is obviously not only humanity that visits this shore. Other creatures are attracted to the harmony and beauty of this beach. The sometimes mischievous, sometimes cruel animal spirit within merely relaxes enjoying the delight of the planets offering this morning.

Another approaches, the young man from the day before comes still seeking his answers after finding no solace in his sleep he has risen earlier than he usually does hoping to find what he needed to find. His breath rises from his mouth, like a spent ghostly spirit in the lifting coolness. It hangs for a moment around him then vanishes into a new life cast back into the planet that gave it life.

Spotting the glittering pawprints of the coyote, glistening like precious jewels, enticed he follows and passing some rocks he spies the coyote sitting on its haunches.

Wondering if the animal is injured, he walks closer.

The coyote, unmoved, studies the approach of the human, knowing this person is a member of a race that has killed, trapped, skinned many of his brethren. Whispered from the elderly that raised him: beware. A snarl breaks his lips.

The man stops and squats onto the backs of his legs. He smiles somehow knowing the animal is okay and not wanting to alarm or confront it. They know too much has gone on between their races to allow for closer intimacy.

The man marvels at the coyote's peace, at the vivid blueness of the sky, pureness of the white sands and at his own calmness. His smile begins to droop as a tear, born from the raindrops of his soul, slowly, like a raindrop dribbling down a leaf etches his face.

He has experienced sadness, known joy. Now he enjoys serenity and all of its final questions.

The coyote drops his grimace and relaxes. Being a baser creature yet it understands the human has not come to bring it any harm. It has merely come, like itself.

After a while the coyote stretches its front paws and languidly rises, water drips from its fur while sand falls with every step it takes. Calmly the animal walks to the edge of the yellow weeds, ready to return to its own realm.

As it is about to enter the grasses he stops and turns his head to study the human one last time.

The man looks up and back sensing the stare. Eyes lock and each in its own way smiles, sensing the solitude and peace of the other. It is enough. Like brothers, each turn and breaks the bonds held in their reflections returning to their own worlds.

Each will reach its own fate and taste its own life. Each will eventually die. Yet always that look will remain etched, like aboriginal drawings on sacred rock in their memories to dance in firelight cast into times embrace.

Wes' Echo Harp

The tall, gaunt figure was conversing with the police officer as I steered the tow truck in behind them. Decked in a worn-out army jacket and dirty jeans, his unkempt hair and scruffy beard told me all I needed to know.

Being on call for the RCMP in this area meant I sometimes came across some grizzly scenes, but fortunately not this time. The dilapidated Volvo 240 had seen better days, with screws adorning the back fender to keep it in place from the cancerous rust claiming it. The rear license plate was gone, rotted off by the looks, and was obviously the reason he got pulled over. What a fool! Probably penniless, you'd think he'd at least stolen another plate, or perhaps he didn't even know it was long gone back down the road.

I waited for details from Tom Johnson as I began to pull my chains from the tow truck.

Of course, there was the possibility that he was a down and out honest person and either he hadn't noticed or wouldn't consider stealing a plate from another person. He glanced my way, looking concerned, and in that brief stare from his drawn eyes, I knew he was an honest man.

Funny, I come across a lot of souls while driving my tow truck; some victims, some unfortunate and unlucky souls, others scrupulous, and some unscrupulous. He, I could tell, wasn't any of those.

As I walked up, he stuffed the ticket, meaningless to him, into one of a dozen pockets where it would stay, either to do things like start a fire, make a scratch pad, or pick his teeth, but never to be paid. He stepped to the trunk of his car, opened it by unhooking a bungie cord, and pulled out a well-worn knapsack.

Tom approached me as I watched the guy. "Hi Charlie. How's things today?"

He always said that I replied with my standard response. "Oh, could be better."

"He said he had an in-transit permit for the vehicle, but the only one I could find expired two years ago. Probably one of those living-off-the-land types, most likely never worked an honest day in his life."

I think based on all he's had to deal with being a police officer, Tom was more than a little cynical with those he pulled over.

As I watched the man pull articles from his trunk, I sensed that wasn't the truth. "Yeah, the real hippie type, that's for sure," I reassured Tom.

"Take the car to your impound yard and I'm sure it'll be yours after a month. Can't see him coming back to pick it up," Tom chuckled.

"Yeah, for what its worth." I chuckled.

I watched him rearrange things in the trunk of his car with a sad look on his face like he was letting go of an old friend and I smiled apologetically at him as I attached the magnetic lights to the top of his car. I watched surreptitiously as, after removing clothes from the pack, he replaced them with what I saw to be bits of junk: old books, a toy car, a drawing covered crumpled cigarette pack, a broken ceramic figurine, and, curiously, a single brown sock.

"Hey! Got a cigarette?" he asked, looking my way.

"Sorry, don't smoke."

Returning to his packing, the final item to be secreted away was a bent and beaten harmonica. Before sending it to join the others, he rubbed his fingers across the metal surface lovingly.

A long-forgotten memory resurfaced in my mind's eye; my grandfather and his harmonica. The curlicued script on the age-old box proclaimed it to be a Hohner Echo Harp, and he'd give it the same loving look every time he pulled it out to play with it.

"Can you play?"

"Nah," he said. "I got it from an old friend. I always wanted to learn but just haven't got around to it." He re-packed the harmonica, lay it gently on top of his other memories, drew the drawstring tight, and secured the flap. "Are you heading north?" he asked.

"Yeah, for about thirty k's before turning off."

"Mind if I join you?" he asked, and without waiting for a reply, hauled himself into the passenger seat.

"Definitely an odd one," Tom observed as he walked over.

"Yup, that's a character all right." I prepared to tie the trunk back down with the bungie cord. A quick glance revealed he'd left a few trinkets behind, almost as if he no longer needed the stuff. Intrigued I knew I had to ask what all that was about.

"Going bowling tomorrow night?" Tom asked.

"Most likely."

"Great. See you there." He waved and walked back to his cruiser.

I rechecked the tow cables and climbed into the tow truck. "Well, we're ready to go." I buckled up and he just sat there lost in thought. "I suppose I should introduce myself, I'm Charlie McFadden."

For a few moments he didn't answer, just stared into the darkening sky.

"Wes." Then silence. After a few moments he asked without looking my way. "Been towing long?"

"Just the last four years." I replied. "You been living like this for a while?" I asked, without thinking. Usually, I'm not very blunt with people, nor do I care about their business, and felt somewhat foolish for asking. But he intrigued me.

After a lengthy silence he finally said, "Only the last twenty years."

My turnoff was coming up quicker than I wanted it to be. "Isn't twenty years a long time?"

He turned to look right at me. I felt his eyes sinking into my soul. "Not if you like what you're doing."

"As opposed to not liking what you are doing?" I blurted out just a little too quickly.

"Kinda. Four years can feel like twenty if you're not happy."

"I didn't say I hated what I'm doing, did I?" I replied too quickly, too emotionally.

"I can't answer that for you." He pulled out the ticket and began to pick at his teeth. "But it shows."

I signaled and began gearing the old girl down for the approaching exit. His car tugged at the chains and the smell of diesel fumes filtered into the cab. How the hell did he know?

More than intrigued by this fellow, I asked. "You interested in staying the night?"

"I suppose." Although I noticed he made no move to leave the truck as we were nearly stopped. As if he knew I'd ask.

The rest of the way to my compound he was silent, while I had a dozen questions to ask. But didn't; respecting his silence.

"The meal was very good, ma'am." Wes said as he rose from the dinner table. We'd only talked sparsely during the meal. Marg smiled as she began to gather the dishes. She took compliments very modestly. Wes sauntered over to the antique cabinet and I followed, coffee cup in hand.

"This looks fascinating," he said, indicating a cigar case. "Must have quite the story behind it." I picked up the case and opened it, revealing quite some of the cigars left unsmoked. I thought it perhaps odd that he'd honed in on the one item I treasured most above all of the others.

"Yes. How did you know?" I replied. "It was given to by my good friend, Ashok, at my stag. I'd known him for years; he was a real off-beat type. He was East Indian, and one of those characters you never knew what he was going to do next. Said he'd had the cigars blessed by a Hindu Rabbi, or some such thing, to bring me good luck. They were only to be smoked when I was uncertain of the future. He said I had to be really clear on what I wanted to have happen or to concentrate on what I wanted as I smoked it, and whatever was on my mind would come true. I didn't believe him at the time, but he assured me that he was very serious."

I paused for a second, recalling the bitter taste of the cigars. "The first one I had the day before our wedding, and we've had fantastic thirty years together. I had one cigar before signing a business deal for my first company and sold that for a tremendous profit. I had another before my son was born and the last one I had before Marg went into the hospital for a serious brain operation a couple of years ago. They'd only given her less than a twenty percent chance of living."

I closed the box lid lightly rubbing my hand over the embossed surface, like he'd done with the harmonica. "I've only got six left and I'll treasure each one."

I replaced the case in the cabinet and we settled in front of the TV. We began to watch a football game together.

Still puzzled about the Echo Harp I asked, "So, tell me why you keep a harmonica that you don't play."

His eyes began to well up, the first sign of any emotion I'd seen from him. "About ten years ago I was hiking the West Coast Trail on Vancouver Island and the first night I set up camp along a beautiful part of the beach. There were others there, along with a little French guy, Marso, who barely spoke a word of English. Instead, he entertained us by playing his harmonica. I can still see his bubbly personality coming to life as he danced gigs and played."

I watched Wes' eyes dance with the fires of life as he recalled that story, picturing him laughing as he watched Marso.

"Two days later we came to a bunch of people milling about a cliff's edge. Marso had slipped and fallen to his death. He had mounted the wall to play his harmonica and apparently just lost his footing. It wasn't even a long drop, only a foot or so, but he must've hit his head. I noticed something gleaming in the rocks and found it. His harmonica." He pulled the harmonica from the knapsack he'd kept with him. He attempted a few blows but all that emitted was a flat, buzzy noise.

"I guess he could have used one of those cigars," I mildly joked.

"Yeah, I guess he sure could have."

He paused and began to speak in a quiet tender voice. "Good memories are very precious to me. So, when I get something to hang on to, I do, and this way I can look at it to cheer me up." He patted the knapsack almost tenderly.

"But even good memories you can't hang on to forever."

"I know; and don't. Eventually I get over it and leave it behind."

"Leave it behind? I don't understand. Are good memories that hard for you to get?" I was puzzled now.

Turning away from me so I couldn't see the tears again welling in his eyes, Wes told me about his past; the beatings by his dad, the school bullies, and the verbal abuse from his mother, a constant in his life. His only true friend was his dog, and he'd found that dead, apparently poisoned by the neighbor. His childhood was hell so no wonder he hung on to good memories like a baby clinging to a bottle. We talked into the wee hours of the morning.

In the morning, I knocked on the door of the guest room to invite Wes down for breakfast. After a while of silence, I knocked again and opened the door a few inches. "Wes? Coming down for breakfast? Marg makes quite the good feast!". But no one answered. Opening the door fully, I found the room empty. The bed was neatly made, and no sign remained of the odd character of the day before. Marg had asked me once why I managed to attract the oddest ones into my life. I remember joking back to her, "Managed to attract you, didn't I?" That was about our only big fight.

Downstairs, after the usual great feast to set me on my day's work, a beam of sunlight flashed at me from the antiques cabinet. Curious I investigate; the sparkle of light glinted from inside the now-open cigar case. Only five cigars remained; nestled in the empty place where the sixth had been was an old, battered, Echo Harp.

Marg was still bustling about the kitchen. After donning my work clothes, I poked my head around the kitchen door for the usual "see you later hon" and her answering smile lit up the morning as usual.

I strolled out into the yard to where the compound was. I didn't have to look to know that where I'd parked the Volvo was empty. Funny, I must have left the keys in it last night. A glimpse of that quirky stranger popped into my mind's eye; Wes's sauntering into the sunrise, smoking my cigar.

What was the old expression? "And the band played on..."

Were-Lovers of the Ethereal

I staggered from the house party into the backyard more drunk or stoned than I cared to admit needing fresh air.

A growl broke the rhythmic pounding of the music. I stared into the red eyes of the massive dog, chained in place. He growled again, even more menacing. I'd had enough dealings with animals, being a vet, to know this was a male, a proud male.

Shuddering more from the welcome cool of the night air than fright I stepped closer wanting to see this three-quarter wolf dog that my friend Jim had owned for the last three years. Lips pulled back in a sneer revealing bone white fangs that knew the taste of red meat and blood, probably wanting mine.

It lunged to attack the heavy chains holding it in place. I held my hands up displaying peace as I took a few steps closer and squatted on the cool wet grass just out of his reach. "Hi fella, you look mighty upset. I'd be too if I was tied up all the time."

It stood there growling.

I'd been close to animals my whole life, preferring them to the company of humans, which is why I loved being a vet. I guess the physical and mental abuse suffered in my childhood had a lot to do with it. Humans? Why would I say that word?

"I bring you no harm, hairy one." I study its rather unusual long pointed ears I see its tail begin to wag as the growls lessen in severity. A sign that even if it was abused it has begun to trust me. Remarkable, I know dogs are very psychic and it obviously senses I mean no harm.

"Hey Lisa. Come on back inside, the joint's just rocking," hollers my current boyfriend, Dave. For a male he's okay, very caring and sensitive to my needs, especially in bed. For now he'll do but I'll keep looking for a Mr. Right. My life is complete with my studies and my vet work, for now, but there is someone out there, I know.

Memories of last night, doing dishes after dinner, come to mind. He walked up to me from behind and began to run his hands along my body, his breath hot on my neck like a rabid animal. I felt his urgency and we made love right there in the kitchen, my hands still wet from the soap water. *Ah, delicious.*

"I'll be right in, just give me a minute to cool down."

The door clanged shut as the dog growled. His long ears peredk up as I return to just the two of us. "I've read that wolves are mythical creatures. Many Celtic people and First Nations believe they carry wolf spirits with them. Intriguing you are the first one I've met."

It growls again.

"Ah, cut it out. I mean you no harm and you?"

I pause as I edge a little closer on the grass. It glares at me, trying to intimidate me. Teeth glinting in the moonlight, so close and menacing, like Dave last night.

I've been told the eyes are the doorways of the soul. "I've read that wolves have a special sense. They can comprehend things, people around them, at least on their level. Some native legends speak of the wolf as a haunted creature. It howls to the moon looking for its soulmate. Others speak of it as all-knowing and wise." *Maybe I needed to howl to the moon to find mine.*

I look up and catch, in the briefest of moments, something cross its eyes. A blink and it's gone. *What had I seen?*

It just sat there, not letting on, like it knew what I was saying. "You are neither of those, aren't you."

"Lisa, we're going to get some pizza. Are you coming?" Dave yelled from an open window.

"Yeah, hang on, I'm coming."

I returned to the crazy ruckus inside without looking back and as we climbed into the car I heard a desolate howl break the air. Above the moon hung, waiting.

I hadn't heard any wolf howls for real before, but this one sounded different somehow, with an eerie reverberation to it, like someone was speaking through another voice. I shook my head. Maybe that just was the effects of the marijuana I smoked earlier.

During my quiet time at work on Monday I researched what I had on wolves, which wasn't much and ran a google search.

I was puzzled, and the ears bugged me. In all the pictures I fanned through none had ears like his.

Somehow, I came across some pictures of what were supposed to be werewolves and there, staring at me from a comic book, of all things, Werewolf by Night. I saw his face imaged back at me. The face reminding me of what I'd seen briefly in his eyes.

I hit print and took that image home.

That night I returned to Jim's on the pretense I think I lost an earring out in the backyard. He was busy and let me look. I stared at him sitting on his haunches as he returned to growling, a natural state of being for him. This I already knew.

"You're not a werewolf, that I know. Jim has you chained up for years at night to keep his backyard safe from all the crazies around the neighborhood."

It glared at me intensely.

"Only is there a crazy inside?"

It continued to glare at me.

Somehow, I knew this was a ruse. "So, what are you?"

Jim came sauntering into the backyard. "Wow, this is incredible. You're the only one that has that effect on him. Other than me bringing him food, he is never silent. I rarely take him for walks anymore as he freaks out on everyone around him. I used to take him for many long walks in the woods, at least there he seems at some semblance of peace. I think he likes you."

"I think so too." I just had to know why.

"I've got to get something from the shed. I'll leave you two to bond some more. Wow, crazy." He shook his head as he walked away.

It glared at me, not with the murderous red intelligent eyes of the were beast from the comic book. There was something else there. I've stared into the eyes of enough animals to know the difference of being alive and intelligence. This being held something different in its gateway to the soul. Something it kept locked inside. That much I knew.

It growled louder.

I wanted to run my hand over its long dark hair, to pet him.

Its growl lowered an imperceptible amount like it knew what I thought.

I saw Jim returning, got up and pulled an earring from my pocket. "Thanks, Jim I found the earring."

"No problem, come by anytime."

I left knowing something important. It could read my thoughts. But whatever was inside would not reveal itself to me. Was it so scared of humans? It liked Jim although he was a hard master. But he had found it weak and appeared to be beaten at the side of the road and brought it home.

Or did it hide some terrible secret inside?

That night the comforter was soothing. It was late. I stared at the cover of that comic book, like I was staring at him. But the eyes in the comic book were full of rage and hunger. I shivered and rolled over shutting off the light.

The thud of four paws, a continuous rhythm on damp earth. Invigorating. My tongue lolls out to one side. Saliva flings free, mixing with the evening dew. Fingers of wind comb through my fur, stroking the muscles underneath.

On I run, only the constant thump of my heart and the thud of my paws interrupt the still of the night. I glanced to the moon. It shines back with the eerie hard white of splintered bone. A macabre voice screeches out in the darkness.

It is my lover, him. A warmth surges through my loins, I gallop on. On to that hideous growl.

On a high boulder he stands, serenading the moon.

I stop watching that proud figure. Neck back, tips of its pointed ears highlighted in the dim light. Mist rises like the hunger from within his throat as it howls voraciously again, for me.

I return the growl, responding to my own hunger within.

He turns, the redness of his needs glaring at me, hunting me down.

I awake with a start and stare at the cover of that comic again. As I go to flip the cover over, the beast turns and leers at me with hideous misshapen teeth.

I scream and it is on me in a flash. His fangs sink around my throat, his claws tear at my bedsheets. My cry, only a gurgle escapes as his member enters me. Claiming me.

In the morning, I struggle to rise. Every bone cries out, stop. Leaning over the sink I spit out whatever remains in my heaving guts. My eyes are hollow and sunk into their sockets. On my neck are little white scars, jagged pinholes in a row. Blood stains me between my legs. I feel so weak, whatever this creature is, it has drunk and feasted on my soul.

The next night again.

I walked into Jim's yard carrying a twenty-two and chain cutters knowing he has gone for the evening. My clothes are baggy, I've lost nearly ten pounds. I will not endure this hell for another night and possibly couldn't survive either.

Overhead, fittingly, is a full moon leering down like a bleached skull.

I squat down, keeping the gun within easy reach. As we begin our tableau the wind picks up trashing about tree branches, there is more than one storm raging tonight.

It sits there with that low growl in its throat and I can imagine a near smile.

"Have it your way or begin to explain what you are. I know this much, I know you are no wolf. And if you refuse to speak and wish to continue this charade that's fine." I reached for the gun and put it on my knees. "I will not allow you to feast on my soul, another night. So talk or reveal yourself, or die, you son-of-a-bitch."

I had sworn a long time ago that no man would ever violate my body, not without my consent. No human man nor damn creature either.

Those eye slits that shone with a murderous rage opened looking subtly different like the heavens of space suddenly exploded, visualizing millions of worlds and of horrors I couldn't even begin to comprehend.

A light rain began to fall. Vapors rose from the wolf's body beginning to sizzle like in outrage at striking something not Gaia born.

A mist rose and began to swirl, condensing. Soon I was staring at a mass of solid throbbing ethereal cloud of gas that began to beat with a life of its own.

The wolf covering fell aside, still breathing but drained of its soul and I stared at the essence of this alien being as it solidified. Powerful, manly, humanish, shimmering for a second on two thick solid muscular legs.

In a blink it surrounded me, swept me into arms of steel. I tried to struggle, too late.

Perhaps last night I could have fought it off, but not tonight. It had grown in strength and I had weakened.

Only this time it slammed me to the earth. I gasped for breath, and it opened its eyes to mine nearly touching and everything fell away to blackness.

I was on a spaceship. The heat intense, my legs buckling as I was being tossed around, buffeted by entering the atmosphere, we were crash landing, why didn't matter. All of us aboard were about to die either from the crash or the ship about to erupt in total flames becoming a meteor. I gagged, air thick with acrid burning plastics and other fibers. I opened my mouth to scream only to inhale intense scalding heat leaching my breath and moisture from my throat.

I stumbled over one of the bodies of the others around dead. Some kind of gelatinous substance spewing from its mouth.

Another jolt sends me flying back against a panel of video images scanning the earth. I struggle to maintain control. My flesh begins to boil in the heat.

Through the view screens I see the earth racing up to hit us in greeting like bugs slamming into a windshield. It hits buttons searching, scant milliseconds are all that remain.

One screen focuses on a female wolf in her den, looking pregnant giving birth.

The mother howls in pain as he hits a button, vanishing as the craft explodes into a fireball.

She looks up at the fires streaking across the sky. Soon six puppies lay beside her and one stares as well. Its ears longer and pointier than the others.

I gasp able to breathe again. The mist is gone. The alien is gone and Jim's wolf-being sits there content with that low growl in its throat.

Had I dreamed this?

It sat there with those eyes that bespoke of the stars it once belonged to and wanted to reach for again, imploring me. I stood up and walked up to that beast. Whatever it was it couldn't speak to me, not in any language I'd ever understand. With one hand I reached out and stroked its long silky mane. It and I knew what must be done.

With the other hand I pulled back the trigger and fired over and over.

The chain fell to the ground with nothing to hold it up right. As he rose to the stars he gazed at me with a thank you grin and was gone, his voice howling to the night.

"Go find your others." I smiled, a tear trembling on my cheek.

On nights of the full moon, I often find myself sitting outside on a hill staring upward. In the distance I hear a far-off cry from the heavens, of him. I still feel the thud of my paws, the wind in my fur and the wetness between my legs.

War Zone Within; The Eyes Don't Lie

Just outside of the city's boundaries the busy highway traffic zipped relentlessly by the twenty-four-hour Esso truck stop. Our favourite haunt. The three of us whiled away the overnight hours sipping cold coffee and picking at French fries drenched in gravy, reading novels or discussing last night's hockey game. We didn't spend much; didn't have much to spend! But the waitresses liked to have us there. A lot of truckers, lonely men, I'd come to realize, and bikers as well, came in on the late hours of the night and somehow we helped them feel safe. What we could have done if any had got out-of-hand I've no idea but perhaps our very presence put them off trying their luck.

The bell jingled above the door, alerting us to the fact that someone had entered. We never openly looked round, just kinda snuck glances out of the corner of our eyes, just in case the newcomer was paranoid or something or just easily offended. Some people like to be easily offended; gave them an excuse to start something.

This guy was muscular, a few days of growth adorning his chin, smokes poking from his jean jacket pocket waiting to be lit. Inadvertently I caught his gaze and the look of death and war zones emanated my way. I looked away quickly; after all, I've read that the eyes don't lie.

The bear-like man glanced around the small fifties-style diner, sizing it up in a moment like a man on a reconnaissance patrol, ready to bolt, take cover, or get rid of what was before him at whatever expense.

I looked away as I caught his eye again. At sixteen I didn't know nor understand what the depths of war did to a man's soul.

He squatted on one of the stools around the diner, back to the wall, not prepared to relax in one of the four booths like we did, with the twenty-five cent juke box machine begging for someone to feed its throat.

Wayne and Dean continued eating their cooling fries. Wayne, a fan of westerns, reading Louis L'Amour. Dean, a saucy thriller novel. I put my sword and sorcery novel down onto the cool laminate surface, knowing the battle within this man was beyond anything I'd ever read and, hopefully, would never have to experience.

He glared at the waitress who had approached him and, in a deep voice, asked what pies they had. I knew the answer, the same as it had always been in the two years we'd been coming.

"Apple, laison, chelly, bluebelly," sang from her whimsical oriental-accented voice.

"I'll have apple pie and coffee to go," he spat, looking up my way, knowing I was watching. War zones erupted, jungles he prowled in once: Vietnam, Korea stalked in his heart, where one click, one crack of a branch in the stillness, meant life or death. I had never known such a feeling. The only tension I'd experienced was kissing my girlfriend Shelley and hoping to get past first base. His eyes rang of men dying and guts exploding in machine gun fire as friends vanished never to be talked to again. With death in a masquerade of justice, pirouetting in sadistic poetic grace, sauntering elegantly between branches of jungle forest looking for the next to claim.

I knew he'd broken necks, slashed throats, and seen more horrors than in any gory sword and sorcery novel. Like an overcoat in warming comfort Death clung to his backside, clutching at his senses, on a moments vigilance waiting to strike.

Growls of Harleys pulling into the parking lot echoed out in the dark. Three bikers strolled in under the jingle of the bell, bearing patches on their backs of some gang they belonged to like emblems of a battalion. It was obvious they'd been drinking and were spoiling for a fight or some kind of trouble. The bar at the other end of the block haad just closed for the night and often had many fights erupting from it. This wasn't a clean part of town.

One staggered and bumped the man as they walked by, not apologizing. He said nothing, nor moved, not needing to instill bloodshed tonight.

"Hey, buster! We usually sit there in these stools," another barked. The waitress's hand shook as she placed the coffee and pie before him. He caught the fear in her eyes, ignoring the bothersome bikers, like flies on a hot summer day. If they'd simply walked to another stool all would have been chill.

"He told you to move the fuck over! Do it, or I..." the third blurted out fuelled by his superiority through male beer-induced bravado. He was much bigger, with a larger gut than the others, but it wasn't to do him much good; he never did get to finish his sentence. The man spun around on the well-greased rotating stool and one hand blazed backwards nailing the rude biker between the legs. He rose, grabbed the second biker by the face and hammered it into the marble top. The third he booted in the ribs and I fancied I heard bones crack.

He glared outside in case more were coming in as the three bikers crumbled in pain. One puked up the beers he'd downed earlier.

"I'll just have the coffee to go."

I shook, hoping he wasn't coming our way as he stared back at us.

I knew he could have killed the three just as fast if he wanted to. He grabbed the paper cup full of scalding, steaming coffee, and rose, holding it in a steady hand that had no mercy or feelings left in it. I knew silence was a virtue with him with a memory of instilled training and horrors I'd never know nor hopefully ever have to experience.

The waitress came with sugar and milk, staring at the three moaning, crumpled bikers.

"I like it black, straight up. Good coffee," he said, taking a sip of the still-scalding liquid, "but I'll pass on the pie."

He stared my way, threw a dollar coin on the counter worth four times the current price of the coffee, stepped over the one retching up, and disappeared into the night like he'd done in the jungle. Uncompromising, invisible.

In that glance, the lifetimes he'd endured came to me naturally, like leaves falling from trees, carved into the soul of this man, never leaving him, bearing it forever.

What I'd only read about, he actually lived. After all, the eyes don't lie.

Don't Cry Jack, Daddy Will Save You

Andrew stared at the video terminal. It had been six months since this voyage to Mars had begun and he was more than a little bored. "Okay guys, what say we check out the hometown gossip. Ran out of any other headlines to view."

Only the voices in his head replied; there was no one else on the ship. His mind was home to multiple personalities, each with their own abilities, and each had learned different skills. So he was a one-man Mars expedition. True, he only had the physical power of one, but the benefits of such a small craft outweighed that fact.

Peacefully he sifted through the articles until he came across one that stopped him, grabbing his full attention.

"Henry J. Johanston was found dead in his home this morning. Police believe this to be an apparent suicide. Henry is the father of famous Andrew B. Johanston, the fourth person to attempt to land on Mars.

Henry was alone. Long time residents will remember the scandalous charges brought against him in 1989; charges of sexual abuse on his children and ex-wife Silvia. He was found innocent. Henry and Silvia quickly divorced after the trial. Silvia was later charged and found guilty of abuse on her children. A year later she was killed after getting into difficulty while swimming with some friends and drowned, which was rule accidental.

Andrew had not been living at home when all of this had come out. Reports, however, neither confirmed nor denied that Andrew was suffering from a mild case of MPD (Multiple Personality Disorder). Whether this assisted with his training is not known."

"The bastard beat me to it!" Andrew spat with a voice not truly his. He flipped through the other news stories trying to concentrate but couldn't. Slowly the anger subsided and Andrew returned to his normally relaxed state.

That night as he closed his eyes, ready to do what no order human being had ever done, he tossed in his sleep. He was to be the first human ever to step onto the surface of Mars.

The walls of his mind's council room shook with rage.

"I say!" spoke Frederick, the third personality, "I say we dump the bloke and damn them all to hell."

"I don't know, we shouldn't be so harsh," Jessie replied. His long locks of golden hair were beautifully styled and his dress flowed around his feet as he walked, so petite, to the witness stand. It was a rather odd situation. The personalities, although residing in the one body, all had their own appearance, as if they could project it onto themselves somehow. When the dominant personality, they even saw it in the mirror.

Jack-in-the-box stood up from his seat in the jury box. "He's coming to get me; I just know it!"

Andrew saw his bedroom. A flash of fire filled his insides as the weight of his stepfather slowly lifted from above. He screamed in pain. The obscene pink thing hung, satiated for now, as something sticky spilled from him covering his sheets. A grunt of satisfaction was all that was said as he left the room. Andrew cried in agony, laying curled in a fetal position.

Footsteps, softer ones, entered his room. His mother.

"I told you a million times, Andrew! If you mess the sheets you have to clean them yourself. Now take those down to the laundry and put some clothes on first." As he rose, she smacked him across the head. "Can't you ever be good?"

Caliph felt the strength of his horse's loins as he crashed into the council room. Drawing out his sword, he stared down at the judge. Weakly he stared up. "You have sworn to protect us. This is protection." Caliph waved his sword at Jack-in-the-box as he stood there sobbing. The others that felt pain joined in a chorus of lament.

"I have sworn never to harm others. I seek only adventure and excitement. But I have brought one who has no such qualms."

Big Ed shouldered his way into the council chambers.

The judge looked up. "He is not fit for this room nor desired to sit on this jury. He is dangerous." The judge bellowed as loudly as he could, his voice, though, no longer carried the booming authority it once had.

The drugs had weakened him too much.

The rest were stunned. Except for Caliph and Nathan, the rest had never seen anything such as this before.

"You aren't allowed to speak; you are not on this council." The judge sighed wearily.

"Go to hell! I've been kept quiet for too long. I got rid of them, or should I say we should have offed the other one."

The judge started to protest but Big Ed drowned him out as he continued. "I am tired of your weak leadership. You can't control this council, so how do you even think you can protect the young ones."

A chorus of agreement shouted back. The judge knew he was right. His job was to protect the children. He had not done so and knew he hadn't the strength to do so now.

"I say we give power to someone else," Black Ed added as the cries gathered in intensity. "I say we banish you to the back chambers and elect a new judge."

Not having even the strength to bang his gavel the judge rose and slunk from his chair. His robe flowed like tears behind him as he disappeared into the darkness.

Much argument and discussion followed. Without the judge's influence chaos ruled.

As morning neared and ground control tried to waken Andrew, they were stunned to see him sobbing in his bed.

It was Joey crying. He only wanted to die. The hurt would never go away. The pain was always there. Someday he would make it go away, forever.

Denise Sutton rolled and grabbed her phone. The incessant buzzing that had disturbed her sleep at the ungodly hour of three am finally ceased as she answered the call. "Hello?"

"Hi, Doc. We've got a problem." George Walters, the head of NASA Ground Control, barked into her half-asleep ear.

The sound of any man's voice calling at this time of the morning would usually have been met with a few expletives, since her husband had left her for a younger blonde three weeks before. Denise bolted upright in the queen-sized bed. How someone as obnoxious, crude and vulgar as George could have ever made it to the head of NASA was beyond her.

He continued. "Tom hasn't responded to any calls in the last three hours." George spat out, panic tinging his normally in-control voice. She knew he had twenty-four hours in which to land the first man on Mars, after three previously failed attempts and twenty astronauts dead.

"Is he alive?"

"Yes, vital signs are active, but showing some amazing fluctuations."

"Damn! Okay I'll go to my screen. Send me all of the videos and his vitals since last contact."

She grabbed her robe, tossed an instant coffee pod into her machine and sat down before the monitor. As she waited for the coffee to brew and video records to be received, she went through the vital signs that George already had forwarded. Tremendous heart, pulse and blood pressure changes. A beep interrupted her thoughts; she punched in a new security code and fast forwarded through the sent videos. She stopped when she got to the point of seeing Andrew reading the news. She called George on her Bluetooth as she sipped probably the first of many coffees.

"It's from his hometown paper."

"Didn't I say I wanted to see everything before Tom got a chance to read it?"

"Yeah, but it's only his town's paper. What can possibly be in there? Bake sales, the Jones cow got loose, or the next Legion bingo meeting, that's what!"

Denise searched and found a copy of the last newsletter posted on the front page of the paper. "You ass George! His father's death is in that article."

"Yeah, so what?"

Denise ground her teeth in anger. *Bloody stupid chauvinistic male bastards.* "Listen real close you pompous ass. The reason that a psychiatrist like me was added to this mission and not the others is because Tom has MPD. And in the reports I sent you, it stated, that if someone is notified with the death of their abuser, they often go into relapse."

"Sounds like psychobabble bullshit to me, Doc. All I know is I've got twenty-four hours to land this baby."

Denise guzzled down her coffee, no time for a shower. "Set up my private room and I'm on my way. I'll explain when I get there."

"Hello, Andrew? Do you hear me?" Denise queried. After a moment of silence a small almost feminine voice broke the quiet.

"Andrew isn't here. He's the guy behind the big desk, isn't he?"

"Yes, he is."

Denise scrambled to recall who this might be. "So, Amanda, are you scared?" She knew Amanda was a twelve-year-old girl who often played alone.

"Yes. I'm scared. But it's too bad really. That judge was such a cool looking guy."

"Look Amanda, this isn't the time to fantasize about the judge. I would like to know what happened to him."

Denise watched as Andrew turned to face the monitor. The face of girlish innocence dropped quickly replaced by a haughty look of nearly royal bearing. Frederick sneered and spoke in his impeccable English manner. "I believe I can help you, milady. You see, this cad, the judge fellow, has been given the heave-ho."

"What?" *God, had he regressed that far.*

"And I for one am glad he's gone. He was such a common bore."

"Ah, Frederick, can you tell me how the council got rid of him?"

"Quite so. You see it wasn't one of us, but some new rascal named Big Ed. I believe he's related to Caliph and Nathan. But enough of that. I'm off to find a suitable cup of tea on this vessel."

Big Ed? That was one Denise had never heard of before. Which meant not only had Andrew come totally unglued, but he had created a new personality or had suppressed this one.

Denise switched screens until she saw Andrew rummaging in the kitchen area. "Tell me, good sir. Who was responsible for the judge's demise?"

The figure with his back to the screen stopped. His shoulders drooped. Gone was the righteous bearing of a blue-blooded Englishman. He merely stared, blinking at the camera. No emotion, no personality, it was the Dead One, a personality Andrew used when he was sometimes being abused. A quick switch and Andrew's faced filled with tears and he fell to his knees and began sobbing in a little boy's voice. The one she knew. The one was Jack-in-the-box, a strange little boy who held much of the pain inside. Tears streamed down his face and he pulled back into a corner, hugged his knees to himself and began to cry.

"He's coming! Don't let him touch me, please!"

"Jack? Listen, there is only you on this ship. He can't get you here!" Denise didn't know if they all aware of his dad dying. She switched screens zeroing in on his face.

She knew the pain that wracked this child's body and had seen and felt it many times before as a child herself, which is why she went into this line of work, in order to help others.

"Jack-in-the-box do not cry. Jack-in-the-box do not cry. Jack In The Box only spring out. Daddy will take away the pain."

Denise listened as he sang that rhyme over and over again. It was a rhyme Andrew's dad would sometimes sing as he tried finding out where Andrew was hiding and was always followed by an episode of sexual abuse and knew he'd sing that to himself for hours. She knew Jack-in-the-box was too ingrained into Andrew's personality and had to get someone else to take hold.

She rose and grabbed another cup of coffee and, as she squinted at its bitterness, she wondered who to get to come forward into Andrew's mind as George came striding up.

"So, what's the scoop? I got a hold of the big guys and they're finally telling me the same thing you said earlier. That our man has MPD."

He stopped his macho bravo act and stared at her trying to grasp really what was going on. "What exactly is MPD?"

Why did she have to go through this now, damn it, but she knew if he didn't truly understand he could possibly help. "Often, highly traumatic events will promote the behavior of dissociations, a psychological or behavioral defense, usually in persons that have a biopsychological defense to disassociate, as many children can do. Also, if that person's psychological environment is chronically permeated with traumatic events of one sort or another, then that individual instinctively resorts to disassociation as a self-defense mechanism. Repeated constantly it leads to the formation of multiple personalities."

"What kind of overwhelming traumatic events are we talking about?"

"Usually mental and sexual abuse, often accompanied by dysfunctional behavior around love and affection."

"What in the name of Sweet Jesus is going on here? Do you mean to tell me we've spent billions of taxpayers' dollars sending a fruitcake to Mars?"

Denise cared little about George and, except for the fact he was head of NASA Ground Control, she'd have dumped her coffee down his shirt. Drawing a deep breath she fought to remain calm and explained. "As you are fully aware, this mission has failed three times already and this is NASA's last attempt at a manned landing. I was familiar with the psychological aspects of this mission. I had also discovered that one of the top astronauts was a fairly stable person with MPD. He had the abilities of several top professional experts inside him and in essence can do the job of several people.

I helped Andrew to reintegrate his personalities. Did you not read the psychological report I put together for this mission?" She grabbed her breath trying to go back to her more in control voice. "All twelve of his personalities sit on the jury. Only one can speak at a time and the judge interprets this information and presides over all to determine the best course of action. His decision is final. The judge is very rational and will call forward only those personalities that are suitable for the situation. Andrew is the judge and in many respects Andrew is really thirteen different people. Each personality has its own strengths and weaknesses. I also implemented a drug program to stabilize and control Andrew. The benzodiazepine sedative triazolam, to allow for the ascendency of the judge's personality. Ethchlorvynol, which produces central nervous system stimulation and helped the judge feel more in control. And lastly lithium, to suppress bipolar disorders and decrease the frequency of manic episodes."

"Well, that's just Jim Dandy! Yeah too much of that report went way over my head. So what the hell went wrong?"

"You let Andrew read about his father's death. The death of an abuser can often trigger massive regression and relapse. I put that into his file as one of the precautions to not let him encounter."

"How the hell are we supposed to know he'd wig out reading the local news?"

"It was in his file that you were supposed to read." Having enough of George's belligerent behavior Denise slowly poured the rest of her coffee onto George's leather shoes.

"Hey! What the fuck?!"

"Until you decide to talk to me in a more civil tone I will not respond to any of your questions. I'm heading back to my room. Don't disturb me under any circumstances, I've got to see what I can do to piece Andrew back together and I'd advise to sit down and reread my report." *You ignorant prick,* Denise wanted to say as she walked towards her room. She tried to very quickly dump her emotions tied to George. Something she had been very good at with her ex. Too good. Her concentration needed to be on finding what happened to the judge and try to get Andrew's personality back together. As she opened the door to her room she glared back at George dabbing the coffee off his shoes. "And get someone that can make a respectable cup of coffee!"

"Hey, Doc; all I care about is getting him to plant the UN flag, say a few words, and run a couple of tests. I don't give a damn which one of him does it just as long as he does. The rest of the trip home I can handle. Your job is to guard his emotional well-being and get Andrew back on line. We've only got twenty-four hours to initiate a landing or I have to scrub this mission. I've failed twice already and I sure as shit ain't going to fail a third time. So, I don't care how you do it. Just do your job and get him back together."

"You pompous bastard!" She gave him the finger as she slammed her door shut and stared up at the display of over a dozen video screens that were located all over the Mars lander. She felt bad for the rude gesture, but she rarely let out any emotions at work or home. No, actually that felt really good. If this mission wasn't so important she'd have quit right on the spot rather than take orders from that ignorant excuse for male belligerence. Of course, it would also end her career and she loved doing what she was doing.

George stood there smiling as the coffee puddled around his feet. All of the others in the large operations room looked away, some smirking for what she did. *God, she looked stunning when she got excited.*

Denise breathed deep and sat down before her monitor display. Okay now to concentrate on how to get this landing back into operation. The main screen was blank. She glanced across and caught Andrew in the bathroom applying what looked like make-up to his face. His hair was tied back with a barrette. *Where had he stowed those away?*

"Hi Jessie."

"I'm not Jessie, I'm Alice!"

Alice? Who the fuck is Alice? Another personality he'd kept hidden. Crap how many did he have that I didn't know about after all the years working with him?

The coffee began to turn in her guts as Alice talked about the operations she had to order to fully become a woman.

Jessie she knew was a transexual, apparently Alice was or wanted to become a woman. Somehow Jessie was suppressing Alice this whole time. This is bad. Somehow, he'd been layering one personality over another.

A couple of hours later Denise rose from her chair and went out to get another cup of coffee and a sandwich. George appeared almost magically as she sipped on the coffee ready to go back to her room. "Well, how's it going Doc?"

"Bad. He's layered at least three personalities that I'm not aware of."

George looked at her, puzzled.

"Layering is a process by which some MPDs suppress certain personalities by other known personalities. These are usually more undesirable personalities."

"So, you're telling me he's like a three-level fruit cake. We can see the top layer, but God knows what's underneath?"

"Yes. Crude, but good assessment."

"And this judge fellow?"

"I'm about to find out. Now excuse me. This is coming to a critical point in the venture." She grabbed a ready-made sandwich and headed back.

A brooding face with eyes of pure hatred stared at her from the screen as she sat down.

"Ed, I presume."

"Yeah, I'm Ed. Big Ed to you. Nathan said you'd come looking for me. I said so what? Nathan is only a sissy anyways."

Big Ed reminded Denise of an adult version of Nathan, wwas a malicious troublemaker. He had suppressed Big Ed, who was his adult version and who was criminally minded. "I'd like to talk to Nathan."

His face softened a little, almost un-wrinkling its hatred. The piercing eyes were replaced by unemotional coldness. It was uncanny, sometimes how each personality could look so different from the others on the same face.

"So! If it isn't the Doc Lady. Say, get laid lately? It would help you ease up a little!"

"Nathan, we're not here to talk about my private life. We're here to talk about you."

Nathan imitated Denise's words as she spoke.

"Where's the judge?"

"I told council he wasn't needed anymore, so we gave him the boot. Those drugs you put him on only made him weak."

"Gone? But you can't! He's the judge."

"So what? I got sick of his bull. I'm running the show now. Who needs this council room? It's all bullshit."

"Listen to me Nathan and listen carefully. I know you don't want to die and if we don't get someone who can run this ship all of you are going to perish on the Martian surface." She knew Nathan had an evil heart but she also knew he probably wanted to live. Some of the others she knew would have been happy to crash on the planet's surface.

"Okay bitch, I'll get the twins. They'll know what to do."

The twins, known as Enable and Integrator, were the reasoning centers of Andrew's mind and one of the main reasons he was elected for this mission. The twin could and did outwit and outthink most of the other trainees for this mission. They knew the ship, its abilities, and what to do if something came up. They were like mental Siamese twins and it was impossible to tell which one was actually talking. Andrew's head would sometimes shift to the right or left slightly as they talked.

"Where are we? And..."

"What is the difficulty?"

"If you didn't know, the ship is about to land on the planet's surface, and one or both of you are needed to plant the flag before leaving."

His head moved left to right a couple of times as if the two were having an intense discussion between them.

"Easy! I can handle the fine adjustments and..."

"I'll handle the others."

"Agreed." He sounded like both voices were speaking at the same time, even though they only had the use of the one larynx.

"Together we'll hold consciousness until the landing sequence is completed."

It was eerie when she could hear both voices talking at virtually the same time. She knew the ship was now in good hands, paged George to let him know, and decided to lay down for a quick nap. She was beyond exhausted and would need some time thinking about how to re-integrate the new personalities. Denise set the alarm for an hour and closed her eyes, mentally exhausted.

The pounding on the door made Denise jump. George burst into the room. "He's done it! I mean they've done it."

"George, didn't I say I don't want you in my room?" she blurted out before the fog had lifted from her brain, the realization of what he said finally hit home. "What?" She blinked in shock. "He's landed?" Her elation was like a little child on Christmas morning opening presents.

One of the assistants ran up to the open door behind George. "Ah, George and Denise; there's something strange happening on the surface."

George ran from the room and Denise looked to her screens. She saw a figure dancing and parrying with one of the electric antennas like it was a sword.

Caliph thrust his sword into the guts of the monster before him. A strange planet meant strange monsters to fight and even more fetching princesses to rescue from these heathen Christian infidels, she knew.

He sprang forward to a rocky outcrop. Unable to judge the right amount of effort needed on this planet's weaker gravity he slammed into the rocks. A boulder rattled free and came crashing down onto his leg. Even in this lesser gravity Denise estimated that the rock probably weighed nearly a hundred kilos.

Denise rose from her chair, ran her fingers through her hair in a comb-like fashion at an attempt to tidy herself, then decided she didn't care how disheveled she looked and entered the silent control room. Her communications didn't extend to the suit Andrew was wearing.

"We're sunk," George spat, and threw his headphones across the counter.

"Vital signs are stable, but fluctuating," someone from a console yelled out.

"He's only got fifteen minutes of oxygen left." Another hollered.

"Unable to tell if he's cut himself," another said. She knew his self-sealing suit would reseal itself, but if he was bleeding, he could possibly drown in his own blood.

"Are we on Global TV?" she asked.

"Yes," George burst out. "I've got to contact the president now." Knowing his life was becoming total shit in front of the entire world.

Denise ran her hands through her messy hair again trying to think. "Okay put an ad on and get me a headset; I need to talk to him," she yelled, trying to think who could possibly get him out of this predicament. There was one that Andrew possessed. The one personality she feared.

She grabbed the headset. "If you can hear this give me a growl. The body is dying only you can save it."

The closed eyes fluttered. In all of her years of psychotherapy and dealing with MPDs this was one she'd banned from the council. Yet it's strength, cunning, daring and agility was greater than most Olympic athletes. It even ate mice raw.

A growl rent the air as his eyes sprang open. Pupils widened, nearly filling his eyes. The sheer cunning raw animal power seethed beneath those eyes. Many in the room gasped or looked away, not expecting such animalistic rage. Deep breaths filled her ears and his lips opened trying to show fangs ready to tear something apart.

Lone Wolf, as she called him, had returned. She'd never experienced as beastly a personality in anyone else.

Notified that something was going on, George left the president hanging mid conversation and stared at the screen, shocked at what he was seeing. "He sounds like a cornered dog! Good God!"

Denise ignored him, she had to keep intensely focused or she lose him and he'd tear the suit apart. "Wolf, your body is dying. You must free yourself. But the leg must stay. Hear me? The leg must stay complete."

George blinked in total disbelief.

"Ten minutes of air," someone yelled out.

She knew his heavy breathing was using up the air faster than normal, yet this canine personality had to perform like he normally would consuming air and nutrients faster than a man. She also knew that like a trapped beast it would rip its leg off in order to free itself.

Hands began to claw at the suit as more snarls rent the air. His heavy breathing fogged the visor.

"No Wolf! The rock! Lift the rock!"

He glared down and, using its paws, the creature of the night attempted in vain to budge the boulder.

"Damn! It has the strength but can't use what it thinks are paws as hands." Denise closed her eyes trying to figure out what to do as a shy but strong voice broke the air.

"Take it easy there fella. I'll help."

A snarl ripped free.

Thank God billions weren't watching this. They'd never believe it. Hell, I don't believe it!

"Jethro will help you. I'm your friend. My dad tortured all of our pet dogs for fun, so I never kept any, but I've always wanted a pet wolf to protect me. So, none of us wants to die."

Jethro was one of newer personalities, shy and not very bright.

Cautiously one hand lifted to the growling beast. It slowly sniffed at it and then made to lick at it.

"What the shit is happening?" George blurted out.

Denise lifted her hand to silence him.

"Yes! The two of you together can lift the rock," she whispered into the microphone. Somehow this personality had the courage to speak up and she knew it could merge with the other one to become hopefully one being.

"Okay buddy, let me borrow your strength to lift this rock, but you must pull the leg free and promise not to bite me. I'll give you some treats when we get back."

A quiet growl greeted Jethro. His large hands gripped the rock, and, grunting and with sweat dripping down his face, the rock began to budge.

With a loud howl the beast pulled its leg free. "Good boy. Now I'm taking you back to safety."

For all intents and purposes, it looked like he picked up the wolf into his arms, As he did so, it cried out in agony. He began to lumber back to the ship; for the observer it was as if he was holding his arms around empty space.

This was a good sign. If Jethro could merge with this terror then there was hope others could as well. Maybe she could pull this tortured man back together again.

Everyone in the command center cheered.

"You are so fucking awesome!" He bent over. "I could kiss you"

Denise pulled back and held her hand up. "Kiss me and I'll have you charged with sexual harassment!"

More cheered at seeing George being put in his place.

"Okay, I concede. You, lady, are one helluva broad!"

"I'm your colleague and expect to be treated like one. Now go tell the president." She ordered him, her boss. "I've got to get him settled down in the ship and see if we can get those twins to begin lift off."

As George left and Denise walked back to her room, smiling wholeheartedly for the first time in years, the others gave her a standing ovation. Which was as much for standing up to George as for the success of the mission.

"Can you get someone to get me a coffee? I've still got a lot to do."

Amid the cheering the older red-headed lady looked at her, "No coffee; I'm breaking open the champagne to honor the heroine of the hour!"

The Doctor To The Rescue!

Mark Huang; superb dentist, lousy criminal. Concerned about a Mr. Jones, a very strange patient of his. He thought he was an alien. I asked why?

He replied with, "he has four more teeth than has ever been recorded on a human."

"And that makes you think he's an alien? Are you kidding me?"

I asked him why he doesn't just sneak into his house for a poke around. I got short shrift about the perils of breaking and entering!

"Well, Frank, if you're so good at it, why don't you go along? You can take this mysterious Doctor friend of yours with you!" he challenged me.

"Doctor who?" I hear you ask. Well, just The Doctor. As a novelist, I had regaled Mark with tales of my adventures through time and space with The Doctor and I think he thought they were just fiction. This was the first inkling I'd had that Mark might actually believe me!

That is how I wound up outside the mysterious Mr Jones' garage with my trusty terrier guard dog, Sparky, and a pouch full of various Endodontic hand files Mark had lent me as I had neglected to grab my lockpicks. Well, I didn't think I'd be needing them to drink wine with my dentist!

In about ten seconds I heard the audible click of the garage door unlocking. I scooped Sparky up in my arms and stepped over the threshold which triggered a slight but shrill alarm, followed by a flash like a thousand light bulbs. I fell to my knees onto damp grassy earth and bathed in sunlight and tropical heat. "What?"

Suddenly cast in shadow I fearfully raised my head to be greeted by a very quizzical stare from a living, breathing Stegosaurus! Okay. So, Mark was correct. His patient *was* weird!

"How many times have I told you not to go on those wild adventures? Well not at least without me!" My wife, Jen's, voice echoed in my head as I hit speed dial one; The Doctor. A zap from his Sonic Screwdriver and my lowly Android phone could call anywhere and any-when. Only will it work in whatever-hundred-thousand BC?

A screech rent the air above me and I fearfully looked around to find I'm surrounded by a pack of Stegosaurs and Pterodactyls flying overhead. Not what I expected to find in a normal suburban garage! A fifty-six Ford Thunderbird yes, Pterodactyls, no.

The stench of rotting meat assailed my nostrils as I spied Sparky tearing into the massive pile of dead something just below me. I hauled on his leash, nearly gagging on the stench. "I just hope you're not allergic to hundred-million-year-old dogfood," I scolded him. Who'd have thought terriers would love dinosaur meat?

More cries as two carnivores, T. Rex or Allosaurus types, broke the jungle bushes and tore into one of the herbivores. Obviously, lunchtime. Hopefully neither Sparky nor I were next on the menu. A six-inch-long tooth lay discarded nearby; I grabbed it to show Mark later, or more likely for moral support. I breathed a huge sigh of relief as I heard the familiar "vworp, vworp" behind me.

"Sure is hot and humid in 200 million BC, give or take an epoch or three," The Doctor remarked, as he tugged at his bowtie. "Now, it is usually *me* taking *you* on travels into danger and excitement, not the other way around, Frank Talaber."

We both stared around and watched the two giant carnivores, possibly Allosaurs, feasting on a Stegosaurus carcass as I explained everything. He flicked his sonic screwdriver on and scanned around. "The residue seems to indicate that this is a device used by a Draconion, masters of disguise. Your dentist must be very observant; they usually blend in. However, they aren't a peaceful species, so I think we need to get back in the TARDIS and skedaddle pronto before..."

It was too late; a metallic click and a strange buzzing filled the air. A being shimmered into view. The Doctor grabbed me and dragged me behind the stinking carcass. "You know how I tell you 'everything's going to be fine' even when I've no idea whether it will be or not?" The Doctor said, fiddling with his ever-present bowtie again.

"Yes," I replied.

"Well, everything's going to be fine!"

The being, dressed in upper-body armor, pulled a laser from its side and stared at a dial on its arm. "Yup, just what I thought! Your dentist's alien *is* a Draconion, and he isn't in a picture-taking mood."

The alien trained its laser in our direction just as my small terrier leapt from nowhere and ripped into his leg. Caught off guard, the Draconian looked down, confused, screaming as Sparky tore into him. It dropped its laser in shock and flicked a button to remove its helmet in order to better see his attacker.

"Good God!" It wasn't human, or even mammalian in nature. It was some sort of reptilian; similar to the Allosaurus, but smaller, more refined, more ...

... more evolved! The alien stared up as something large blocked out sunlight as one of the carnivores thumped past us. It had left its meal and moved to attack.

The Draconion bent over, swatted Sparky aside reaching for its weapon. Too late. The huge Allosaurus reptile snapped the screaming being just above the knees, lifted its head straight up and swallowed the alien whole, luckily ignoring us. All that remained were mere shins and blood-filled boots.

A yapping filled the air as Sparky ran up to us, tail a-wagging, as The Doctor smiled and scratched him behind the ears. "You are the most annoying, most troublesome, most incredible little dog in the universe. Let's get you and your inquisitive master home!"

My wife, Jen, came to me the next day holding the six-inch-long tooth I'd put into my pants. I had some explaining to do!

Thesaurus and Raven Stew

"Memory. The retention of thought." The crowded Banff tavern was full of chatter and laughter, but the elderly lady sitting alone in a booth seemed not to notice as she flipped through her dear old friend, a thesaurus. "Memory: remembrance, retention, reminiscence, recognition, recurrence, recollection, afterthought. See thought, past."

Iridescent breezes strewn in beguiling summer fragrances swept seductively over the rhythmic slapping of ocean clawing away at shoreline and rock in salty repose. Above it all rises the clop, clop, clop of dropped pebbles tumbling over and over.

Troy bolted upright from his sleep, the same haunting dream, yet again.

A wooden sign, proclaiming 'Ol' Irish Pub', swayed outside to mountain breezes. Inside dark-stained wood absorbed the gaiety of tin-whistled folk songs and the chattering of patrons laughing and carousing, overriding the elder as she muttered to herself whilst flipping through the well-worn book in front of her. Her only other companion is a black, tattered baseball cap, with red unreadable stitching, plunked unceremoniously down on the table. She pulls at her meal of chicken and fries with a slow devouring grace, oblivious to the noise around her as if nothing else mattered except her and her memories.

Becoming aware, that was the problem.

Goosebumps stole across Troy's naked body as he grabbed a bathrobe and staggered out onto his balcony overlooking Kitsilano beach. Mists, hiding the view of Vancouver harbour, hung in elegant draperies of white rising lace. Early morning light lessened the greyness as he lit a cigarette and slowly exhaled. The crows, always hanging around, hidden in escarpments of cedar and spruce boughs, were strangely silent. No irritating harsh cawing cracked the stillness.

Mists and crows. Damn! Is it me, or does it always seem to be fogged in when I have that dream? Shivers stole away at the pleasure of nicotine's timeless embrace.

I've grown to hate them both.

The girl he'd brought home from the tavern last night was gone. What was her name again? *Oh yeah, Suzanne. How funny.*

Troy took a long pull from his smoke and tried not to remember back to the time of someone with nearly the same name. His mother. And that summer over twenty years ago when they went to Rose Spit, Haida Gwaii's desolate tongue of land. He was ten, part of a happy family, back then.

That's the difficulty. Memories; the past. She hadn't any, the elderly lady mused, as she mulled over her thoughts seeking deliverance from the words within her trusted old friend. It struck her again, that was the problem. The past.

"I reckon she's a bag lady. Look at her! She can't possibly pay her bill," one blonde buxom waitress sneered to another.

"Well, I don't intend to get stuck with it. Between food and the four glasses of wine it's nearly seventy bucks," the second waitress replied, pulling on the hand pump, filling her latest order for three pints of draft.

"Look at the way she's dressed. Those threads must be years old; I don't think she's changed them for a month. And that old book she's got. How can you read the same book over and over again? I can't even flip through a magazine twice, let alone—"

"Read a book? Bet you've never read a book in your life." The manager walked over. "Go attend to the other customers and leave the old lady alone. I hear she rents the old Crawford cabin on the edge of town."

Dad called Mom an eccentric writer. Nuts is more how I'd describe her sometimes, to my friends, but that's why my dad loved her. Even in the face of the worst disasters she created, often unintentionally, Susan always managed to be cheery. Rose Spit wasn't nearly the craziest place Mom took us to research her next book, but it did cost us an SUV, a thirty-kilometer walk... and her.

We were near Massett, along the top of the islands, when my parents had picked up a young hitchhiker. Heather looked lost and stranded. I was mesmerized by her, and I think my parents were too. She looked First Nations; long jet-black hair, with several strands braided around each other, under a tanned exterior that spoke of long lazy days in the sun. Something in the way she talked drew you in and held you in the gaze of her large brown eyes. Ragged clothes lent to the suggestion that neither they nor she had been washed for quite a while. Her face lit up when Mom asked her if she knew how to get to Rose Spit.

"I just came from there. It's magical. The beach is full of crystals like discards from a magicians' drunken convention of miss-brewed hops and defunct spells. How they glisten in the light of a full moon and sparkle as you walk." She danced in her seat, barely able to contain herself. "In fact, did you know that's the location of Raven's legend, where he opens the original clamshell to release the first Haida natives into this world?"

Mom was scribbling frantically in one of her many disheveled notebooks as we all looked at her with the blank stare of clay slammed butt end onto a potter's wheel, glimpsing occasionally up from her new Haida Gwaii baseball cap that dad had just bought her. "Raven is the Haida's main creator god. When picking around in the clamshells on Rose Spit he heard some funny noises coming from one of them. He opened it up and out wriggled these strange two-legged beings. Too scrawny to eat, instead he watched them until boredom or hunger took over and left his new toys to run around on the beach to evolve." She stopped and glanced at Mom with a soft coo in her voice like a contented pigeon. "I could guide you. I know where the best crystals lie in this magical realm of

'Islands on the boundaries between worlds'; that's what Haida Gwaii means you know." Her eyes sparkled as she talked animatedly, drawing my parents in with her enchantment. I sat bemused and forgotten in my seat.

Mother's eyes widened.

Dad said, "No way on Earth are we going there," but I knew better.

Sure enough, before the day was over, we took off on a twenty-odd kilometer drive over a deserted beach, passing only a shipwreck, rolling dunes and a spit of seagrass-covered sand. Bouncing and jostling in the backseat, I wanted to throw up, as the vehicle lurched drunkenly over yet another sand dune.

"You know how the Haida got their name don't you?" Heather piped up.

We of course assumed it was because of the islands. She laughed, "No, the Haida soon became great warriors, the most feared on this coast. Matter of fact, they sailed their giant cedar canoes up and down the west coast, raiding villages, taking booty and slaves, usually women, to help keep the blood of the tribes fresh. Early in their travels they set upon the mainland, near Bella Bella, and when the scouts of the village spotted them. They ran into the village yelling, "Hide our women."

My parents laughed, "'Haida' women! Get it?" Mom giggled.

I nodded in agreement, gulping as we passed a final radio tower. Like a helpless passenger in one of Christopher Columbus' voyages, waiting for the inevitable, we left the edge of our known world in the sinking sun like Columbus sailing away from the edge of the known world.

As we jostled in our seats, I caught Heather staring quietly out of the window. Lost in the reflection of glass something dark and soul-less stirred. I slid further against my door and clutched its handle. There was something darker to Heather than mere braids and big eyes.

"If the tide is out far enough you can walk for ages on the spit, while the surf pounds on either side of you," our hitchhiker enthused as she returned to her chatty self. I didn't want to walk for ages, I wanted to go home.

Where the grass ended, we drove down onto the strand of Rose Spit. I knew it was a mistake as we lurched onto the rocks. Heather's eyes shone darkly as my mom's excitement hummed all around us. A kilometer later the tires started spinning and suddenly the world was going nowhere.

"Damn!" Dad cursed as we floundered in soft sand that became softer still as the tires dug deeper into it. We scrambled out and pushed and pushed, yelling with relief every time the vehicle lurched forward a few feet, only to bog down again.

"Looks like we get to spend the night on the beach," Mom gasped, making the most of things. She rearranged her long brown hair, sweating under her proud new baseball cap, black with red letters proclaiming, 'A Fellow Watchman Of Haida Gwaii', bought earlier that day in Skidegate.

I slumped against the fender and glanced over my shoulder. Fog was already creeping in from the ocean, dark and heavy as the shadows gathering in Heather's eyes. I knew this much ... I didn't like her, didn't like her at all. All of this was her fault.

Our tent was pitched among the piles of driftwood, above the high tide mark. Dad cursed under his breath as we gathered enough wood to start a fire and form some sort of makeshift protection against the elements. Unloading the SUV, and saving what we could, we watched the encroaching sea slowly swallow it up. Mom disappeared up the beach with the girl, looking for crystals. I remember Dad cursing about women and the trouble they'll get you into, yet in the same breath saying how much he loved my mother. I wondered why they were worth all the trouble.

The old lady sipped at her wine and summoned the waitress again. "I'll have another one before I go."

Back at the bar, the blonde slammed the glass into the dishwasher. "Shit! That's the fifth! I don't like this one bit. I've seen the old Crawford cabin, no lights on at night. Someone told me there's a squatter living there. I reckon it's her. She'd have saved herself a bundle if she'd just ordered a bottle to start with."

"You're right! What was she thinking? Sure don't make much sense to me." The other waitress shook her head.

"Thought. Mental activity." Nouns: thoughtfulness, recollection, cogitation. See judgment, intellect; reasoning. The old lady smiled to herself. "It's true some things just have no rhyme or reason."

Later, huddled around the campfire, the girl told us another tale of Raven. "He has a stone that he keeps in the back of his throat. It grants him immortality, without it he'd lose his memory and begin to age, eventually dying. If he loses it he needs a host body to keep him alive longer until he finds it again."

"Once a very foolish Haida prince challenged Raven," she sneered. "To try and save his people who were dying of smallpox plague."

"That's true," my mom interrupted. "I just read about the horrible plague, brought on by the white men in 1867. Wiped out nearly half the population of natives along the coast."

"Yes, she's right. This very stupid prince thought Raven could save his people and the two fled here, to Rose Spit and the boundary between worlds."

"I think the prince wasn't stupid, but very brave to tackle someone as powerful as the mighty Raven." I commented.

Heather puffed up. "Yes, well, I guess it would take some amount of bravery for the prince to work up the courage to attempt what he did." She frowned. "Only Raven had been outsmarting natives up and down the coast for centuries."

"I'd read he'd been given the gift of unending appetite for his gluttonous behavior," Mom interrupted.

"Well, yes. He had a rather healthy appetite from what I gather." Heather glared at my mom and that darkness passed in her eyes again. "My legs have cramped; I need to walk a bit."

Once Heather was out of earshot I turned to my parents. "Don't you think her odd?"

"No, I think she's quite sweet and chatty."

Dad nodded. "Perhaps we should keep her and trade you in. I hear girls are way less trouble than boys."

"Ha ha! I don't like her," I spat, and stomped off in a stew. I knew I was right. Only why couldn't my parents see it? Had she placed them under some sort of spell that hadn't worked on me?

As I sat behind a large log I heard that sound for the first time. Clop, clop, clop.

I poked my head up and watched the girl as she picked up and dropped pebble after pebble.

I approached her as the sun was gobbled up by a black cloudbank roiling in, and it finally dawned on me. I knew why she was here. "You know what? I bet there wouldn't be a better place to hide Raven's stone than on a crystal laden beach."

"Yes!" she hissed. "The vile prince tossed it onto this beach and ran into the boundary. Or so goes the tale."

"And I'll bet he's been looking for it ever since. Raven, I mean."

She nodded sadly.

I walked back to my parents and huddled in Mom's arms, saying nothing. We shouldn't have come here.

I woke to the sound of the clop of rocks being dropped over and over once again. The last night of the full moon, it hung white and bloated, casting an eerie light to fire up the shifting patterns of crystals by the thousands. As I walked, formations of light drifted in and out of view like runway lights to a landing strip, running for kilometers into the dark. The boundary she talked about.

I knew I shouldn't have left the security of my parents, yet I did. The sound of rocks dropping stopped as I took a few more steps. The grate of stones crunching underfoot behind me. I turned. Smoke hung from the smoldering campfire and, rising through it, a shape of blackness incarnate, wings unfurling to a wide, wide span.

I stumbled against a large clump of fleshy material, warmth rising from it, and stared up into the piercing eyes of a six-foot Raven.

"How tight in there." He stretched his frame, wing joints cracked as he flexed.

"That's what you were doing earlier, wasn't it. Searching the beach for your stone. No wonder you were happy to lead us to Rose Spit."

"Clever boy. You know my secret, now that is a shame for you," he clicked.

As Raven took a step closer a shimmer cracked the darkness behind him. The image of a warrior, a native warrior, flickered.

"The girl. The fire." Words whispered in the heavy air.

Raven glared in the direction of the voice. "The prince," he spat.

"Throw her! Now!" The prince's wavering ghostly figure leaped at Raven.

Without thinking I grabbed the rubbery husk of Heather's body, and, gagging, threw it onto the embers of the fire. My parents never awoke as flames seared the sky.

"No!" he screamed, tumbling with the apparition. I ran as the stench of burning flesh filled the air. Mist, like tentacles from an octopus, pulled and pushed me, this-way-and-that, protecting me from Raven's razor-edged talons. Wings flapped, swishing close in the darkness, caws seethed into the night as shadows danced over the glittering shoreline. Spitting gravel and flinging crystals upward

I dove several times out of his clutches, the native warrior fading in and out, directing me on, into the crash of surf closing in, ever closer, on both sides. The thin tongue of land, retracting away as I ran into whiteness and the arms of Rose Spit. The boundary of timelessness.

"Past. Gone by in time. Past tense: yesterday, days of yore, times past or gone by, olden times, auld lang syne, the good old days. See priority, oldness."

"She's just a crazy old broad," the blonde waitress scoffed. The other looked at her, then back at the old lady. "Hope I don't get to be like her at that age."

"Live fast, love hard, die young, leaving a good-looking corpse owing more than you came in with. That's my philosophy." The second laughed.

"And that book! I sneaked a peak at it, you know, it's a thesaurus. What's she want to keep reading that for? I'm still in college and the only thing I use mine for is to keep my bookshelf steady, otherwise it'd probably fall over."

"I guess it's a matter of priorities."

"Well, you take care of the old lady. Me, I'm talking to the hunky dude in the corner."

That was the problem, she thought, staring at the tattered black ball cap, trying to read the stitched lettering she'd picked at over the years. As if trying to dig into the past. One that lay buried.

I remember falling through gossamer curtains of silk and mist, ending when haze parted and hard ground abruptly halted my fall. My head bashed onto the rocks.

I sat up and felt the gash on my head, only instead of blood oozing out a strange whiteness filled my hands and seeped all over the ground, forming first just a puddle, then expanding into a large pool, far too much to have come from me. A shape rose in a white tower of ivory and took on a familiar avian shape. I jumped and shrank before the image as eyes opened and mist oozed from a large white being. It stared at me, a white bird with eyes of kindness. So unlike the dark version I was running from.

"Don't be afraid. Raven will not enter this realm. You are safe here."

"Then who are you?" I gasped.

"I am Raven before he became Raven," he said. "Before he became cursed with black feathers, greed and an insatiable appetite."

"That ghost. Was that the prince that took Raven's stone? What was his name again?"

"Prince Kiidkayaas."

"But I thought he was trapped in a Golden Spruce tree."

"I was."

"But. You are..."

"You know, not all incarnations are the same in your world and mine. That is why the prince could defeat Raven. There are many inexplicable things in life, as you will begin to realize. Some will be answered, some not."

He told me of many things, including a special lapis lazuli rock I'd find under a stump next to the fire. "Keep it hidden from Raven and you'll be safe. Now you must go," he whispered, and I awoke beside my parents in the morning. A kid's crazy dream?

After we hiked out of Rose Spit, Mom disappeared the next day. She said she was just popping to the washroom and never came back. I remember dad telling the police about the black baseball cap with red lettering, in case it washed up. We reported both disappearances to the RCMP, but to my knowledge neither she nor Heather were ever found. Dad searched and searched but it was like the earth just swallowed Mom up and took her away. I remember getting the same eerie vibes from her as I did from Heather before she disappeared.

I never told Dad about my experiences there, should have perhaps, but who'd believe me? And maybe it was my fault she disappeared, I realized years later.

Dad never dated after Mom left, and began to drink alone late at night, sometimes holding pictures of him and Mom. Shortly after I went to university, the doctors discovered Dad full of cancer, but I knew he quit living after that trip and died of a broken heart. The cancer only shortened the agony he was living through, so in some ways it was a blessing.

Blessing: sanctification, consecration, absolution, the laying on of hands. Memories of talons touching her and absolving all before came back as she sunk into his eyes.

The waitress sauntered over as the perceived bag lady rose and collected her belongings.

"Don't take off without the bill, will you dearie?" The blonde smiled artificially as she handed it to her. The old woman looked at her a moment before pulling out a pen from her pocket and wrote quickly on the back of the slip of paper. "Where's the washroom?" she asked.

"Ah, to your right, behind the bar. But I do need the bill taken care of first."

The bag lady pulled a hundred from her pocket and handed it to the waitress, along with the bill she'd just written on. "Keep the change, dearie," she called over her shoulder with a smile, as she shuffled towards the exit, pulling low the tattered red-lettered Haida Gwaii cap.

The blonde gaped at the hundred-dollar note before yelling, "I said in the back! Didn't you hear me?" 'Crazy old broad,' she tried to whisper under her breath.

"I heard you, all right. But I didn't say I wanted to use the washroom, did I? Just wanted to know where it was." She walked out the front entrance into the darkness with a surprizing soberness and straightness.

The waitress read the scrawled message on the back of the bill.

Youth. Condition of being young. Nouns: puberty, girlhood, callowness juvenility, immaturity. See posterity, newness.

"What the...?" She ran outside but the old lady had vanished into the night.

During the rest of her shift she kept pulling the old lady's bill from her pocket rereading the words scrawled on it. The next morning she pulled the thesaurus from under her bookshelf and began flipping through it.

Cool mist-laden air stirred as Troy butted out his smoke and stared back into his condo. He caught the door ajar to his curio cabinet. From the mist-shrouded trees a raven cried out as he absentmindedly scratched at the small white reminder from his trip on the side of his head. He didn't have to look to know the Lapis Lazuli stone was finally missing. *I knew he'd find it one day. One of those inexplicable things in life, but at least I know I'll get a decent night's sleep now after all these years.*

Havens of the Heart

A breeze born of spirit stirs lands, curiosities, and sails of the heart, awakening souls clenched tight under fears walled foundations. Spirit winds' evocative calls gather to these rock-scoured beaches all those souls that respond.

Like seeds of various genealogies, each one is different, disconnected from the others. All are deposited in the secure pod of Haven by the Sea.

All thrust into the here and now and for a brief moment, their lives are sheltered from the revolving world. Winds born of South Pacific Isles, smelling of salty decay and ancient Mariners breath, stir deep the wells of the past.

Under the guidance of the warmest of hands, the caringest of hearts, and the cleanest of intentions, all are gently pried open.

Set in place by man's hands or nature's touch, cedars anchor earth to bedrock separating diamond blue sky from emerald forest. To soothe and comfort, allowing the fire of souls aflame to tread the pathways and tremble in forbidden fears. Tears flow, glistening like dewberries on knifed swords of angers release.

Dammed energies are released and flung free to flow. As everything must flow, into the cradle of the sea, into the nether of space, into the grace of the universe.

Finally, all stand as one, with the innocent gaze of children with aged eyes at life's new meanings; reconnected to the passions of their soul.

Another spirit breeze stirs time and place, billowing unfurled sails and gathers into its arms these rejuvenated seeds. Seeds vibrating with life's deep breath and scatters those seeds back to the lands hence they came.

Each forever different, changed from within, to sprout their own paths and destinies. Each linked to each other by invisible spirit threads of memories of yesterdays and tomorrows to be relished. Relished like the sweetest of fruit nectars that dribble down trembling throats and are held in the same reverence as one would gaze at aboriginal drawings on sacred rocks.

Windsong's Calling

Based on a true incident that happened in Haida Gwaii (formally the Queen
Charlotte Islands) off the western coast of British Columbia. A man, Grant
Hadwin, cut down a very rare Golden Spruce to protest against
logging. The Haida believe there is a prince trapped inside the tree and
that is why the leaves have turned gold in sorrow for this prince.
This is his journey after awakening.

Thick sap oozed from the Golden Spruce, congealing like blood. The death chant of Gordon Chatwick's axe shuddered through the tall tree. Amidst this forest of varying shades of green, the Golden Spruce was unique. A precious jewel to the natives with oral stories of a prince trapped with, while its needles of gold were viewed as a hybrid to the scientists.

The axe bit one last time, cutting past the cambium membrane. Gordon paused to swipe at the sweat burning his eyes. The chainsaw done the bulk of the hard part, his axe would finish it off. There was only an hour of darkness left before the chance any tourists would arrive and discover what he'd done. But before that, the winds would pick up and send the ancient Golden Spruce crashing to the earth. His opposition to the continued raping of the planet's resources would soon be complete.

Overhead, the tree groaned under its own weight, protesting its demise. Sap flowed down its gouged sides, sticking to Gordon's boot as he moved. *Damn, this goop is everywhere. Never seen a tree bleed this much. Then again, I've never cut a Golden Spruce. Good. This will get their attention.*

Gordon pinned the note he'd scribbled to the base of the trunk. The handle of the axe stuck to his fingers as he gathered his knapsack. Every step was hampered by the gummy sap sucking at his feet.

I got this stuff all over me. Better burn my clothes back at camp. The public will

not let this damage go unnoticed. The fight to save the forests continues.

The Golden Spruce cried out in agony. Haunting, piercing screams of an ancient being having its existence ended splayed the air. Splintering cracks echoed as the wind increased.

Gordon swallowed hard, the iron taste of fear clinging to his mouth. A former logger, he'd cut down many trees in his day, but this was more like murdering a living being. "Oh God, I've killed something beautiful." He rushed to its aid, trying to support the groaning trunk.

Muscles strained, tears streaked the sweat on his cheeks. *It is alive? What have I done?*

As mournful cries rang out into the echoing forest around them.

With his hands covered in warm sap, and the winds picking up, it was too late for remorse. "I'm so sorry." He retreated to the bank of the Yakoun River, where his kayak waited to whisk him to the ocean waters of Masset Inlet as he heard the death kneel of the ancient being and a loud thud echoed throughout the forest.

In the vanishing darkness, the sap was congealing into two body-shaped pools. Solidifying and expanding like bread dough, filling with more substance than the sap itself could ever provide. The fresh aroma of spruce spread thickly across the glade, mingling with other smells that didn't belong. Putrid, nauseating odors of animals decayed during eras forgotten in the vaults of time.

Shapes began to emerge in that soupy muck. One was taking the lines of a human, a young male. The other was leaner, more avian. Feathers adorned this one's body. Long black feathers.

As if the spruce tree sensed its demise, it secreted more sap from its wounds. Time, to a species whose lifespan was measured in seasons and annual growth rings, now became fleeting seconds. The sap that provided its energy flowed like a watery vein into the two still objects, filling them, imbuing them with substance.

Both cocooned forms jerked and kicked at the same time, struggling to grasp at the strings of life, of breath, of leaving an arcane reality and entering a former one. The figure bearing the feathers kicked violently; it, of all beings, had been tricked into being trapped in this tree. It had to be the first to emerge. It had to be. There was no other way.

The other, a young First Nations male, fought more to fight the madness, the insanity haunting his mind. He'd spent many lifetimes trapped in dimensions not meant for people.

A final cannon-ball crack shattered the morning as the wind gusted and the Golden Spruce stood, disconnected for the first time in its life from the earth. The umbilical cord severed, freeing the two trapped within.

The male's lips parted, and for the first time in nearly a hundred and fifty years, he cried out.

Prince Kiidkayaas cried out, gurgling on amniotic fluid, a black wing tore free from the ooze. With a horrible sucking sound, Raven stood up on his two spindly legs. The prince continued to wail as Raven shook himself free of the gooey sap. Raven had landed himself into many predicaments, but to be trapped inside a tree wasn't something he ever wanted to do again. He hopped over to where the prince was now fighting to escape from the cloying webs.

"Caw," he crowed. "So, you thought you could defeat me, silly boy." He leaned forward, deftly plucked down and tore into the prince's body. A gush of blood spurted skyward as he yanked the beating heart from the lad and flung it into the forest, where it landed in the bough of a cedar tree. Needles, still falling from the crash of the Golden Spruce, fluttered downward in a sticky mess, covering the heart. It pumped its last few beats, spewing its last crimson droplets. The prince's lifeblood mixed with the sap oozing into the folds of the cedar.

Raven watched the body convulse in its last few shudders. Satisfied the prince was dead, he sauntered over to where he had flung the heart. He hoped to devour it and the soul of its owner, thereby not only ensuring his victory, but also gaining the spirits and attributes of such a brave warrior. Alas, the scattering of needles had somehow carpeted the heart. He flicked some fallen leaves and too impatient to search, Raven cawed to himself. He didn't have time for this as his stomach growled deeply. What he he'd give for a decent meal.

"No matter," he thought. "I've won, after all this time. I've won and defeated you, brave prince."

He snickered as he sauntered back to his adversary's messy remains. Robbed of their soul, they were quickly congealing and soaking back into the earth, returning to the puddle of sap that had temporarily infused them with life.

As spruce needles continued to fall, he searched for the reason he'd originally become trapped in the Golden Spruce with Kiidkayaas, squinting in the dim light, unable to spy the shiny rock buried in the mire. His immortal stone ... where was it? Did the prince realize how close he had come to winning? Raven shuddered. He'd almost lost to one of the people that he, Raven, had himself created. What irony, he crowed. But then his life had been full of ironies.

Frustrated again, he stood up straight and sniffed the air. Late summer, the winter spirit winds would arrive soon. Only something in the air was different. The scent of metal ore sang to the Raven's nostrils as he strutted around the base of the conifer. The Golden Spruce had been felled by human means. How grand this tree had grown since he and the prince had been trapped in it. How many cycles of life had passed? He glanced around, noticing the crush of moccasin prints in the soft earth. The tracks of the one who had cut down the tree?

Still, something hung in the air, something unusual, unnatural, but first he had to find the one that had freed him before he told any others. A trail of crumpled vegetation led him to the heavily wooded banks of the Yakoun River, the brine of the ocean filtering in as he squinted across the waters, where the first rays of sunlight, brilliant in their hues of vibrant pinks and reds, tried to penetrate the mists. A slender canoe, with its lone figure, bobbed. The craft had just exited the freshwaters of the river and entered the brackish currents of Masset Inlet. Raven's immortal stone could wait; first he had some more pressing business to attend to.

Time to reward this one for freeing me, he thought, closing his eyes. His sleek body shimmered and shifted, shades of white and brown bubbling to the surface as Raven transformed himself into a large bald eagle. With a hunting cry, he flapped his new wings then lifted skyward, reveling in their sheer strength before focusing on the odd-looking canoe below with his yellow hunters eyes.

Gordon stared in awe as an eagle screamed its shrill hunting cry from the vicinity of the felled Golden Spruce. Smiling, he marveled at its grace and magnificence as the bird rose. Cunning, efficient hunters, bald eagles could lift many times their weight in prey. They had a regal, don't-dick-with-me haughtiness in their yellow eyes. This one turned in a lazy circle rising with the wind currents until it began its descent, towards the kayak. Too bad he didn't have his camera with him.

"What the ..." he muttered, his smile turning into a frown of bewilderment as the predator swooped down towards him with ever increasing speed, its wings folded in.

Trepidation ripped through him as the eagle's sharp cry again broke the serenity. The largest eagle he'd ever seen, sporting a six-to-seven-foot wingspan, and the killing machine was diving straight at him. Gordon froze in fear's icy grip, his fate shimmering in the glint of razor-sharp talons and the steel-eyed depths of the hunter's chilling yellow gaze. Terror, the sheer panic that numbs the mind and steals away at will, pistol-whipped him.

This can't be for real.

The size of the raptor was fearsome. He raised his paddle in scant defense, hands sweaty, slipping on the paddle grips. There was no place to go except into the water and he didn't have time to untie himself from the kayak. For a split second he peered into the emotionless stare of the predator's eyes and knew how it felt to be prey.

Adrenaline flooded his system, time gearing down, slowing to a crawl.

Wood splintered the air.
He cried out as talons crushed into his chest.
Blood sprayed the kayak and the waters of Masset Inlet.

Red gore and bile cascaded up the human's throat as he went limp. Raven lifted both man and canoe skyward, claws ripping the canoe's skirt away from the dangling body, letting the unfamiliar vessel tumble to the sea. No canoe he'd ever seen had such a skirt, but people of the Far North had craft called kayaks, with similar skirts on them. Was this a fellow from the northern tribes? If so, what was he doing here?

He made a large turn over the inlet, shook the figure once. His talons had accurately penetrated lungs and heart, and another rain of red peppered the calm blue-gray surface beneath. Certain the human was dead, Raven released him. As the body hit the water, he noticed for the first time that the male, his face and hands, were extremely pale of skin, not the darker husky hue of the Haida.

Lungs pierced, the corpse sank below the waves into the arms of those living beneath its waves. He was theirs now, in the realm of the Kushtakas, the sea otter people.

Weariness seared his wings as Raven headed back towards the Golden Spruce. He glided most of the way, each stroke from those enormous wings a huge effort. Tired, why was he so tired? With a thump, branch groaning under him, he settled on a cedar by the river's edge, closed his eyes and struggled to change back to his true self. Slowly, the feathers of the eagle flushed to black and the majestic white plumage on his head shimmered and darkened. Razor talons and mighty wings shrunk until he was himself again. *So hard*, he yawned as weariness sucked at his consciousness.

Raven's eyelids fluttered as he fought to stay awake. He'd been in limbo for so long, perhaps that had made him weak. Weak and hungry, but then again, he was always hungry. It was his curse in life to have an unending appetite.

I need sleep first, he thought as he steadied himself on the cedar limb, he sniffed the air again. Something was definitely different, not right, though he still didn't know what it was. Surely things couldn't have changed that much since he'd last walked this land? How long had it been?

He wasn't used to tiring so easily. The shape changing had taken much energy from him, too much. This would have been as easy as picking ghals from the beach before. Hmmm. Delectable blue mussels and clams, preferably cooked over someone's open fire, preferably stolen from that person, since Raven didn't know how to cook. In fact, he feared fire. Smart things, the humans he'd created. How much smarter had they become since his entrapment? Not crafty enough to out-think me, he thought with a smile as he dozed off dreaming of juicy clams and other delicacies, cooking in a pot over a hot flame.

Freed from his body Prince Kiidkayaas floated in wisps of mist and light above the carnage. This was his soul essence. Was he dead?

His heart had landed with an unpalatable splat in the secure bough of a great cedar. Golden spruce needles had rained down covering the heart like a warm blanket, hiding it from Raven's gluttonous hunger and keeping it from drying out. One last act of protection from the dead Golden Spruce? If Raven had devoured his heart before his soul could be released, he'd be part of Raven now and his life ended. Kiidkayaas sent a mental 'thank you' to the great tree spirit for saving his life.

The prince stared at the scene below: the tree cut down, his body soaking back into the soil. What had happened? His body wasn't real flesh and blood, but was composed matter from the spirit of the spruce tree. Someone or something must have released him and Raven from their arboreal imprisonment.

Weary of fighting, Kiidkayaas stared heavenward; he wanted only to go to the land of his ancestors, to join the rest of his kind. His people ... what had become of his people? He'd been unsuccessful in his quest to save his village and that could only mean one thing. He continued to gaze upward, troubled, as his heart dissolved, merging into the sanctity of the wood, back into the earth that had spawned him.

Where were his people? If he was truly dead now, he would soon find out during his journey to the afterlife. Feeling a tug from below, he feared already that it was too late. As he tried to lift himself from the clearing, he saw the tenuous threads of spirit, of <u>waangaay</u>, reaching up anchoring themselves to his heart.

First one, then another, and another ... the threads wound around his soul. Tugging, pulling him down. It was indeed too late.

As his heart dissipated, Prince Kiidkayaas tried to scream but couldn't of course. He had no mouth.

He swirled down, dragged into the confines of the great cedar spirit all around him as memories of his old life, his old ways pulled at his sight like the pitch of coal tar shimmering on moonless nights, gloom in its most insidious foulness. Blackness of no substance, no energy, no being, sucked at Kiidkayaas as he sank into its unknown depths. The life as the favored prince of the southern Haida, the totems lining the beach that spoke of family lineages, how they used to terrify him as a child, now little but memories. He dreamed of winters snug within the longhouses, pungent smoke curling up through their center holes. Rain, always raining, drumming on the roofs while his people feasted on the gathered summer's bounty. Most of all, he dreamed of the potlatches and the ceremonials.

The dances, the songs and the spirits came together during those cool, wet months. Spirits, drawn to the din, hiding in the corners until the dancers could draw them out. Chanting endlessly, until the spirits possessed the writhing bodies. There, as here, the air was unmoving and thick with spirits. Somehow, he knew this was where he was now. In their realm, where they normally lived, in the darkness. In the spirit world.

Memories of his former life, of his way of existence, cowered in this sea of dark reality. He knew this wasn't the afterlife, otherwise his ancestors would have been here to greet him. The warrior-born turned. Nothing above, below, or in front of him. No earth, the mother that nourished him, which his body would someday return to. Nothing. Complete and utter nothing.

Ethereal winds howled past, reminiscent of eagles' chants. A hawk's cry died on the stillness.

He closed his eyes and allowed his mind to quiet in its panic. He no longer bore the body of a prince, but his spirit still reeked of dignity, of fearlessness, of pride. His soul stole at the solitude. He closed himself to senses that held no use here and curled within. Until he simply quit being and just was as ethereal winds evoked sadness peeling through unending canyons of ebony. Kiidkayaas floated and bobbed along, a seed borne on harsh winds. This way, that, on the whisper of worlds adrift in interstellar currents. Pulling at him, tearing, transforming. Finally crumbling, like bones baked to dust under a sun's brutal gaze. Fingers of breeze tore at each sundered section and stole away. Scattered, flung into the sea of dark nothingness. Somewhere a tear floated. A dream, gone. All that remained of what once was, washed into the ether.

****

The sun rose higher in the sky, Kiidkayaas stirred awake.

Awake? How long had I been out?

Sun's energy stimulating him like a tonic that spread from his needles down through his trunk into his roots.

Roots, leaves?

It hit him. The Golden Spruce saved me. I am now part of the earth, transformed.

He felt the solid strength, the pride of solidity, the thickness of his skin. *No bark*. Birds twittered from his high branches while insects crawled among his bark, feeding themselves, and worms oozed through the dirt, wiggling past his roots.

Splatters of water startled him as a cloud burst its rain overhead. Refreshing, liquid beads of life ran down his branches or dripped from the tips of his needles to settle in a circle of moisture, absorbing into the soil where the ends of his roots lay. Content at last. If he retained a mouth, it would be smiling a most satisfied smile.

Nothing mattered here; even time was a memory. Simple solitude and serenity, the calmest peace he'd ever enjoyed settled down into the chambers of his soul.

Born of stillness, connected to the spirits of the sky and the earth.

He touched both, knew both, felt both circulating around him. He could no longer see with his eyes, since he had none, yet he saw in other ways.

In the shifting of the clouds overhead, of the winds that bore the sghaana giidas. In the world as it moved, the approaching season, the ascent and descent of the sun. So many new things out there that he'd never truly experienced before, yet for now, none of that mattered.

Kiidkayaas soaked in the reverent worship of the awakening sun's energy. Invigorating, stimulating. Every day the same satisfying sensations tingled every nerve and limb he possessed. What a glorious way to live.

But this morning something odd happened.

Was this what woke me up from many years of slumber?

It was not caused by a passing breeze or the landing touch of a bird. What had grazed by him he could only describe as conscious matter? Or at least, whatever had flittered past had the same tenuous characteristics as a thought. A different kind of thought to those he'd had before, but wasn't all thought the same? All he knew for sure was that this entity of thought, of consciousness, wasn't his.

He knew the direction. It came from below. But from what and from where? Again, it happened again. At this very moment, he felt it once more.

Gone now. Something had been there, just then, dancing away quickly. Was this another new sense, one he'd never had before? Had this been happening regularly, but he hadn't noticed it until now?

Kiidkayaas crowded all of his remaining senses, his rationality, what remained in this form, into his roots. He had many parts, and he realized that the individual parts of him at the tips of his roots all perceived reality in exactly the same way. He drew himself up into his spine, and once again, something whizzed by. It was easier to detect that time. The essence resembled a current of intangible water flowing through the ground, as if the earth was a river of transportation. He, though, it was he who was in every root tendril. Thousands of him, all connected, all part of one. If this was conscious perception, then others were out there.

Kiidkayaas pulled all that there was of his mind back up the trunk into his needles. Thriving on the tingling energy, gorging himself, he forced himself downwards in a burst of concentration. This time, one of his parts slipped through the soft root endings and kept descending until it encountered hard bedrock. He anchored himself there.

Something insubstantial streamed by in the inky darkness. Startled, he shot himself upward, back into his roots. How could he describe it? It wasn't him, but it was like him.

Did other bits of him exist? Or were there others, like him, out there? Through every sense he possessed, Kiidkayaas stared all around. His strength was too diluted right now; he had to concentrate on absorbing the sun's energy. He'd ponder this later, when the sun settled down for the day. When he would shut down his limbs and withdraw his consciousness down into the bowels of his roots, content in the sensation of being fed. As close to sleep as he used to experience it.

But for now his roots tingled as first one, then another, then more and more of these logical ruminations, as he called them, whipped by. He remained still, curious as to why he hadn't noticed them until today. These weren't spirit beings. They were different. Like that thing that had floated by when he was attached to the bedrock. Like bits of him, drifting along. Was it simply that he was aware of them now, couldn't perceive them before, hadn't the capability?

He reached down into the soil. Water leached from the surface, oozed past him. He could feel the intake of minerals seeping in from his root tips. The ground, the dirt was part of him. The soil he was pulling life from, he realized, was ancient remnants of him, horribly ancient bits of him.

Once this soil had been trees, like him. Now changed, altered, becoming him, another tree, the circle of life. Other forms of flesh and bark, dozens, millions. This was in essence another river of immaterial existence.

Life, but not any kind of life he knew now. Who was it? What?

He slipped into the soil, only a small portion of him. It was easy to do, this way. Other sections of him slipped through the ends of his roots. Just then the ticklish sensations of the others slipped by. Kiidkayaas grabbed onto them and sped off, attaching himself and wrapping himself around their embrace. Together they flew through the earth, their thoughts becoming his and his theirs. Stunned realization made Kiidkayaas let go.

It made sense, he knew now.

****

It was morning once again. Kiidkayaas felt himself being drawn upwards into his branches again. He looked all around in disbelief as the sun warmed them and dried the dew from his bark. Sheer happiness sank in.

He was no longer alone. Millions of others were out there, like him, or at least similar to him. Everywhere. A great crowd of him. If he could have smiled, he would.

The life energy of the sun extended farther than his needles and bark, though. It reached into the very ground. Spread across the earth, it was bits of him, of others. At last Kiidkayaas had begun to understand this new sense of his. Untold millions, all trees, all like him, all connected to their brethren by the remains of the ancient ones, the ones that were alive on the earth once. Now they were the soul on the surface of the planet, coating it like a skin, alive but not alive. Alive, breathing, and his to gain sustenance from.

The ancient ones were feeding him.

Also they were his to travel. These pathways, all connected, all belonging to and composing the creature called earth. All at peace.

In the darkness memories of riding Raven came back and how he got to be here trapped in the Golden Spruce for hundreds of years. He listened from one of the cedars as the tourists and the guide talked about the event, his memory hazy still.

"So, Prince Kiidkayaas of Sghaan Gway set out on a quest to find a shaman who could cure his people of the mysterious sickness." One of the tourists asked as they loaded back into the boats that got them here.

"In a place called Ttannu where many had already died, as I mentioned he met a man called Kungii of the Raven clan who said that the shaman, Kteilta, had left the village to head north for Llaanas in search of the shaman and sorceror, Xatsinoo. In exchange for food Kungii would lead the prince to this powerful shaman. But during the journey Kiidkayaas and his slave Wago tricked Kungii into revealing his true identity to the slave and the prince: Kungii was in fact Raven, the great transformer and trickster. After a great struggle during which Raven, with his sharp talons, wounded the prince grievously, Kiidkayaas managed to reach in and steal Raven's immortal stone, which as I have said sat at the back of his throat. Now, you see, the wily prince could force Raven to take him to find the shaman, Xatsinoo, the only one who had the power to cure his people."

The memories came back to him of flying on Raven's back ...

Flying with Kiidkayaas astride him, Raven watched a drop of blood spin away into the clouds and guessed the prince's sides were still bleeding where his claws had pierced him. He could bide his time until Kiidkayaas lost consciousness, but already his wings grew weary under such weight. And besides, that would be too easy. After all, Raven had a better plan, one that wouldn't involve carrying such a heavy burden on his back. A fate a little more fitting for an arrogant prince who had outsmarted Raven and dared to threaten his life.

Snow began to flutter around them, and the prince's knife tightened against Raven's throat. "Where do we fly to, Raven? I grow tired of this game."

"Patience, dear prince. You know that we are bound for Llaanas. There lives the shaman and sorceror, Xatsinoo. As I explained, the shaman you sought, Kteilta, was heading north to find Xatsinoo, only I fear he may have been struck by the same illness that has plagued Ttannu."

A hacking cough came from the prince. "Yes, I remember what you told me about Xatsinoo. Now hurry. I tire of your prattling, and I am cold from this snow that is falling."

Raven clicked his beak in satisfaction. The snow he had called down was weakening Kiidkayaas, disorienting him. "Indeed, the snow becomes thicker. The north suffers many snowstorms, but we must hope this one is not too bad. You are after all dressed for the south. Hide among my feathers and they will help to keep you warm. I would fly faster if we could stop to eat."

The prince hesitated before he gave his shivered response. "No landing now. Keep flying. You'll eat when we meet this shaman, this sorcerer, whatever he may be. Not before."

Raven smiled at the slur of Kiidkayaas' voice. Soon the snow swirled until they could barely see in front of them, but at last he tucked his wings in and landed. Winds howled around them as they set down in snow that reached up to their calves, at what looked like the head of a valley.

"I see no village. This had better not be another one of your tricks," Kiidkayaas said as he dismounted, his skin blue from the cold.

"Ah, but you must be careful, dear prince. Xatsinoo has a spell in place to hide his village, and if you look for it you will become cursed."

"Spell, no." Kiidkayaas shook his head, which Raven guessed would be getting foggy from the numbness and the loss of blood. "What now, Raven?"

Raven eyed the leather pouch around the prince's neck. He was sure the boy had tucked his immortal stone in there. "You will need to cover your clothing, as a southern prince would not be welcome here. And these will give you some protection against the cold." He moved to a rock and produced a fur cloak, a headdress, and a pair of moccasins.

As the prince donned the offered clothes, thankful for protection from the biting chill. Raven slipped the skin of an old man over his feathers, transforming himself. Then Kiidkayaas stopped as he spied Raven glaring at his pouch, which he'd lain on the ground when his numb fingers struggled to fasten the heavy cloak. He snatched the pouch up and placed it back around his neck.

Raven shifted his glare to the prince. "We shall approach Llaanas on foot, so as not to arouse any suspicion. Tell anyone who asks that I am your grandfather."

He turned and began to strut towards the village. The snow had already started to drift, and before long the prince was lagging behind.

"Wait," he cried, "I can't keep up to you. My legs are stiff and refuse to bend."

Finally, Kiidkayaas looked over Raven's shoulder. As he did so, the raging snowstorm suddenly diminished, but instead of any village called Llaanas, he saw ahead only the waters of the Yakoun River.

He faced Raven, knife in hand. "There is no village. You have tricked me." He grimaced in obvious pain.

"Ah, brave prince, you should not have looked so hard. There is a village here and now you will have a very long time to look for it."

"What?" He tried to move and realized he couldn't. "What is happening to me?" He looked down at his feet. Tiny roots were spreading beneath them, anchoring him to the earth.

Raven cawed. "I have tricked you at last, foolish prince. The spell is not in looking for the village. That would be too obvious. It is instead in the moccasins."

"E-i-i!" Kiidkayaas screamed his agony. He couldn't pull his feet from the moccasins as the roots had begun to grow up into his soles and into his flesh. His skin was taking on a mottled woody hue, reconstructing his flesh from the ground up into bark, blood gelling into sap, slowing his mind. Pain transcended pain as his body thickened.

Raven flung his human skin aside, transforming back into himself. He plucked the pouch from the paralyzed prince's neck and quickly swallowed the stone that he found there.

"Safe," he crowed at the doomed warrior. "No one out-tricks Raven. I would have helped you, prince. Helped you to find the only shaman who could cure your people. But you are far too arrogant for your own good. A little time spent thinking about such behavior will perhaps teach you a lesson."

Kiidkayaas stayed silent as the wood converted nearly his whole body. Just as bark was forming over his visage and he was nearly consumed into the tree, he slowly stuck out his tongue. Nestled in the crevice of his mouth was Raven's lapis lazuli stone.

"It is not I that is so foolish, Raven. I too can play tricks. Turn me back to what I was." The words came out with great effort as the bark grew over his face.

"No!" Raven screamed and spat the fake immortal stone from his mouth. He looked up but it was too late to reverse the spell he had cast on the prince. The spruce tree he'd created had nearly petrified the prince and the immortal stone.

Raven had doomed himself to die.

He leapt for the small space where Kiidkayaas's face remained and flew inside the spruce. The trunk bulged outward for a moment before solidifying again, black feathers fluttering to the snow, adorning the ground. Only the voice of the snowstorm whistled through the forest and across the waters of the Yakoun River.

"That summer, the spruce tree containing Raven and Prince Kiidkayaas sprouted golden needles. All who could sense such things knew a great sadness emanated from the Golden Spruce tree." Tom smiled at his audience of paying tourists. "The same Golden Spruce Tree, recently cut down on the Northern Island."

****

Kiidkayaas seeped his essence through his roots, trying something different this time. Each part of him that oozed into the muck stayed separate and began to travel, moving apart then contracting, pulsing like a heartbeat. Venturing out farther each time, wanting to know his limits. On every contraction every bit of him returned. Perhaps there were no limits.

In the meantime others went streaming by, all flowing like a river in one direction, past him. A piece of him joined the flow, allowing him to be swept up in the ethereal energy. He contracted again.

Again, many parts of him joined the stream, the flow. To where? Or was there a destination? Was it a journey with an end, or just an experience to be shared communally? He continued, enjoying traveling with the others, until it became serene, meditative.

Other parts of Kiidkayaas expanded out even farther, some encountering the roots of other trees. Many he recognized as being cedar like him, but several were foreign. Different species, he guessed.

The ones that were cedar interested Kiidkayaas. Cedar, he realized now, was what he'd been drawn back into after being released from the Golden Spruce tree. His prison for so long, yet comforting, familiar; a sanctuary, a home. It was the Golden Spruce that had knowingly used a cedar to save his life after Raven had torn out his heart.

He circled around the tiniest root tendrils. The ends were open, like his. Did he dare? Could he enter another tree, another being?

He sent one of his parts into the root and upwards it flowed. He stared up the shaft ... it was open to him. The host came down, and they communicated without voice. One of the senses he'd not understood until now. The other's language was more basic than his, its thoughts simple and clear. But then, this being had never been Haida, never been other than a tree, and this was fine. Still, he felt friendship, no other feelings, no hurt, no sorrow. Only peace, a gentle peace. Contagious, infectious, all around him. He sensed the other trees would be the same as this one, creatures of simple serenity.

Thanking his host, Kiidkayaas contracted again, returning home to the cedar tree that held his spirit.

****

One part of Kiidkayaas stopped on his journeys through the earth which he loved so much to do. Something wasn't quite right. He'd joined the stream of thought with all the millions of others as he had on his last couple of expansions. Many he couldn't communicate with, but the cedars' thoughts were so close to his he could comprehend them. As for the other beings: trees, animals, ghosts – he wasn't sure what they all were – in this river of harmony, Kiidkayaas simply enjoyed their presence. Perhaps later he could begin to understand them.

Each time he felt more comfortable flowing farther than before. Until the surges of ethereal life bypassed an area, tingles from the cedars shivering him to stay away. He stopped on the edge of the flow, the rest of the entities curving around him. There were no physical boundaries before him, only an absence of life. Yet none of the others dared to venture forward. Curious, Kiidkayaas moved ahead anyway.

The others continued past; they did not come to where he was as he inched into this new space. An area where no thought traversed, where no flow happened. A vast field, devoid, erased of life. Only silence whistled to him, like death dirges amongst gravestones.

He looked up. Roots. Here, there were roots like every other place he'd visited. Except these appeared different. He peered closer, examined one of the trees. It was cedar like him, and the ends of its roots were open, or more accurately, frozen.

In a scream of never-ending agony. An unanswered wail of terrified silence. Urged to flee, instead he moved cautiously up the roots into the stem, terror translating into every atom, crying. Escape! Run!

> Instead of the tall runway of the trunk, he stared skyward into stars. The rest of this tree was gone, cut off. Its heart, its essence, torn away.

Only a scream, on lips that didn't exist, went on forever.

Kiidkayaas flowed out of the dead cedar and swam about the empty field. If he'd had hands, he'd use them to cover his senses. Abject screaming penetrated through every cell of his matter. No wonder no one came in here.

The next time he expanded outward even farther and found more, tens of thousands, perhaps millions, in these vacua. The whistling madness was too much, too hard to set aside, too hard to find a place of peace within.

Only massive, callous destruction could cause this.

Kiidkayaas contracted, and on his next expansion he too refused to travel the dead zones of frozen screams, where the haunting visions of terrified tendrils shrieking on and on stayed with him. Instead, he avoided them and continued flowing along as the rest did, becoming one, enjoying the serenity, the meditative calm. Yet every time he had to swerve or felt the constriction of funneling into bottlenecks where the others refused to flow, Kiidkayaas felt a twinge of regret, and of guilt. The earth could and would rebuild itself. Seeds would eventually sprout and begin new life, absorbing decay. Was there nothing he could do? Perhaps having a greater consciousness wasn't such a gift after all.

****

In the morning Kiidkayaas expanded outward again. Near the edge of another bottleneck, he stopped. A cedar on the fringes of a zone of frozen screams caught his attention, as the serenity in its roots replaced by shrill screaming. This one was still alive, but in terror. He had to put aside his own terror and find out what was causing this madness and put a stop to it. The heart of a warrior born called out to him and the prince swam up into the roots, shrieking vibrating everywhere. He wanted so much to comfort, to console. He moved up the great vein and a terrible shudder ran through the tree. The host ... where was the host?

Another tremor, even greater than the first, scared him. Heavier vibrations shook the cedar. What was happening? An earthquake?

Finally, Kiidkayaas spotted the mind of this tree. It sat huddled, petrified amongst its needles, seeking to do the impossible and escape into the nether space through the very tips of its branches, as far away from the source of its demise, too terrified to attempt to flee via its roots. He moved closer to the tree spirit, the quaking easing, another shudder ran rampant through this once serene creature, which screeched an agonizing cry of death as a crack blistered the wooden skin. Kiidkayaas streamed towards the roots. He had to leave this tree, before it was too late. The stem split away and hovered momentarily in the grip of space, the connection to earth and life severed.

No escape now.

Fleeting death, unthinkable to beings who measured breaths in decades, entire seasons in seconds, struck like a lightning blast. Kiidkayaas wailed, as he had heard so many others wail in the dead zones and shrilled in frozen terror as the cedar crashed to the ground, taking this part of Kiidkayaas' soul into death's dark dimension.

Kiidkayaas contracted. Several of his own branches shuddered and dozens of boughs paled, needles falling away. He knew now why the ones in the dead zone were so terrified. But what had scared them? What caused the vibrations? What could cleave these trees into two? He trembled. What if this were to happen to him?

No, he had to put a stop to this. This was not natural, nor was it the way to end his life. Whatever these were they caused the dead zones, he knew it.

He wanted to age, to feel the bark thicken on his surface until it got too heavy to bear. Wanted to collapse into the forest and return to earth's cycle, only to spring up and begin the whole process again.

He expanded once more until he reached the cedar he'd just been trapped inside. Staring up at the roots, he saw the part of himself that had died trying to escape, locked in the horror of his own demise. Keening in its agony, sundered from the chain of life, no voice to shriek its pain. Already other trees nearby bore grimaces of screaming silence.

Kiidkayaas swam to the nearest living tree and went inside; up its roots he swam and into the trunk. From the topmost branches he spied the cause of this destruction.

Creatures with round feet and metallic bodies. Pale-skinned humans, versions of the way he once was, stalked the woods. In their hands growled beasts of metal with teeth like a shark's, the voice of a grizzly bear and the voracious appetite of raven himself. The pale-skinned humans merely touched the boxy creatures to the tree's surface and the caterwaul of a dozen mountain lions in battle shook the earth with the fury of Thunderbird himself. Bits of bark ripped into the sky like snowflakes in a violent blizzard. In seconds, the box beasts with their voracious appetite had bitten deep into the heart of each tree. Another bite on the other side and another casualty fell, its back broken. These tribe people did not take the time to have a ceremony, thank the tree for its life, giving the being within time to leave, as his people did before they used the tree for building a canoe or totem. No, carelessly they slaughtered the defenseless without regard for the carnage ravaged on the life-forms within.

One approached the still-living cedar that contained Kiidkayaas. He bent to his task, concentrating on his work, and the familiar violent shudders returned as the box with teeth ripped its way into the trunk. Kiidkayaas looked down. A thick, high branch jutted out below him in a direct line over the logger's head, already splintered along its surface, threatening to break away.

Shunting his fear aside, with all of his might he concentrated on the limb. He knew what he must do.

A groan escaped him. A cry of pain. More splinters appeared on the branch. A crack shattered the air. Kiidkayaas bellowed in agony and triumph.

The logger looked up.

Killing part of what he was, Kiidkayaas tore part of his essence from himself.

The man screamed with nearly the same terror as his victims had displayed as the limb broke away from the cedar above him.

Earthward crashed the huge branch, slamming into the ground with a sickening crunch. A mist of red sprayed the mortally damaged tree, the air, and littered the forest floor with its gruesome coating. The metal box creature grew silent, falling away from lifeless fingers.

NO.
Shattered the serenity of the earth.
NO.

Came from everywhere at the same time and Kiidkayaas was yanked from the cedar by some powerful, invisible force. He struggled but it was no use ... he was locked in a grip of iron. Whatever held him was far stronger than he was.

When Kiidkayaas contracted, that part of him didn't return. He trembled, fearing something was wrong.

Really wrong.

Kiidkayaas slammed into the bedrock. He struggled to rise, but something held him in an inescapable grip.

YOU HAVE CONTRAVENED THE BASIC LAW OF EXISTENCE.

Echoes from everywhere. "I was defending myself. Trying to save others," he thought to whatever was out there.

NO. THAT IS NOT ALLOWED.

"Why?"

BECAUSE YOU ARE A TREE. THAT IS THE WAY OF YOUR EXISTENCE. THAT SHALL BE THE WAY OF YOUR

EXISTENCE UNTIL YOU RETURN TO THE EARTH, TO BEGIN AGAIN.

A light penetrated the darkness, revealing shapes ... huge, incredibly old beings shouldering out of the inky background. He was in a cathedral of lofty trees, surrounded by them. Just around them circled the revolving flow of the river of energy and thought, where he swam so often.

These were the very ancient ones, the oldest trees on the planet. They towered into the sky. Trunks thicker than he could ever imagine floated into his vision: a giant stunted sequoia, some looming redwoods, massive cedars, stout firs and gnarled, sturdy spruces.

Combined, they spoke again in a common voice. WE ARE THE ESSENCE OF DIDA CWAA NANG QAARUNS.

The essence of the spirit being who travels up in the woods.

YOU BROKE ONE OF THE BASIC LAWS OF EXISTENCE. A TREE CANNOT SAVE ITSELF, NOR OTHERS. IT IS ONLY A TREE.

THE SAME AS ONE OF US. WE ALL MUST DIE SOME TIME, IN ORDER TO RETURN TO THE EARTH, THE MOTHER OF US ALL. TO BE REBORN AGAIN AND CONTINUE THE CYCLE. OUR ONLY RECOURSE IS TO RETURN YOU TO THE FLOW OF THE EARTH, TO BE REBORN.

"Wait," Kiidkayaas thought defending himself. "Yes, I, too, was reborn with Raven when the Golden Spruce was felled. I was once a Haida, a warrior, but no more. I was not reborn as a prince of my people; I've evolved into something different. So I am more than a tree. I've talked to many of the others, but they do not reason. They do not think. They exist only as trees, to be fed in the morning by the sun's light and rest at night, content, in harmony with the earth and the flow of life and peace. I am not like that! I think. I retain that from my former life. Like it or not, I am more than a tree."

For the first time in eons, dissension broke the ranks. Mumbled comments flew back and forth.

IT IS DECIDED. YOU ARE UNIQUE. YOU ARE MUCH MORE THAN A TREE. MUCH LIKE US, YET YOU CANNOT BE ALLOWED TO RUN AMOK. YOU ARE YOUNG, NAÏVE AND SPONTANEOUS. WE WILL BE WATCHFUL OF YOUR DEVELOPMENT AND WILL ASSIST IN YOUR UPBRINGING.

Kiidkayaas screamed as he began to spin around, whirling down a siphon, into the darkness that he knew all too well.

The sun rose over the crest of the mountaintops, kissing a new day, its light penetrating the darkness cast by a forest of green. Deeper, ever deeper, until the low-growing foliage surrendered to its warm touch.

The ground shuddered as something beneath the surface moved. Life roiled, unfolded, and sprouted. A cedar bud, so much like him, opened its first shoots to the giver of life, the sun. A newborn. He felt his essence funneling down into it.

All around this new cedar tree birth circled an incredible crowd of other, very old trees. So it would be: they would teach him, show him what they knew and keep him within their protection and watchful eye. At the same time, they formed a jailed enclosure all around him. He could still stream across the earth at night, as before. Yet knowing whatever he did, they would be there, watching. They now had the ability to stop him instantly.

He couldn't conquer the elders.

Why would he want to fight? To remain a warrior, an old part of him cried, answering his own question. That essence was still there, that warrior pride of being Haida. But he couldn't fight them all.

For now, he was satisfied to rest and observe, to let the sun feed his being and his new soul. Every night and morning, Kiidkayaas returned to the cathedral to watch himself, this new part of his being. This part being reborn. He felt protective, like a father to a son. These were the only words he could use to express what the elders had said. This new part of him, his son and himself, were one and the same. His son, the cedar bud, grew, apart and yet connected to him. As were the elders. As were all things. Connected to the universe.

Content for now, Kiidkayaas relaxed and enjoyed the ebb and flow of life. But under the gaze of watchful, benevolent eyes, the silent tendrils of confinement suffocated.

****

Curiosity driven, a part of Kiidkayaas travelled to Sghaan Gway, his old village. He rose past the roots, into the trunk of a cedar, and looked around.

Nothing.

He darted from one tree to another.

Nothing. The bay, the rocks, the feel of the soil, all were the same. There, near the beach, stood a group of weathered remains. Trees, silvered from the constant leaching of sun and rain.

No, totems. The poles of his ancestors, capped with ferns and mosses. The one in the center he recognized. His father's totem, standing before the spot where his father's longhouse once stood. Now only fragments amid grass and tall cedars.

His father's pole that told of his great potlatch. It stood with four others, some askew, all worn, faded, returning to the earth they had sprung from. Wind whistling through the mortuary boxes. The village, his people, all gone. The shaman Sayaayuhl had been right; his vision had come true. Kiidkayaas turned to leave and spied another totem, upright but nearly buried in the woods. He moved closer. This one he had never seen before. It hadn't been erected before he became trapped in the Golden Spruce. Half-finished, clumsy looking, hewn in a hurry, it bore only two figures. Carved from the cedar was the image of a human, his hands around Raven's neck. Raven's claws dug into the human's sides.

Eyes of death and desperation adorned the human. Familiar eyes. Raven's eyes glared, contemplating the human's fate. Raven, gloating.

Prince Kiidkayaas felt his gaze being drawn back to the human's eyes.

Why did they seem so familiar?

His eyes. The human was him. The him that no longer remained. He stared blankly at the totem, searching within himself for something he no longer possessed, for emotions that formed no part of him any longer, beyond his grasp, relegated to an earlier incarnation. The village, his former life, all seemed so distant, so inconsequential and forgotten. Gone to the circle of life. What good is a prince without a people? Where have they gone and what has happened to them? Spirit winds howled by, under the earth, past the roots. Calling.

Beneath roots anchored to the earth, the mother of us all. *They are very strong here.*

A whisper broke their constant murmur. Kiidkayaas listened for a moment, distracted from the scene before him. Again. An odd whisper of something different that he'd never heard before.

Other sounds broke the background buzz. Calling.

Another whisper and inside where there should have been no feelings, no remorse, a prick touched his soul and he bled.

A part of Kiidkayaas didn't return as it flowed to the edges of the smallest of the roots. He listened, searching for that whisper again.

Father?

Kiidkayaas slipped past the others and settled down in the whistling region of the screaming silence. He had to think, *how to find my people? I know I am no longer human, but my soul is still tied to those that were my family.* The dead zone of logged trees, where so many still screamed their pain and horror to the earth. Here, there was no one to watch him, no one to spy on him. Here, as thousands wailed in open-rooted horror, he was alone.

Shutting out their voices.

The multiple being known as Dida Cwaa Nang Qaaruns could read his every thought and did. Yet the reverse was also true. Perhaps Dida Cwaa Nang Qaaruns didn't realize that Kiidkayaas could read all of their thoughts, or that he knew eventually he would mature and become part of this incredible multifaceted spirit. That in itself was a great honor.

While studying Dida Cwaa Nang Qaaruns, Kiidkayaas had learned much about the universe and how earth's connection to it worked. He had also discovered that this ostentatious creature, too, had broken the natural laws of the universe. And not once, but on several occasions. One of those occasions had created the rare Golden Spruce tree that eventually Kiidkayaas had become. This was something that Dida Cwaa Nang Qaaruns had not expected, but when the natural law is broken, unnatural things happen and hence that led to my creation. *Was this done on purpose?*

Kiidkayaas contracted and pulled all of himself back in. *It is time to evolve once more if I am to find and help my people. I sense this is the path I must take to make this happen. To become one like the Dida*

Cwaa Nang Qaaruns or a familiar to them. Then I can't be under their control and I can somehow help my kind.

It was time, like the seasons to evolve once again. He stilled his soul and if he could, took in a deep breath and let serenity of the earth seep into him.

Allowing ethereal gusts to howl past, reminiscent of eagles' chants. A hawk's cry died on the stillness. The warrior-born closed his eyes allowing his mind to quiet in its panic. He no longer bore the body of a prince, which now seemed like a former imprisonment. But still bore its fighting soul.

There were others, many others in this peaceful darkness. Memories of a former life, of his way of existence, cowered, shrinking away in this sea of dark firmament.

What he was or was becoming? The prince didn't know, except that he knew he wasn't dead. No body but a spirit that still reeked of dignity, of fearlessness, and of pride.

The mother earth that nourished him in ways he couldn't even begin to comprehend. So hard to focus, he closed off senses that held no use here, yet there were new ones instead?

Was this evolution?

He simply quit being and just was, his soul stole at the solitude, allowing prevailing winds to peel him through unending canyons of ebony. Floating, bobbing along; a seed of aura borne away on harsh breezes.

This way, that, the whisper of worlds adrift in interstellar currents, pulling at him. Evoking sadness, tearing, until, like bones baked to dust under a sun's brutal gaze, he finally crumbled. Fingers of draft tore at each sundered section and stole them away. Scattered, flung into the sea of dark nothingness. Somewhere a tear floated, before being whisked away.

A dream, gone.

All that remained of what once was, washed into ether, once again.

Forming anew.

There is no death,

> *Only a change of worlds.*
> *Seattle [Seatlh] (1786-1866)*
> *Suqhamish Chief*

A Scratch In Time Saves Nine

On this cool spring night, Medbh stepped out into the dim moonlight and dug a hole in the earth to relieve herself, when a loud boom erupted from the clearing, she had left. Silicone webbing exploded over the nest the others slept in, curled around each other to keep warm. Two other booms sundered the dark. Bress, the large dominant male of the pack, let out a large roar, disturbed at something interrupting his sleep. He spotted the lone Hu-man clad in a protective suit several feet away. Beside him, two Pit Hybrids snarled, ready to protect their master. Bress immediately launched into attack mode and hurled himself at Derek without thinking. The Hu-man commanded the canines to stay and took aim at Bress as he thundered towards him, snarling his rage.

The females of the harem tried to escape the entanglement of the ropes as Derek aimed at the slavering feline with the massive lion Esque head and pumped two shots into its chest. Blood and spirit sprayed heavenward and the massive male collapsed dead to the ground, skidding towards the man, tongue hanging out.

"Gotcha! You'll make a splendid trophy. The others will make for a splendid enjoyment before I skin them." He fired darts at all nine of the females and they collapsed in drug spasms, quickly succumbing to its effects. All except one.

Arianna, my love, and, like me, first born, staggered up onto wobbly legs, fighting off the effects of the tranquilizer darts. She proceeded to tear apart the net restraining them. "You can't do this! We are the dominant rulers of this world."

Derek smiled at her and pumped another tranquilizer into her. "Not anymore. The United Planets Council has decreed that you are declassified as a barely intelligent and very aggressive feline species and may be hunted. I have one of the first licenses. This world is greatly needed for its natural resources and any wildlife considered dangerous must be wiped out in order to protect the investors."

Arianna snarled, collapsing, fading from reality. The rest had succumbed to the drugs as he grabbed his plastic twist ties and began securing their hands and feet together before the effects wore off. "You I will leave for last."

He flipped Arianna over, grasping her heavy breasts in his hands. *Breasts I loved to nuzzle against at night as we made love.*

"God, the others, they are right! You are soft and delicious. I'll have many an evening of pleasure before your head joins the others."

Medbh stood in shock, wetting herself again in fear, hearing everything he said and wanting to attack him, but unable to move in complete shock and the knowledge that either his weapons or the Pit Hybrids would easily defeat her. How many nights had she and Arianna made sweet love to each other? Bress let the women in his harem pleasure each other before mating. It aroused him and the others wanted to be in his den willingly because of that.

The Hu-man took out his large laser cutting knife, sheared Bress' head away from his body and tossed the bloody head onto his floating land-speeder craft that hovered in the air behind him. "Your head will make a fine trophy for me to brag about to the guys."

She bent over, silently sobbing. She wanted to attack and tear into this man. She was one of the few that had their ancestor's warrior blood like Arianna. She wanted to come to the attack, but knew now was not the right time, as she stared at the weak thin claws on her paws and knew to do so would have her end up like the others or torn to shreds by the canines. Gritting her teeth she slunk into the woods. Ancestral memories began to whisper inside her head. She had to regain her ancestor's abilities; abilities that had been stripped away many generations before, but which now she could have again.

Medbh ran back to her ancestral grave grounds. She knew what she had to do. Memories ran through her head from very many generations ago of savage warrior females ruling the world. In their calm moments they realised that the uncontrollable bloodlust would cause their extinction and it was decided to splice their DNA with that of the more docile males. Only the druids and the mystics at the time went too far with their DNA transfer spells and over generations the once-docile males became larger and somewhat aggressive, and the females became timid beings made only to simply forage, supply babies and give pleasure to the Lord of the den.

Medbh, running in fear and anger, felt the need for vengeance growing stronger inside, urging her to release the spell. Through the trees she tore, leaves whipping at her face, the memories of what she had just witnessed spurring her on. She knew that she alone had to get her love back. That is all that mattered. That and revenge.

Dawn was breaking when she finally reached the ancient burial grounds of the ancestors, and she collapsed, near exhaustion. All around the remains of the warrior queens lay. She cried out, releasing her misery into the sacred earth, and it answered, energising the instilled memories and...

A spell began to recite in her head. This was etched into the blood memory of the first-born females of the packs, as she and Arianna were, in case they were ever required again. The terrible events of this night had been the trigger.

Medbh began to source all of the herbs that had been purposely grown around the grounds and she sat to light a fire. The flames' heat lit up the darkness, taking away the cold, as she spread the needed herbs in front of her. She scratched the historic sacred symbols on her arms, deeper ones over and under each breast, drawing the life-giving milk which mingled with her blood and dripped into the fire, igniting it further. She put the two most sacred symbols of the ancient Ogham druidic language onto each virtually hairless cheek of her face.

The final herb, Nepeta Cataria, she sprinkled around her. The drug-like fumes, so compelling to her species, pulled her deeper into a trance, and she threw the last handful deep into the fire, calling out to her ancestors to fulfill her need. As if answering the call flames erupted and smoke quickly filled the night air, flooding her and the clearing in thick waves of ancient mists. Shapes began to shift in the heat and haze and she breathed in deeply inhaling the fumes of the ancestors, clouding her vision further.

From the misty fog several figures emerged. Clan members of generations past.

"I am Morrigu, the Warrior Queen. You have called for vengeance on those who would abuse and slaughter our kind."

Behind her others stood, muscular arms crossed, all females.

"She, Arianna, is my love, my heart. She means everything to me."

Medbh explained what happened. How the interlopers to their world had abducted the love of her life and declared the Lycran unfit to live to rule or even dwell on this world.

"If it is vengeance you seek, it is vengeance you'll get."

"Inhale our spirits' essence into your soul."

Medbh inhaled deeply, allowing the spirits to enter her lungs and being. Electric sparks erupted all over her sleek furry skin. Hairs began to grow and thicken, harden, becoming nearly armor-like. Claws lengthened into sharp talons and her ears elongated. Fangs grew and eyes enlarged and wounds earned in battle after winning over their enemies etched into her legs and arms. She felt herself growing in height and she knew she was becoming a warrior female like the ones in the smoke. She breathed deeply again, awakening to the new sounds and smells by virtue of her enhanced senses; noises of squirrels scratching up a tree, a bird's wings beating in the air high above came to her ears; ears that once were used to alert their species to the slightest sounds of danger when on the prowl. Nostrils flared at the new smells, the sweat off a bee working pollen from flowers, pine exploding into the warmth of the morning sun's heat. She opened her eyes catching glimpses of dust floating across the field and of ants scurrying to their home. She ran her hands along her thighs, revelling in the muscular feel, and her tongue licked at salty lips and sharp fangs. All her battle instincts were sharpened.

"You will need the weapons we once possessed to defeat this one. They are near here in our crypt, buried with the remains of our clan."

She rose effortlessly and spread a green blanket of leaves, damp from the morning dew, over the fire, extinguishing it. "Time to retrieve our weapons to begin the hunt to reclaim our dominance."

Medbh let out a high-pitched caterwaul to the sky and tore off on all-fours running to the stone cairn faster than she ever had, relishing the fluid muscles, the memory of Arianna driving her on.

The next night she scouted around the artificial plasticised structure the Hu-man had erected in the clearing. The two large Pit Hybrids slumbered atop of a skin, licking at it like it was sweet chocolate.

With her acute vision she didn't need to get too close. The smell of the Hybrids made her grit her teeth in anger. Through the windows of the strange dwelling she spied Bress' head, already set on the wall, together with that of Oceana, one of the harem. She flexed her now-mighty talons in rage. She knew the Hu-man had a defensive shield around the building and to try and break in would be a massive undertaking, especially with the guard dogs outside. So he would have to come to her.

The canines seemed to doze off, their bellies distended from gorging on the meat that once was encased in the skin they licked at. The markings she knew. It was, or had been, Oceana. A red mist seared her eyes as she gripped her sword. She deftly moved over to the floating land-speeder he had taken the bodies of her clan away in.

Medbh charged the ionic shield of her ancestors and arced a blast of light at the vessel.

It exploded in flames.

"What the...!" she heard from inside the building.

Instantly lifting their heads the Pit Hybrids sensed her presence and spotted her; they charged like Bress had yesterday, thundering towards her snarling in rage. She stood her ground and drew another of her ionic swords from the leather weapons holster over her back. They leapt at her and in midair she slashed at both, searing them in half, as Derek ran outside in time to catch his pets gasping their last breaths as flashes of sparks highlighted Medbh.

"What have you done? Who are you? You will die horribly for this damage, vicious bitch. This expedition has cost me nearly my life savings."

With the door to the building open she inhaled deeply, the others were still alive and, by the scents, Arianna as well.

"You have no right, they are mine now. I claimed them by hunting rights." He flicked a switch and his protective suit surrounded him in a blue glow. Another switch commanded a small hyper-scooter to float out to him.

Medbh ran off as Derek approached the bloody remains of his canines.

"I'll get you for this! Do you know how much these two cost me? The best money can buy, bred for viciousness and hunting abilities." He mounted the hyper-scooter and tore after her, knowing the base was safe as he turned on its force-field. "Now you will be mine."

He tore after her at full speed down the trail.

Nearly two kilometers later he caught up to her. Or rather, she slowed to allow him to.

He fired from his hand-held laser. Medbh spun around, dodging the beams, and, retrieving a spear from her holster, flung it at him. It wedged in the mechanics of the craft causing it to come to a grinding halt, skidding harmlessly to the ground.

She approached cautiously as Derek struggled to free himself from the wreckage. "You hunt us not for meat or sustenance, but for your sport and sexual pleasures. Or worse, purely for a trophy to hang on your wall." She snarled in rage.

"Yeah, that is my right. I paid a lot to be here and take great pleasure in the thrill of the chase and the rewards after." He licked his lips vilely at the sight of such a great catch as her.

"Then I shall take great pleasure in the thrill of the chase as well and in the end, of your head adorning my sword."

"What? You cannot do that! It isn't right, it is inhuman and against our constitution." He flinched, showing some fear for the first time.

"I am Lycran and yes, I will take great pleasure in mounting your head and displaying it to the rest of your kind, as you would in doing the same to my kind."

"Over my dead body! You'll be my biggest trophy. Go to hell!" He raised his laser and fired at her.

She twirled and let the blasts ring off her shield, reflecting the beams back at her enemy. He screamed in pain as the beam returned and penetrated his force-field, searing his hand, melting the pistol into it.

"Bitch!" He tried to stem the flow of blood, picking bits of metal and flesh from his hand, screaming in agony.

She sniffed the air. "You smell of fear, prey. Now my hunt begins."

Derek's eyes widened, knowing he had to get back to the base where he was safe, and in order to get more weapons to come after her, cursing that he had brought only the one laser gun and a small semi-automatic pistol, which he knew now would not penetrate her shield. "I will return and hunt you down. I don't give up!"

"Neither do I!"

The blue aura of shielding still glowed around him. Medbh, knowing that without being able to use his own laser weapon against him as she just had, decided to retreat. To think. Her sword alone would not penetrate the force-field. She backed into the forest and watched him scuttling off to his base, nursing his wounded hand.

Medbh snarled and sniffed deeply. She tore through the forest, her claws clicking on the cool earth, mind working feverishly.

Earth! Of course! Got it.

She ran ahead, skirting around him, and found a large, mainly-rotted log that had fallen across the trail. She tore into it, crawled inside and waited.

Several minutes later he came to the large log blocking the trail and went to step over it. As he did talons raked easily upwards through the rotten wood, rendering his flesh, and tore at the controls on his arm. The blue shimmer around him flickered out. His protective shield didn't surround him entirely or it would sever his connection to the earth and he wouldn't be able to travel on it.

He grabbed the small pistol and fired back at the log. Medbh had already crawled out and slunk away into the forest. "Damn it, she's fast." Bloodstain flooded downwards over his chest.

"Now the hunt truly begins." She licked her long tongue over her fangs, relishing the battle. *This is what it once was like for my ancestors.* Voices whispered back from inside; "*yes*".

Derek ran down the trail as fast as he could, panic clenching at his heart and mind.

She came out of nowhere again and ripped her claws across his face. He screamed in agony and fear and fired at her again. Only, like before, she was gone, and the bullets merely tore apart leaves and branches.

He slowed, taking the time to watch all around him.

From above she fell like a silent blanket of snow and tore open his back. His vest fell away held on only by his arms. "You can't do this! It violates a dozen civil codes of the United Planets Council."

"I can and I will! Your Council has no powers over me. You have violated my race and will pay the price."

He spun, firing everywhere, hoping to get her.

She appeared, standing proud and defiant, about ten feet in front of him, eyes of fiery rage staring at him. She put down her shield and crossed her arms, pulling two swords out of her holster. He aimed at her, firing volley after volley. With stunning speed she flicked each shot away with her swords until a loud click filled the distance between them.

Click, click, CLICK.

"Damn! Empty!" He went to pull another clip free, too late, as she strode forward and slashed him side to side across his legs with her ancestral swords.

Unable to stand with muscles cut away, Derek collapsed forward to the ground. She slammed her clawed foot into his back and lifted his head.

"Please!" he begged.

"I give you the same mercy you gave Bress." Her sword ripped across his throat and she pulled his head away.

The rest of his body went still as the vapors of his life's soul rose from him. Medbh inhaled and drew his soul into her lungs. "I add your being to mine, and now I go to get that which means the most to me; my Arianna."

When she got back to his cabin, the shield was off, its power source depleted. It didn't take long to find the others, still restrained with ties, locked up in cages. She guessed some would have been sent away to be sold on markets; for what purpose she dared not explore.

Medbh used her swords to smash the locks and slashed away the plastic restraints, releasing them all.

"You're free, and safe. I have triumphed."

Arianna stared at her in surprise. "Medbh?" She recognized the voice, but not the muscular being before her.

"Hope you like my new look!" she said, as they all walked outside the enclosure. She wanted to destroy it, but would come back later to learn more of these Hu-mans before doing so. The others of the harem all sobbed at Bress' head on the wall and they took it down. He would be buried with respect later.

Arianna took her aside as they did. "What happened? I heard voices and saw visions in my head, mentioning the old ways of our race, but I was helpless."

"When I ran away the old memories came to me. We knew a long time ago that if we continued in our warlike ways we'd have decimated our people and our world. So the mystics perfected a solution that reduced us to what we are today, docile, loving beings. Only some were nervous of us being without defences, so they perfected a potion and injected into some of the first-borns, to run through the generations into each of their first-borns, like you and me. If ever needed, the knowledge would awaken and allow us to call the ancestors to us."

"Like now, as a defence mechanism."

"Yes, protecting us if needed and called upon."

Arianna eyed her up. "You're even sexier as a Warrior Queen," Arianna said, and leaned over to kiss her. "My heroine."

"I will repeat the regrowth ceremony on you, and any other first-born females of our race who have received the calling. Many ancestors reside in me, and we will begin the process of bringing our true Lycran selves back in order to seek our return as rulers of this world. And I am aware, somehow, that this can be only a temporary state of being, should I wish it. It is like an armor or weapon that I can don if need be. I am able to shift back to the old Medbh whenever I want."

"I kinda like the warrior. Now let's reclaim our heritage and our rights to our world."

In Calleigh's Arms

In the cold of the night, I remember... as old fingers of frost etch their way across windows scratching at ghosts of memories gone by.

As I enter into Calleigh's arms once again my life now spreads beyond any realms I have ever encountered or dreamed of.

Birch wood crackles in the fire as I enter her realm again.

"I'll have a Merlot." Years cascade by dragging me down memories roads as her voice, a ghostly visage of the woman I met on our first innocent date, disappears into dreamtime. I learned recently how Celtic Wiccans seduce their desired partners through bewitching incantations of the Cailleach through their eyes.

Sipping wine, becoming the fly trapped within her web once more.

To dream, a chance to live those heady days again in forgotten realms where life is magic and magic... was... unknown.

Her voice pulls me back to us. Naïve, innocent. There were no heroes here. Only victims bound by enchantments. Ones that can never be let go.

We talked endlessly, her hands warm in mine. Synergies transforming, me, us, falling into enchantments that unknowingly existed, hers by carving. I am the prey.

We lived decades together. I suspected nothing, until she told me as she lay dying. Her hands now cold, gone to the earth to reclaim her.

Cailleach spirits, I learned, go to dwell in recluse in Gaia, while their physical shells return into the all-encompassing earth. Further strengthening their hold on our world.

Bastards.

Earlier I cried tears outside that crystalize on frigid earth in the dead of winter, waiting for the release of springs calling.

True love or spell bound trickery? After her passing this realm, I began to research the how and why this is happening.

Again, cold fingers etch across glass, threatening to enter what was once our house. I sit before the flames, silence reigns supreme.

In remorse she begs for me to join her. I cry, I cannot, not yet, my dear. Each sip of red takes me back there to the time of her eyes. The touch of her soft lips. Skin on velvet skin, caressing the memories of us naked in orgasmic splendor.

All I have to live for now is without you, without my heart. My sundered soul lives with her in the cold earth as hers is without mine.

A spell like a double-edged sword can be enacted by both and I made sure that without myself, she cannot go to whatever lands the Celtic Wiccan spirits go to.

One day, my love, one day. If you remain mine, as I did with you. The true test of love begins.

I smile, raising the glass of Merlot, to her picture on the mantle toasting the memories of that first date. Chilled glass rents electricity in my hand while outside hers caresses frigid panes to a time, long ago and memories of us dancing in cosmic lights to the rhythm of the Earth's heartbeat in her arms.

303 JEN

Time's recollections flitter like butterflies alighting from fields of sun-cast flowers as I stop before an apartment building staring as snapshots of a life like Kodak moments blur by, one after another.

I've been here before.

Two children and ... good God! ... my wife.

303.

The building is empty, plywood covers windows. A sign proclaims it's to be torn down as part of the city's revitalization plan to become a parking lot for the new shopping mall being built. The main door is barred.

I walk around to the back. Snatches of memories that I can't quite grasp haunt me.

Did I live ...? Not possible. I'd not seen this street, let alone this building, before today. Yet, I drove here, why?

The rear door is locked. I look around in the empty parking lot. The gray sky threatens the usual rain in Vancouver's wet winters. I walk to two faded yellow lines and stand where I used to park my car.

A Ford; red.

How did I know that?

303.

The faded numbers on the parking stall conjure more reminiscences. I met my wife living here, we had two kids.

The sweet scent of antifreeze and old tar assails me. At my feet a green stain remains, dried like blood. I changed that car's water pump here.

A white panel van pulls up marked Ministry of Transport. Two men get out ignoring me entering the building. Minutes later they come out carrying boxes, loading them into the van.

Why would Transport want to have anything to do with a closed building? I wait until they disappear inside and decide to enter behind them. Boxes lay stacked in the entryway, stickers marking them as building number and apartment number. All marked Ministry of Transportation.

The two enter the elevator. Instinctively I head for the stairs and walk up two flights.

Dropping laundry with my kids, laughing, I've done this before wearing a tee-shirt proclaiming "Nazareth Live", a rock band from Scotland.

A girl whirls around in my head. Blonde, curvy. Her name? Can't recall.

I gasped. We were married. I stare at my bare ring finger. Old indents in the skin speak of truth and vows of unending love. *'Til death do us part*. I walk straight to the door I entered thousands of times before.

#303.

I'm dreaming this, I have to be. This is crazy.

A red paint stain on the apartment's entrance. I smile. *This is no dream*. Touching the red stain, recollections of my struggle to get a red couch in the door and dropping it. The couch we watched TV and made love on. With a deep sigh I walk in.

Four crush marks in the living room indicate where the red couch once was. In the bedroom boxes fill nearly half the room.

A dismantled bed frame made of ornate wood haunts at me. Its memory burned into my mind with each night of pleasure we had.

I tear open taped boxes. Clothes, my clothes, tumble out. Books I've read and forgotten. A chess set with a rook missing. I search for its replacement, a miniature Darth Vader. "Luke, you've been checkmated," I used to say in a deep wheeze.

A lifetime flooding back. Our daughter's first screams, playing Frisbee with my family in the park and vacations in Mexico. A life, my life. It's all here.

But how? I currently live alone in a condo.

"Excuse me, you shouldn't be here." One of the men in the white coveralls speaks. I didn't hear them enter.

"Yes, this building and its contents are private property of the Ministry."

"No, this is my stuff and this is, or was, my apartment."

They pass knowing glances. One pulls a computer from his pocket and punches 303 into its database.

"Name?"

"James McFadden."

"Birthdate?"

"Current Social Registry number?"

"8412 578 0347."

"It's him. Sign here."

Too nonchalantly he hands over the pad. He's done this before, many times.

"Signature matches file," bleeps back the computer.

"You can take the stuff, it's yours. The building will be torn down in two weeks. You have until then to remove it."

Just like that they leave me and return to their job. No explanations, no 'hey what the hell just happened?' Only myself left holding boxes of memories in an empty apartment. My life given back to me, one that I didn't know existed nor lost.

Numb, the next day I return with a rented truck, fill it, and drive to my condo, numbered strangely 303. I've lived here for two years, according to the mortgage papers. Before then?

How is this possible?

The weekend is spent laughing and crying as I unpack old possessions; my teak statue of Buddha, holding what my wife said was a skateboard and half an avocado. Inside subtle fragrances of incense cones persist recalling nights of passion. Jenny comes to me.

This doesn't make sense of any kind. How do I forget an entire lifetime? Like I'd awakened one morning and had it all wiped out.

Could the Government have done this? Some sort of amnesia program. Or maybe I'd been crop dusted on the way to my car one morning with some kind of hallucinogenic drugs .

And the most nagging question of all, where is my wife? My Jenny?

God, I miss her now.

My journals. I used to write everything down; funny, still do.

Frantically I begin to pull boxes apart. They must be here. A heavy carton yields my journals. I sort them and look for the most recent.

Notes two years ago describing the chaos from people wandering around like they've got Alzheimer's, forgetting things. Where they live, how to drive a car even. Websites, I'd jotted down several stating the effects from radiation and radio signal interference from cellphone use and other electronics. Site after site I check no longer exists. All covered up, is this a conspiracy against the world-wide web or some kind of brainwashing?

That afternoon my buzzer rings. Two men from the Ministry stand outside. "We believe you have questions that need answers. Come with us."

I quietly enter the van, wanting answers. A stab of pain throbs across my head as I try to use my cellphone. "Bloody things, someone told me they give you brain cancer."

"Yeah, I was told they're just under microwave radiation strength, can fry your brain just like eggs." He laughs and I ease up, realizing it's just two guys doing their job and I wasn't the first one they had to find. The innocuous sign in front of a building proclaims, 'Ministry of Transport'.

I'd seen such signs never paying attention to them around town.

We enter and a lady approaches. "Come with me."

After hours of reading files on my past life I look up at the lady. "Why are you telling me all of this so freely? And all I really want to know is where are my wife and kids?"

"I'm not authorized to release that information, but I can get you someone who is."

I stare at her fearing, yet wanting, her answer as her cellphone rings.

"It's for you," she says, passes it to me and presses a button. I put the phone to my ear and listen to a white buzzing noise for a few seconds before everything goes blank.

The next day I answer my buzzer and stare at a blonde lady glaring at me. "My name is Jenny McFadden or at least was." Something about her I find exciting. She extends her hand. The touch of her skin is electrifying. We've touched intimately before.

"You may find this crazy, but I had memories the last few nights. Of you and of us. Living in an apartment building on the east side with two kids."

I blink in shock, like something out of a fantasy. Except for one small detail. "Lady, I have no idea who you are."

"You must remember. James, we loved each other so much."

I blink as vague memories flutter and two men wearing white overalls enter the hall.

"Damn, I gotta go. Here's my number, call me."

I watch her drive away as a white van marked Ministry of Transport follows. Tears streak her face, reminding me of a woman I knew with blonde hair. *Jennifer.* I stare down at the card before putting it into my pocket.

The two men in white ask me questions about her. I tell them the truth, don't know.

"Just a second." He dials it into his cellphone and chats to someone for a few seconds.

"Here, my supervisor's got a couple of questions for you."

I listen to a white buzzing noise.

Fresh black tar stings my nose as I glare at the precise yellow lines in the new parking lot for customers enjoying mindless shopping at the new mall. I stare around standing in the void where an apartment building once stood until recently.

Why did I come here? I pull my car keys out and find a crumpled piece of paper with a phone number I don't remember getting.

A touch of a beautiful blonde woman. Intense, electrifying. Is that her number? As I get in my car I stare at the license plate; 303 JEN. Memories come flooding back.

Life's Ruts

Tears streak down my face as I struggle awake to stop the incessant beeping. "Just a horrible dream," I tell myself. I reach to feel the comforting warmth of my still-sleeping wife before rising. Blood red neon informs me it is five-o-eight, July second. The day after Canada's birthday.

I grab my bathrobe and do what I've done a million times before: wash my face, brush my teeth, go downstairs, put the water on for tea, feed the cat, turn on the computer to see the news of the day, stock reports and sports.

Familiar patterns of my daily life, worn deep in my mind like ruts, I do without conscious thought; unable, without great effort, to get out of them.

My first conscious effort is to remind myself it's Monday and I haul the garbage outside. I have a shower, get dressed, prepare lunch, usually a sandwich, some fruit and a tin of soup.

I take my wife tea in bed (yes, I spoil her, but she's English and it's one treat she really loves) and a kiss, "I love you" I say, the horrible dream fading into the void and I leave for work.

So many of us fall into these familiar patterns. Some call them ruts but that makes them sound unwanted. There's something comforting about them that we need, otherwise we'd go crazy, overwhelmed with too much to remember, too much to think of. Like learning to drive a car for the first time. Some incidences do jar us out of them, back to feeling fully awake. It could be something good, like a much-needed holiday, more often it would be the opposite; losing your job, getting divorced or the death of someone dear. My dream, now nearly forgotten, pokes back at me as the engine catches.

The set patterns idea hammers at my mind. The 'what-next' in my life. What am I doing here? Chaos without order. Am I going nuts? My mind is racing, so many thoughts tumbling in.

At a red light I look for a CD and realize I've done this so many mornings, so many times. Ruts.

A large semi-truck pulls up behind me in the slow lane. I know a newer red GMC SUV will pass me in the fast lane, bearing a middle aged man, like myself, drinking coffee whilst driving. I don't, my wife says it's dangerous. She's right.

It does and he is.

"KEB 178," I yell out his plate number as he passes and I am correct. All morning I begin to predict things, randomly, as they pop into my head. This isn't about ruts or patterns. This is about insanity. Have I become clairvoyant? Psychic? At lunch I go to the lottery terminal and pick six numbers for tomorrow's draw. I know I'll win millions, yet it doesn't matter.

Suddenly nothing matters, only the dream.

I check in to see a psychiatrist later in the week. "I'm getting these flashes, insights."

"Yes?" he mutters, seemingly uninterested. "Flashes of what, light? Religious visions?"

"No, more like knowledge. I've been predicting things all day long. I know ahead of time the customers that come into work unexpectedly and who's on the other end of the phone before I answer it. I knew a red SUV would pass me on the highway and his license plate number. At Starbucks I knew the male server would spill coffee on himself. I entered the lottery and won all the numbers, I'm rich beyond belief. I know the numbers of the upcoming lotteries. I know the result of tonight's CFL football game, BC 17, Edmonton 33."

"Interesting", he mutters, almost to himself. "Hang on a second."

He delves in some papers on his bookshelf and brings out a magazine.

"I've recently read an article from a group called IONS, Institute OF Noetic Sciences," he throws the magazine on the desk but I do not pick it up "that prove people can tune into others thought, pickup their partner's wavelength, know what they're thinking. Or strangers even. They can do things like predict who the next phone call will be. This in part explains why there've been many people that get visions of impending disasters. Maybe you're getting in tune to everything around you," he says as he taps his pen to his forehead.

I want to take it and ram it up his nose. This is so much more than picking up a few stray thoughts, and it doesn't explain the bad dreams.

"I know you don't believe me. Write this down and I'll come back on Monday." I give the lottery numbers for three different draws on Saturday. "Do you watch sports?"

"Yeah, baseball and Formula One racing."

I close my eyes and concentrate. "Raikkonen will win, Scott Speed will crash in the twenty-ninth lap. New York Yankees will beat Toronto. The Cubs will squeak by the Red Sox." I've seen it all from newspapers in my mind, like I've read them before.

He jots it all down. "Check with my secretary, but I think we're booked a few weeks ahead."

"After this weekend, you'll believe me. We'll talk again on Monday." I left. I could tell by the look on his face that he thought I was a borderline basket case.

I sit in the park in silence. They say meditation is good for the soul, quietens the mind. Only parts of the dream returns and I've visions that I've tried to give all my lottery winnings to the starving of Africa, the Save The Rare Spotted Toad Society, worked for SPCA, and Salvation Army. I've dedicated my life to religious orders, become devout Christian, Buddhist, Atheist, Communist. Lived a life full of peace and free love in a hippy commune in San Francisco. Made sure I've not killed a single creature, let the mosquitoes have their fill of me until they could barely fly away, bloated and red bellied, "Have a nice life and say 'hi' to your kids," I wince in pin-cushioned pain, watching my arm swell.

All the religious gurus, theologians, spiritual Dalai Lamas claim that we were put on this earth to learn lessons and until we get it, we don't move on. Returning time and again. What is there I've done wrong or haven't learned? Have I done this before? Am I reborn? Reincarnated?

Visions strike me of other extremes; being a good law-abiding citizen didn't help, lives consumed with debauchery, alcohol, drugs, fulfilling every kinky fantasy possible, hired dozens of hookers. Even snapped and went on a murdering spree, ended up in jail and letting the men have their way with me.

And always the horrible dream returns. But through it all there is only one thing I haven't been able to do, haven't tried.

I see him again the next week.

"Amazing! All your lottery numbers and sport scores were correct. You've become some kind of clairvoyant in tune with whatever is happening out there. Astounding! You could become filthy rich or save lives. So, tell me, what are next week's lotto numbers?" he asks.

"I'm already filthy rich. I predicted the winning numbers in the thirty-six million lottery. I'll bet you didn't believe me and never bought any tickets."

He purses his lips. I know my answer. I stare at the hands of the clock calmly ticking away, while my mind screams at the well-established repeating ruts.

"I can't see past Friday," I sob into my hands. "I can only see to the end of next week. Nothing past that. I know everything that happens these two weeks, but no further. And I can't shut it off. So much flooding in."

"There was also a case of a man in Russia that remembered everything, every little detail. He went nuts before he became eighteen." He prescribes some psychosomatic drugs. "These are mild, but they will calm your mind and relax you. Next week we'll begin testing for other factors, possible schizophrenia or go for a CT scan. I've heard of brain tumors or aneurysms causing strange things. I think we need to check deeper into what's happening in your brain."

"Thanks, doc." I crumple the prescription into the garbage as I leave the elevator. He is of no use. The dream will return again, I know it.

Unable to bear any more I do the one thing that I've feared I couldn't ever do. I book a flight on Lufthansa airlines, bound for Germany. I know that it will go down over the Atlantic at 10:20 AM July 14th, the last day of my visions. 'No survivors' claims the papers.

An explosion tears apart one of the fuel tanks as we cross the midway point of the Atlantic. Jet fuel spews upward, flames roar to life. The air masks deploy and I struggle to put it on as the dream comes back to me.

I turn off my alarm clock. July second. I begin to cry.

A-Hunting We Will Go

Sherida opened her eyes. She was alone in a large cellar. She remembered her instructor telling her group in the first minutes of her training, 'expect the unexpected' was the golden first rule. Immediately two explosions ripped through the walls of her classroom and her instructor grenaded into a fireball of flames. Three of the trainees burst into tears and collapsed into helpless bundles. Some stood shocked, and a couple beside Sherida surveyed the surroundings and dove into action, either propping desks up or grabbing whatever they could to defend themselves. Sherida and the two others progressed to the next level as the virtual images faded away and her instructor stood there grinning. The others were sent home.

'Always be aware and wary' became the byline of the three. Memories of those days flooded in as claggy earth called to her from the dark as she began her first training mission on her own. Above wooden boards creaked as if something prowled. The souls of the former trees shrieked their demise above her head. She closed her eyes, trying to focus. *Distractions.*

Thousands of grubs, worms, Millipedes, no longer living in the displaced earth, removed to form this cellar cried from the pits of their souls. An overwhelming cacophony of anger, death and HOW DARE YOU? Flooded her senses.

Three words, humanistic.

A plod of a footstep, behind her.

Another, closer.

A cuff upside the head before she could react.

HOW DARE YOU?

Again, hammered at her senses.

It was spiritual, not alive. Thorough the intense natural voices of the once living entities in this dark dank place, she got it. Not her objective.

Something just outside the perimeter of this place and the earthen walls; something stalked her.

Only this wasn't human. *This was the creature I was here for.*

She willed herself away from the enticement of the trapped spirit. That wasn't her mission here, just a delusional distraction meant to make her fail.

She stood on the warm alive earth just outside the lone hut. She scanned the bushes with her cyber implants. A shadow moved thorough the brush. It was night anyways, but she picked up the large feline stalking her. She closed down some of her sensory array as the noises of birds, grubs began to overwhelm again. The heat sync of the creature wavered and vanished. What?

Sherida glared around. It had the ability to alter its perception field. Hence a very dangerous predator, one rarely seen or taken on this planet. Far more deadly than the Leercat from her home world.

From her left something lunged at her. Sherida spun away, blood spurting along her side and it was gone.

Damn, she rolled into a crouch, adjusted her perception filters. It stalked around her like a Velusian Boxer, waiting to lunge in again after the mandatory eight count or just testing the mettle of its opponent.

She leaped forward somersaulting and swung an open fisted blow at it. A sneer from the black furred cat as she caught it off guard. Slitted yellow eyes opened in an insidious glare as she caught it just below the throat.

Rage hissed in a half gurgle, startled at being touched. More used to being the one doing the attacking.

Sherida spun around again aiming a kick to its head. Empty air answered.

It had moved in a heartbeat.

Claws raced along her other side. The first slash had already begun to heal itself. Only her abilities could heal so many wounds; did it know these cuts would slow down her attacking abilities?

The creature sneered as the smell of hot blood filled the air and it continued to pace around her.

Yes, it knew. I wasn't the first one here to do this.

No wonder it was so dangerous and the last test before graduating from the ranks.

Still many failed, many died. She only had to touch the small disc in her left palm to return her back to the craft orbiting the outer shell of this world. Only that meant failure.

She lashed at it with her laser embedded in her right palm.

It blinked and was beside her. Sherida spun away catching it in the gut. Claws lanced out and slashed away at the laser. Sparks flew and she tried firing again. The creature gleamed evilly at her as mere sizzles answered her request.

It also learns very fast.

The beast retreated and began to slowly regain its composure, breathing deeply.

Good, gives me time to heal. Already the wounds on the left side had stopped bleeding and had scabbed over. The right side had nearly done the same.

Just as she thought that the black-furred creature leaped at her. Sherida jumped aside. Long rakish claws tore down her left side again. Reopening her wounds.

It's playing with me, teasing me and it can read my thoughts. Evil bastard.

The creature growled in return. Hungry for more it ran towards her.

"Play with this." She opened her right palm and a blast of white light hit it full in the eyes. Sherida hammered the blinded cat over the skull and tore off into the woods.

She needed time to think how to defeat this feline. Her objective wasn't to overcome the creature, but to retrieve a crystal from a monument located a few kilometers from her touchdown point. Still, she had been warned there would be opposition to overcome. Now she knew how many never made it past this last phase of training. One wrong move would probably cost her life.

After minutes of running her radar told her it was just ahead. Gaining quickly, she knew the cat was approaching from behind. If needed she would kill the carnivore, but she would rather not. She sensed the cat wouldn't have the same compulsions. What was worse than a killer, was one that toyed with its prey. She ran through her memory banks on the known inhabitants of this world. Only one entry said anything about the rare Panthess. A black feline that mercilessly hunted down all it fed on. One man's journal entry told about being chased for days, losing blood and skin with each attack, until he had nothing left. Even then his final journal entry was that it sat there watching him, with one functioning arm and both legs crippled as he wrote his last words into his journal. The journal survived, judging by the reports of the meager bits of flesh they found, his remains never to be found after he became dinner.

Sherida gritted her teeth as she ran. Even with her augmented muscles the feline was circling in front of her. Almost too late she sensed it ejecting from the dense brush; a swipe along her arm and her implanted return switch tore away. Blood streamed down her arm. *He was making sure I didn't escape. I had about three hours until the ship would move to pick me up. This hunt was to the end.*

It ripped another strip down her back and savagely licked at the moist blood, tasting her. Then spun away. Sherida collapsed, trying to quickly repair herself, but the damage was intense. She struggled to get to one knee. Everything spinning.

It ran in for the kill and instead swatted her aside. *It's toying with me.* She tried to focus and pretended to collapse. Blood everywhere, the beast unable to control its hunger dove to her. The smell driving it on.

She swung around and slammed into its groin, the beast howled in agony and fell to the ground. *You should have killed me when you had the chance.* One of the things she learned in training; don't hold back it may cost you your life in return.

Sherida got up and ran to the base of a large fern that looked like an overgrown fungus. All around the tree lay birds and rodents flopping like they were drunk. She collapsed and slowly began to climb up out of the cat's reach. Her vision began to blur. The smell intoxicating. She shut down all of her olfactory glands.

The creature slunk into the glade. It walked with a slow limp, obviously in pain and growled in her direction, but didn't approach.

Safe for now she closed her eyes and let her equipment take over.

Sherida closed her eyes. Blood covered her body and dripped down the main stem of the tree. Below the Panthess slowly circled.

She didn't know why he hadn't torn her out of the branches and finished her off. *Was it simply toying with me, teasing me some more with torture? Or was there another reason?*

Sheer volumes of pain tore at her mind. *Okay, beta blockers kick in.* She felt her agony begin to subside.

Now, she scanned her memory banks. The new implanted technology within her began to take over and repair her vitals.

Or are you simply waiting until I heal and wanting to toy and torture me some more?

Her olfactory glands were being shut down automatically. *Why?*

'Highly hallucinogenic substance in the immediate atmosphere' fed back in her brain in response to her question.

My bio-mechanisms were protecting me, shutting down my nostrils, as well as heal me. Okay then, what is this tree and the hallucinogenic substance? 'Genus undiagnosed, but similar to a Polyphyletic Fungus. The vapors given off perform aphrodisiac and hallucinogenic qualities, similar in composition to Psilocybin, baeocystin, psilocin and also contains trace elements of Lysergic acid diethylamide only direct inhalation is 300% percent stronger than the mere smelling or taking of the drug'. *Okay, explains why the Panthess is still circling me. I'm sitting in what is commonly called a giant magic mushroom tree that is laced with LSD. That is why it hesitates to attack and most likely will wait until I climb out of this overgrown fungus. Once the creatures mark or begin tracking their prey they use their olfactory senses nearly exclusively. That combined with the ability to read an opponent's thoughts, make them nearly impossible to capture or kill. Okay, shut down my olfactory senses completely and flush any signs of residue hallucinogens from my system.* 'System healed 58% major muscle groups 90%. Basic functions 80%. Flushing of hallucinogens will take three minutes longer.'

Sherida could feel the buzz beginning to leave her mind. *I can't completely hide my thoughts, unless. Can I get a subconscious filter activated?*

'Searching data base, filters active, but for limited time of fifty-eight seconds.' *Just enough time to rig something up for my furry friend.* She tore her shirt from her body and grabbed several of the softer branches, crushing them until the juices soaked into her shirt.

The cat growled loudly and began increasing its pace, obviously sensing or knowing she was up something. *It can't read my mind, but it knows my body is repairing itself.*

Sherida closed her eyes and let her mind go blank. 'Filters are beginning to erode, including olfactory blockers.'

He ain't going to wait for me to heal completely and the beta blockers will kick out soon as well. If I don't make my move now he'll know what I'm up to.

Sherida wrapped up the squishy mess, already her olfactory senses were beginning to fail. Her outer senses were being overcome. *It's bright outside. So before I begin to talk to little animals on tree stumps.*

Sherida leapt from the tree and screamed out, "The only mistake you made is not killing me. So. I'm coming for you."

She ran straight for the beast. One hand behind her back, catching the normally aggressive cat off balance. It was expecting her to flee.

Puzzled the creature paused, unsure of what to do.

"Okay party time, furball." She took one stride closer and flung the wet mass directly into its face. It opened its jaws in rage as heavens exploded and gasping voluminous odors cascaded down its throat and nose. Eyes stinging in acidic agony, it swatted the shirt away and stared at all manner of beasts and winged serpents descending towards it. The beast swatted at empty air, full rage at being cornered by all manner of demons attacking it.

"Unlike you, I go for the throat first. I don't aim to toy with you, nor allow you to be tortured more than needed. I only want to live." Already the sky began to shimmer in iridescent colors. *Crap, I'm getting stoned as well.*

She spun around, the beast only saw a whirling dervish descending in a twirl as her leg crushed his midsection. A fist hammered down, a crack echoed away in the spinning corridors of its brain as Sherida splintered its jaw. One long fang broke away spinning in the air.

All the cat saw was termites screaming, as they swarmed by the millions towards it. Their jaws clacking in hunger, it tried scratching away in terror. Sherida lunged forward catching the fang and in one deft move she drove it deep into the feline's heart. Blood exploded outward, the creature gasped once, took a step back and slumped to the ground. It gasped again as trees bobbed in fury to a heaven-sent storm and fairies hummed an evil song.

Sherida watched the last breath leave the large cat and it collapsed, dead. She stepped back several feet, before releasing her breath.

Inhaling, she saw turtles swimming through blue clouds of soft wool and doves singing to the glory of the sun.

She collapsed shuddering and slept, dreaming of simpler times.

When she awoke to the distant rumble of thunder that her senses told her it was real and not some delusion brought on by the drugs, Sherida scrambled to dig a hole in the soft earth with the broken talon. As the first dribbles began to filter through the trees in the small clearing she patted the soil over the covered animal. Before she thrust the talon at the beasts head as a grave marker she carved a symbol on her shoulder. A talisman tattoo carved from something of the defeated enemy and worn eternally to remember her defeated enemy and hold its power within her, a tradition on her world.

"You should have killed me when you had the chance."

Sherida rose and checked her timer, in ten more minutes the awaiting ship would beam her back up. She raced to the monument and grabbed the crystal on top of it as she heard the growl of another Pathess crack the splatters of her tears and the planets rain somewhere in the background. Only softer in tone. "Looks like someone isn't getting their other half to cozy up with tonight and has begun to look for them."

Her body began to shimmer.

Book Spirits Flowing To Mombasa

"Namdi,will the pump run?" asked nine-year-old Titombe Oduwaze, looking up from the boxes of books he was unloading. Yesterday, the only generator in his village quit working. Sweat poured down his dark face in rivulets. Titombe had already helped Namdi, his teacher, unpack more books than he had ever seen in his life.

Their village, a poor one on the southern border of Kenya, had raised funds to build a library, but had no money left to buy books. Yesterday, a gift from a faraway country called Canada had arrived; boxes and boxes of books, enough to fill their library and more.

Titombe didn't know much of the world outside his village, but he knew Namdi had gone overseas for awhile to another country called England to play soccer and get learnings, as he called it.

"It is a very large country Canada. As big as a ten thousand Kenya's put together and full of white people and snow in the northern parts. They are called Eskimos or some other name their First Nations peoples that I can't pronounce. They used to live in huts made of ice and snow, hunt white bears and listen at night to the hoot of white owls. The air grows so cold, water freezes into stone and the air falls from the sky in sheets of ivory like the down feathers of the ostrich. So cold even you'd turn white after awhile." He laughed. "Now hurry with that last box, your father wants to leave on his hunting trip."

Titombe pondered for a moment, waist deep in stacks of books, covers bound in various colors, others with writings and pictures of images he'd never seen or imagined. "Only they must be smart to make these books from the snow. Snow must make you smart."

Namdi smiled, "it is not the snow that makes you smart. Where I went to England for my football career, they all go to school, their entire childhoods spent learning from these books that are in libraries like we are trying to build. Only I've seen some libraries as tall a Mt Kilimanjaro with millions of books."

"In any case this boy will go to visit these places one day. But first I think he must visit the only snow he knows in order to understand these things you speak of."

"It is a hard journey to the top of Kilimanjaro."

"I will make it, I am Masai."

"So, you are boy, so you are." Achedi, his dad said as he walked in. "These books cannot teach you what I know. Namdi has learned what he knows from the white man's books, I have learned what I know from this earth. Let him have his books, this place," he stamped the ground with his spear. "It is time to go and teach this boy of other learnings."

Achedi and Titombe strolled over to the pump house.

"Any success?" his father asked.

Several of the other tribesmen stood in front of the town's electrical building.

"No power to the sparkplugs, we think." One muttered glumly.

"We will have to send a message to Nairobi to get a man here to fix our pump. It will be a week or two before we will have power and running water again."

Achedi, pondered for a moment. "Tonight, if Titombe and I do not return from our hunting trip build a large bonfire and begin patrolling the village. The hyena's and other predators will become braver in the dark."

Tsvangi, the only man in the village who knew how the generator operated had died last week on a hunt. When they found his body the hyenas had already begun to devour it.

Achedi sniffed the air, "no rain yet, it contains only dust. This is not a good sign."

Titombe sniffed deeply at the air gagged as a fly in his nose lodged itself in his nose. He sputtered, and spit into the dust. "It only smells like air."

His father laughed, "Save your spit, soon might come the time when you wish you had enough water in your body to spit. When you can smell the air, know gazelle and rain when they approach. Then you will start to become a great warrior, not reading these books. They can not teach you these things."

"But father," Titombe tagged along behind his dad. "These books can teach me how to get the generator running again. I can fix these things. Tsvangi showed me how."

"Bah. Even the wisest man here Namdi, can not understand the workings of the generator. Let alone a young boy. No, you will stay away from the pump house until the people come from Nairobi."

Titombe glanced up at the skies. They were empty, parched of clouds like the dried corpses of the village cattle withering under the heat of the sun. The spring rains had not arrived and now everything was drying up. Even the hyenas and leopards, which rarely came near the village, were spotted prowling nearby.

Titombe remembered watching Tsvangi putter around, doing the things he used to do to keep the old generator running. He'd explain his actions to Titombe. But being a young boy Titombe hadn't paid much attention to Tsvangi's words. If only he had listened more closely. Then he would know what to do to get the generator working. Now his mother and sister would have to walk over two miles daily to fetch water for his family.

Worse still, Titombe knew the elders of the tribe and especially his father, Achedi, would consider this a bad omen for the shipment of books they had received.

"But," his father said as they walked, "What good are these books, will they keep the hyenas away? Will they make the rains come? To become a warrior and leader of your people, you must learn to dance, drum and hunt. These are things that make a man a great leader. Not reading books. That is for common men to do, not a royal son of the Masai people."

Perhaps his father was right. Perhaps it was more important to know how to hunt antelope, just like the lions of the Savannah. Still, since Titombe had begun to take schooling this year, he had found his teacher, Namdi Awalumo, to be a smart man. Even if he wasn't Masai born but a Kikuyu, something he knew his father also resented.

"They know very smart things, these books," Namdi had said. "Very smart things, these books." Everything Namdi had learned, he told Titombe one day, had been from books.

Achedi and Titombe sat still in the in the long savannah grasses. The sun sat low; shimmers of heat twisted the horizon blistering the ground in relentless waves.

They'd been hunting all day. Grass, brown dry of moisture, creaked against each other in the hollow rustle of dry wind. Titombe clutched the spear in his hand. Ahead of them a herd of gazelles stood grazing.

"Now, stay still. I'll go around to the other side and scare them towards you. See the younger ones, spear one as they go by."

"Yes, father." His hands sweated as he gripped the spear and slunk low in the grass. His father vanished noiselessly into the undergrowth. Overhead bustards circled, perhaps hoping for prey, too scared to hunt anything on their own. Titombe wished he could be one of those. Soaring high above the clouds, flying away to the snows of Kilimanjaro. Thinking of the lands where white man studied and the air was cold enough to see your breath. Lands where rain froze into white down and covered everything under its colorless blanket.

He closed his eyes and imagined wings that flapped endlessly, putting thousands of miles between each beat, over oceans shimmering in blue until he spotted an alien shore that stretched forever. Glistening in shades of white, vast unending sheets of stillness.

Landing, he shivered, his breath wafted into the air, freezing, so cold. "What kind of place is this?" Words spoken hung and threatened to cascade to the earth splintering in icy shards.

Crystals hung from trees and ran amuck from cliff edges flowing like he'd seen lava run, only slower, so very slow. "I don't like this land." Snow grated beneath his bare feet sending shivers through him. He walked into a vast city until he stood before two massive oak doors.

The doors opened before him, groaning on brittle hinges of steel, he knew if he touched would stick to him like termites on the end of the aardvark's tongue. "This boy would like to be home now, where only the night air can get cold. How does anyone live in these conditions?"

His eyes caught them as he walked in, eyes adjusting to the lack of light blistering off ice and snow. Volumes of books, so high, row after endless row disappearing up into the darkness. So many books; as many as the pink flamingo's that cloud the sky when disturbed in the water or the stream of termites that pour from their towering hills in rivers of flowing insects. A hundred of his town's libraries couldn't begin to fill even one wall.

"How could I ever begin to find the one I need to help my people?

The ground shook, bringing him back to the dust, heat and dirt of Africa.

"Spear one." His dad yelled running behind the stampeding gazelles. Titombe shook his head, all daydreams of white lands vanished in a haze of dust stirred by the ragging animals. Fear sang from their eyes as hooves turned up the parched earth.

"Now, now!" He pleaded.

Heart pounding, he hefted his spear. The thundering animals swept past and around him as he stood mortified. Some leapt easily over him and they were gone in an instant. Dust settled over him in blankets of shame as his dad came running up breathless.

"You must throw when your heart says so. No hesitation. The head gets in the way of a warrior's instinct. Next time it could be a lion or a leopard that runs towards you and makes you his dinner!" His anger and disgust evident as they picked up their possessions and continued to follow the dusty trail left behind.

That night Achedi talked as they sat around a campfire, beside them strung in a tree was a young buck, a tiny dik-dik. Its head hanging limp, blood dripping from its nose and the wound near its stilled heart, where Achedi's spear had ended its life.

"But father the books know much knowledge, they would tell us how Tsvangi fixed the generator. I could know this knowledge and fix it myself."

Exasperated, Achedi shook his head. "There are ways, mysterious ways that books and Whiteman's teachings can never teach you. There are things that these people cannot understand, that is what I'm trying to teach you."

"But what can I learn that is not written in a book?"

Achedi thought long and hard. "When I was not much older than you, we were having trouble with a leopard that was plaguing our cattle. It killed several before we realized it began to hunt our children of the tribe. 'Once a maneater, always a maneater.' My father said and for many nights we were not allowed out. Hungry, the cat became braver and would hunt us during the day. All of our greatest warriors could do nothing to stop it. Our chieftains were convinced that this cat was possessed by a very bad spirit. So, several of us went to see an old witchdoctor from the next tribe. He was very old, I remember all the cracks lining his face, when he talked. I thought his face would break apart, but he was smart in the old ways.

I remember the look in his eyes when he spoke. The way his eyes traveled around, I thought he was crazy, only when he stared at me, I knew his soul walked inside me and I knew I couldn't lie to him, for he knew what I was thinking.

Listening to our troubles he agreed this was a serious matter. So, we all sat and watched as he prepared himself with various incenses, scattered old bones around and began chanting. After a while he grew very silent and still. None of us dared to move a muscle while he stood there wavering in some sort of meditating trance.

After what seemed like hours he opened his eyes and ordered one of our best warriors to stand in the center of the hut. He told him to take his bow and aim an arrow through the open hole in the hut. He reached out and touched the man's arm as he drew back the bow. "I will be your eyes," he said as his hands swept over the man's face and fired his arrow straight up into the air.

"In the morning, go and kill one more young calf in return for this leopard's heart. Go to the Tsayo river. There near the large bend where several boulders rest you will find the large old Acacia tree. You will find this leopard with your arrow in its heart. You must break and burn this arrow the next night."

"I will always remember this because after we killed the calf I went with my father and we walked several miles to the spot the old shaman mentioned. Far beyond the ability of any warrior to fire an arrow and there was the leopard. Dead with the arrow in its heart.

My father broke the arrow and we lit a fire right then and there and burnt it. I remember how all the bravest of our men wanted to get away from that place. They were very nervous to be there and several said they caught glimpses of the old shaman watching them from the bushes.

These are the things that books cannot teach you. Matters that you can not see, only feel sometimes and know here." He pointed to Titombe's chest and top of his head.

"Now sleep."

The next night the tribe lit a large bonfire at the center of the village, and the adults danced around it to the rhythm of the drums. Ancestral drumbeats meant to keep away animals lurking on hot African nights.

"This was the way it had been before electricity had come to the village. This was what it meant to have skin as rich as the land and the same color as the soil of Africa," Titombe's dad told him. "A people created from the earth and forever connected to it."

As Titombe fell asleep, safe under his netting from the ever-present hordes of Tse-Tse flies and mosquitoes, he stared out the window from his room. He watched the moon cast its night cloak of stars, scattering speckles of light that slowly bled into brilliant sparkles across the dark canvass of nightfall. He heard the clang and tinkle of ornaments as his people danced. The throb of their voices falling into patterns of unending chants. He visualized the sparks of the fire rising, leaping in time to the drumbeats. Everything resonating to the soul that pounded known as Africa.

In the distance he heard the cruel cackle of the hyenas. Laughter tinged with madness and malice. Until the generator was fixed his people would have to be careful in the dark. Last night a couple of domestic animals and one small child has disappeared. The villagers were sure now that it was the hyenas that killed Tsvangi.

"Listen more than you talk and this boy will become a great leader," his dad had told him many times. "The creator gave us one mouth and two ears. They are not there just to keep your hair level."

Still, Titombe saw how tired his mom was from carrying the water today. He wished he had listened more attentively when Tsvangi had talked about the pump-house generator.

To become better, he'd have to learn to read and write. "Phhhh," he snorted, and rolled over, swatting at a pesky fly that had managed to sneak under his netting. He drifted towards sleep, lulled by the drums, their old voices pulsing like the hypnotic tread of the elephants that shook the ground. Soothed by the beguiling whistle of hollow winds, empty of rain. Nothing in this land stayed stagnant, even in death. Everything flowed in a cycle to an eternal pattern of life and death. This Titombe's father had spoken to him on many occasions.

Flowing like a river, Titombe's eyes sprang open. Electricity had something to do with flow through the points of the generator.

Some of the books Titombe had unpacked yesterday talked about engines and how they worked. He couldn't read much yet, but they had pictures. His heart knew the pictures would speak to him.

Titombe rose from his bed, dressed and grabbed a spear and a lantern. He knew what he had to do if he was to be leader someday. He lit the lantern and walked cautiously to the new library building.

Titombe snuck into the library and put the lantern and spear down on a stack of books. These books that were supposed to make men smart, he thought. They had made Namdi smart. They would make him smart, even if he couldn't read most of what they spoke of.

The books had an unfamiliar musty smell that spoke to him of oldness and wisdom from other worlds beyond his knowing. Many had pictures of strange places and sights he'd never seen or even imagined could exist, certainly not here in this world that he knew. "I will see these places someday."

After what seemed like hours he stopped in frustration. This wasn't making him any smarter. It was just causing his head to spin in tortured circles.

He prayed to the gods of the lands to guide him like his father and grandfather said to do. To let him be a proud and brave Masai leader like his forefathers. These Men who knew intuitively what to do when called upon to act.

"I will go to the pump-house and trust my instincts. Maybe my father is correct." From just outside the building, the hysterical cry of the hyena broke his concentration. He laid his head against a stack of books. He would sooner sleep here than chance the hyenas. The generator would wait until the morning.

Titombe turned the lantern to low and laid his head down on the books. As his eyes closed the flames flickered, dancing in the shadows creeping in from the haunting corridors within the books.

Titombe dreamed strange dreams and traveled to faraway lands. Countries surrounded by water, where it was always foggy and a man of letters wrote of jilted lovers who would die for each other, and of mad kings and ravens. He met many others, from different lands, like the men who painted fantastic visions on the inside of celestial rooftops and carved graceful statues. They all called themselves book spirits, dwellers from the pages of the books. Like the rivers traversing the land, they flowed out of the books and told Titombe of many things.

Among them he met a strange bearded white man who made paintings of beautiful women with enigmatic smiles and talked of mysterious machines he'd build someday, all scrawled on his backwards written notes.

The book spirits talked to Titombe like a father to a son. They whispered of astonishing journeys and incredible secrets, all hidden in the books he slept on.

"Trust." They whispered as the town's folk chanting and drumming reverberated through the brick building and shadows of strange lands danced within library walls.

Titombe lifted his head from the books he slept on. The Collected Works of William Shakespeare. Michelangelo. Leonardo Da Vinci.

It was still dark outside. Half asleep, Titombe walked over to one aisle and pulled a book from the shelf, the one these learned men and his instincts had shown him in his dreams. It came out with a slow hiss, like the spell of the lion as he waits in the long grass for the right moment to strike. Poised, coiled and hungry.

The book was about engines. Titombe flipped through the pages, guided by hands not his own, until he came across a picture of the electrical system.

Somewhere he heard a sigh, as enigmatic as the beautiful woman that old white man had painted. Titombe shook his head. What am I doing here holding this book? He stared in disbelief at the picture in the book in his hands.

That's it! Tsvangi had said the points of the generator's distributor were like a dam. When the points had walked to the top of the mountain they would open, allowing the pressure to build behind them. When they closed, the strong current would release in a huge rush to the spark plugs, just like the floodwaters that must run to Mombasa and the ocean. The trick was to know how much water to release.

He tucked the book under his arm, turned up the light on the lantern and ran from the library. This book had the answers to the generator.

The lantern clanked in his hands nearly as loudly as his heart pounded in his chest. As he rounded the last corner to the pump-house, a growl tore away his excitement chilling him to the bone.

From the eerie edges of the dark, calling his name between white razor-edged glints of death, came the laugh of the hyena. He stopped. The light of the lantern flickered off the walls of the buildings. Not one but two hyenas broke the cover of darkness. Their jaws slavered as they approached. He froze. The hyenas split apart. He was trapped between them.

They would tear him to shreds before he reached the pump-house door if he ran.

"Be brave," a voice from inside spoke. "You must show them you are Masai." The beat of the village drums sang in the distance.

He straightened up and held the lantern before him. The hyenas stopped their advance. They were hungry, yet wary. They were not the ones to show stomach for a fight, being more scavengers than predators. Still, Titombe was trapped. The book would not help him much here, his father was right. He should have brought the spear he left inside the library.

No one would hear his cry for help, with the drums pounding in the background. He had to act.

Titombe set the lantern and the book on the ground before him. His shadows wavered against the building's reflections.

"Yes," echoed voices said, "dance, our son." For the first time in his life, Titombe began to feel the compelling beat, began to understand the message of the drums. He moved to the rhythm of his heart and danced as his forefathers had danced, many nights around fires and under African moons. His shadows grew immense, filling the walls. He picked up the book and pounded on its cover like a drum yelling a chant. Stiff and jointed at first he soon fell into an ageless fluid movement. His feet stirred the dust, and from inside, the fierce pride of his ancestors took over. His heart answered the call of the drums becoming lost in the celebration of being alive, of being warrior born, of living in this land that made him and all of his people that way.

He looked up into the moon-filled sky and cried aloud to all that could hear. If he was to die now, he would die as a Masai warrior. Turning, Titombe prepared to leap into the midst of the hyenas.

Only darkness stared back at him. They had slunk back into the dark.

Brother hyena was hungry, but not that hungry. They had no desire to tackle the warrior that danced with ancestral spirits in his heart. Easier prey could be found elsewhere.

Titombe picked up the lantern and approached the pump-house. His ears listened for the slightest sound. The ripe scent of hyena still lingered in the air. Corners of dark shadows could still carry death's call.

He closed the door to the pump-house behind him and setting the lantern on a ledge, he breathed a sigh of relief. Sitting cross-legged, Titombe flipped through the book until he came to the pictures of the distributor and the points. Red arrows showed how the rivers of current that Tsvangi had talked about flowed. He remembered those rivers now. The book also showed him how much the points had to be opened. Small, like the gap in a crocodile's teeth. He grabbed the tools he had seen Tsvangi use many times and lifted the cap to the distributor.

Done. Titombe closed his eyes and hit the button to the starter. The machine turned over a few times and with a lurch, belched to life. It chugged and sputtered for a minute before unflooding itself and settling into a steady purr.

Lights flickered and burst into brilliance, engulfing the village. The drums fell silent and the dancing stopped. Titombe heard the footfalls of the villagers running towards the pumphouse. Yelling, laughing.

Achedi was among the first to throw open the door and stare, bleary eyed at his son. Titombe stood in front of his father with the book tucked under the crook of his arm.

"How?"

"Namdi was right, father. The books do have knowledge, father, great knowledge to fight off the hyenas. But I had to use what you told me, this heart and this head. Father, I will learn to read these books and become very smart." By the frown on his father's face Titombe knew he didn't approve.

"My son, you already are smart." His dad laughed and hugged his son proudly to him.

Titombe stared up at Namdi, standing behind his father. "Here, I'm afraid I borrowed your book. But this boy had no time to wait for school."

As he strode from the building, the villagers cheered him. The next night, as the streetlights once again kept the nights boundaries away, the village held a celebration for Titombe. For the first time, he was allowed to dance around the fire as a man would, to join with the ghosts of his Masai ancestors.

Titombe stopped dancing for a moment and sniffed the air. He turned to his dad and they spoke at the same time, "the rains come."

In the darkness hours later, he heard the rumble of swelling clouds and amid the crowd of dancers, Titombe spied an old, white-bearded man beaming at him as he sat before a painting of a young woman in the clouds gathering. The old man from far away lands of cold ivory raised his paintbrush and as he stared at Titombe he drew that secret smile, that only the two of them knew, on the beautiful lady.

As they walked back to their hut Titombe spoke. "Father, I want to leave tomorrow to climb that mountain." He pointed to Kilimanjaro.

"But, why my son."

"To make igloos and snowballs and dance in whiteness."

His dad pondered for a moment. "These books, I think, teach you crazy things. Only the bravest of warriors travel to the top of that mountain and return." He stared down at his son and instead of seeing rejection he saw determination. They stood under a lamp, in the background the hum of the generator from across the courtyard echoed. "I think it is time this man must rethink his matters regarding books. Perhaps in order to be a great leader in these times one needs to know more than what is inside here. And also trust what one reads and puts in here." He patted his son on the head. "Tomorrow, I will take you on this journey."

Sylvia's Sun-catchers

White glistens off the ocean's waves crashing to shore like a line of marching angels crying to heaven in thunderous silence. The distant lighthouse blinks its one eye at me as I watch an old man playing with his white dog on the beach. Decaying tang of salt air wafts indoors as I shut the window of Amy Tan's room. Comforted by the eerie presence of all these authors cradling me, I walk down the hall and fade from the ocean's shimmer.

A night in the Nye Beach Hotel in Newport, Oregon. I check in and glance at a cat curled on a chair warming in the sun. "That's Shelley and she's not a mouser," the innkeeper states, "she's a sun-catcher cat. Wherever the sun is, she catches it."

"Much unlike the author," I add. The smell of musty volumes hangs; I'm in a very familiar place. "My friend suggested be careful, this place either comforts you or spits you out."

"Your friend is right. You either love it or hate it here." She smiles.

I hear light sobbing and turn but there is no one there. Mere literary sniffles I assure myself, it is after all an old building. "Do you have Wi-Fi?"

"Phhh. We don't have internet, phones or even TV. Instead, at night, the sound of old bards' footsteps creak in the hall reciting their next novel, and you fall asleep to the lullaby of ocean crashing to the beach. Upstairs, there's games and puzzles to play, along with coffee, tea and mulled wine in the library after ten pm. Will that do?"

I can already taste the sweet tinge of cinnamon and heady musk of cloves going down my throat. "Well as long as I don't have to drink Dickens under the table this is my idea of perfect."

Again, tears on cheeks, shedding somewhere in the backdrop. I sign in.

"I warn you Dickens isn't the worry." She leans closer. "I'd stay away from playing cards with Dr. Seuss. He keeps changing the rules to three eggs and ham and even if you win you don't want to have to eat anything green." She laughs as I grab my bags and head for my room.

I pass Jules Verne as the ocean crashes in the background, hopefully not from his room, and wink at Mrs. Jo Rowling as sparks flutter from wand to wand in hers, The Gryffindor. Should be the name of a hotel not a room in an inn, I mutter. If you haven't figured it out yet, every room is dedicated to an author or a novel and yes I will lie with Amy Tan tonight. Well, okay in her room. As I unpack, my wife is shedding old memories in the Irish pub up the street. She hates travelling and Austen or Hemingway do nothing for her. This was my idea for a holiday.

Gentle cries rent the air calling; I stare down the hallway, no one. I decided to go for a coffee upstairs. On the third-floor little ceramic suns dangle in the library, rooms of unfinished puzzles, sofas and a fireplace. Outside seagulls squawk in mock soliloquy, while the heady robust of coffee keeps me company.

From nowhere, she's there. Tear-filled eyes tremble on the face of a dark-haired lady, younger than me but that isn't hard to do these days, as everything seems younger to an aging man. Smelling of lavender and patchouli perfume, while bitterness oozes from her.

I stare side-to-side, wondering where she came from? "Sorry, didn't mean to disturb you." Eyes of red puffiness radiate her misery. She doesn't answer.

"I was just beginning to wonder if the seagulls were squawking at me. But I see most likely it was you instead."

"At me. Why would you say such a thing?" Eyebrows frown.

"Got your mind off the pain didn't it."

Fire steals through those puffed orifices; I'll bet she wants to rake her nails across my face. As a man I think that always translates to lust. There's nothing quite like a lusty woman, ask Shakespeare or Yeats or a lusty female like Mae West. Or is she simply someone that doesn't back down from confrontation?

"You bastard! Can't you see I'm in pain? Grieving?" Lightning shies from her glare.

I've a live one. "Can't you see I'm here laughing and enjoying my holiday? Good day Lady Whatever-you're-royal-highness-is?" Oh, I think she has a lot of lust inside. Lust is good, makes you want to possess life from death. It drives you to not want to give up.

"Jane!"

"What?" Ah, I've cast rod and I've a biter.

"I'm Jane Stevens. I hate being called lady. My ex used to always say that." She sniffles.

"Whew thank God. For a second I thought you were going to say something like Austen or Eyre. Thinking I'm seeing ghosts and actually talking to one is another wholly different thing." She smiles slightly on lips that don't need lipstick to look luscious. The round doe-like eyes and high cheekbones; add twenty more pounds she could resemble Raquel Welch. Why did so many women think pencils and coat hangers are attractive these days? "Ah, so you've lost someone then." I sip at the deep earthy aroma of my coffee.

"Isn't that why people cry?"

"No, sometimes they cry over a good movie, their pets dying. Some cry over eating the best chocolate cake they ever ate. I knew a lady, err woman, sorry, that cried with every orgasm she ever had."

"What? You're rude." Brows furrow. Eyes widen. Lips pout. I taste the salty pain of her on my tongue, like the tang of ocean crashing outside.

"No, Tom. Rude was my brother. I grew to truly appreciate rudeness from him. He could say things that would make priests blush and nuns wet their habits."

She blinks, caught off guard, mouth agape like someone loudly interrupted turning pages in a library book not knowing what to say. "I, er I . . . Are you here alone?"

"Well, if you call a suitcase, dozens of seagulls, two people on the beach both badly overweight, thin on financial resources and long on lovemaking. A porter who doesn't give a rat's ass about his job and only wants to catch the next Seattle Mariners' game, then I'm alone. Oh, the cat. I forgot about the cat. She chases mice on crutches."

"He what?" The tears are drying away as she grinds the Kleenex in her fingers and another smile threatens to break. She is beginning to think I'm nuts when I already know I am.

"Old friend once said, I've learnt to chase fast whiskey and slow women in my maturity. So you call me alone if you like, but no one is ever truly alone, depends on your perception. It's a big, beautiful world out there. Wait. I think I did forget something."

I pat my pockets, "left it somewhere, now what was that?" I look up frowning.

"Left what?" Jane watches my hands, expecting a cheap magic trick.

"Ah crap! My wife. I must have left her back in the pub." I laugh. Jane tries but fails.

I wait, as she wipes aside her tears on the well-worn Kleenex. "Sorry, it's like being in hell right now."

"Hell passes."

"Feels like forever."

"Yeah, I'll bet they said that at the Alamo."

"You're a weird, off-putting man." She rudely stuffs the Kleenex in her pocket like a heavyweight boxer denied his knockout punch.

"Better than a sad excuse for a happy full of life woman." I grin ear to ear.

Jane eyes fire venom. "I think this conversation has ended." She storms by me.

"I think it has just begun. See you tonight. Mulled wine, fireplace and me. Couldn't get any better."

"Not in a million years." She harrumphs in disgust. But I know she'll be there.

I stare out the third story window, the sun recently set, listening to the dull thunder of surf angels crashing to the beach as the sky darkens. Ocean's coldness licks at me through the single-paned glass as the cinnamon infused spice of the wine tickles the nose, addles my mind and warms my belly.

A sniffle. Jane magically appears again.

"Ah, I see you found the mulled wine they brew every night. Lulls the guests, staff and ghosts to sleep." Well most of the ghosts anyways, I thought.

"Ghosts? You think there's ghosts in here?" She speaks, her face a little lighter, eyes less puffy than this morning, and no tears. Perhaps my tirade helped after all.

"Only good 'uns. Most are probably pondering their next book. Some literary great like Left Me in the Wind, a sequel where he did give a damn and falls in love with the Aunt Jemima housemaid. Or Bridges of Jefferson County, the modern-day version of the story where a travelling camera guy realizes he needs more pixels on his digital camera and falls in love with the blonde at the photo shop, only she's into bondage and leaves him tied up in a hotel room. Or even Frankenstein's Monstrous Inventions, tales of organic experiments gone wildly wrong, in triple XXX of course. Wouldn't want to watch your kids viewing drooling cauliflower cohabitating with lecherous broccoli." I'm on a roll, the wine is starting to kick in.

She laughs with her eyes for the first time, smearing away the tatterings of bitterness clinging to her. The streaks of tears are gone, as well as the lavender and patchouli perfume she had on earlier. Darn, must have washed it away in a shower during the day. No odor, no perfumes, no makeup, this is Jane stripped bare. I envisage what she would look like naked and wet. Well, how I could only wish anyways. She's actually dressed in a simple flowered dress that hangs to the floor, not giving me a hint to the fact that her knees might be knobbled or dimpled. Or if she shaves her lady-garden like so many these days.

"No I was born a little more dexterous than that. Spent most of my life changing spark plugs and oil. They do say mechanics have great hands. As for books and writing, I'm more of a reader. I believe for every great book ever written there's got to be someone or several someone's to read it. Or at least someone to appreciate great literature and clutch the covers after they've read the last page and say something profound like, 'Damn good book. So good, in fact, if I was stuck out in the woods with no toilet paper and had to do a number two, I'd use my fingers instead of these pages. It's that good.'"

She makes a disgusted face, lets laughter adorn her face like bridal lace and chucks her wine back. "Your wife doesn't mind you talking to other women?"

"Oh, chatting is okay, but if the talk turns to baseball and getting to third base, she gets a mite cranky. No, at my age, cheering a beautiful woman up and making her blossom like a gorgeous flower is about as close I'm going to get to open any of your rose-petals I'm afraid. The younger generation only thinks of sex, sex, and sex. I once got slapped in McDonalds for saying lovely pair of buns to the waitress picking up her burger tray. Nobody appreciates good well-rounded food these days. I tell ya."

She giggles and goes to get another glass of wine. I sip mine in slower quantities, knowing warmed alcohol hits you pretty quick. Jane returns and I decide to stir the pot again. "I think this is more you. Laughing, enjoying life, chatting up older, more mature and debonair men, over wine. But if I can ask, your ex? What happened, he absconds with the nineteen-year-old buxom next-door neighbor from the local Hooters restaurant? Turn raving gay, or offed himself in the garage by leaving the car running?" I was never great at being delicate about death, or splitting up, but how can you really approach the subject with etiquette. "Or maybe he died while walking the dog across the street by a . . ."

"Car crash while texting. Only I found later it was to spend the weekend with a co-worker and, yes, she was buxom. Bastard. I thought he was a good'un, as you said. Kind and honest. I would have borne his children someday. Now thank goodness I didn't bear his last name and kept my maiden name. We met here nearly ten years ago."

"Here? Didn't see that coming." For once she threw me a curveball.

"My girlfriend thought it would be cool to attend a writers' convention held here annually. I was into Chic Lit and thought why not. Always wanted to come back here with him, but we never did and now I'm here on my own. Starting out all over again, I'm afraid."

"So you've come to bury his memory or at least pitch it into the sea and let the surf angels take him away to the sun-catchers."

"Never thought of it like that, but I suppose you're right. How do you know so much?"

"Been around. My skateboard is on its third set of wheels."

"Or a long childhood," she quipped back. "Look, you make me laugh and that's quite a gift to this sad woman that was pretty angry with you earlier." She stops and looks at me strangely. "Surf angels? How funny, never viewed waves in that way."

"Yeah, that's the third glass of hot wine talking, makes you appreciate illusions in a better light. But laughter is good medicine, cheaper than Viagra and consumes fewer calories than frowning. Usually makes for better pictures as well. But it's late and I must check up on my wife Cynthia. She's probably still at the Irish pub telling rude Irish jokes or chasing leprechauns, or ruder Irish men." Jane stares at me, lips plump, eyes wide with desire. I have her and if

I were Rhett Butler or Austen's Willoughby or Bridget's Cleaver, I'd reach behind her head, pull her to me, holding her while I kiss those waiting lips. Unfortunately, I was born a gentleman.

"But I must bid my adieus and go find my whisky besotted wife."

"Wait! You said a minute ago something about the sun-catchers. Are they those?" She points to the ceramic suns, etched with native designs, dangling in the corner of the library.

"Yes. The little sun-shaped ceramics you see hanging around here. Me, I take them to be the opposite of the dreamcatchers of native beliefs. These give you dreams and instill the faith to grow better things in your life. Or at least cheer you up with positive karma. I guess they give a little sunshine out to those that need it. Hey, maybe they also give you fantastic writing thoughts. Like, man, after I leave here I'm going to starve myself living off only Can Hardly Soup for weeks on end and write insanely like a madman."

"Don't you mean canned hearty soup?"

"Nope, soup so good I can hardly stand it."

She laughs again nearly choking on the wine, "I really fell for that one. Thanks Tom for cheering me up." She reaches her hand out, I shake it and she lets it hang on my skin for a second too long. Lingering. Like I said if I was dastardly those lips would be crushed to mine.

"You're welcome. Some of my stuff is kinda hooky, but then so am I. The wine has wiped me out and I'm not much for breakfast, especially Cheerios. I'm a late morning type of guy, kinda like get out of bed around two pm and see what the day drags in. I leave it to others to kick-start it. So good night." I leave her pondering, watching one of the sun-catchers as it begins to twirl when the heating kicks in.

I walk down the stairs before she can reply, turn at the last step and look back. She's vanished again. The ceramic twirls, gleaming back at me, I didn't tell her about the other side of them. Cynthia will probably get jealous knowing I chatted up a 'young bird', as she calls them. Still, Jane was in pain. They say even deep hurt is temporary, while madness is a lifetime sentence. Just ask Van Gogh or Picasso. Only madness doesn't hurt as much, unless of course you're trying to express or find yourself. Then there just isn't enough canvasses to paint or water colors to suffice.

I grab the dog instead and go for a walk along the beach. Mist hangs on the ocean's tendrils like in the movie The Fog and begins to drift thickly inland. I wished I had Adrienne Barbeau to chat up on the beach or walk hand-in-hand with. Instead, the dog barks and scatters seagulls. I laugh as the mist curls around us, knowing my hands would sooner be cupping other body parts if I had her in the room.

Jane gets up early in the morning. Looking in the mirror, a smile graces her lips. It was him, he made her laugh last night. She must thank Tom before leaving.

She peruses the gift shop next to the front desk before leaving. "I'm checking out now, but do excuse me." She interrupts the porter listening to the last night's Baseball highlights in a small room adjacent to the desk.

"Damn! Mariners lost again." He shuts off the TV in the private room and comes out to attend to Jane, closing the door behind him. "Sorry about that, not supposed to let guests know I've got a TV here. But screw the owners, I don't really care. We're talking important stuff. It's the playoffs." He glares at her. "Was everything alright? Was your stay okay? Which room?"

"Yeah great. The Hemingway room. Say, are there any more of the sun-catchers for sale or have you sold them all? There were a few out here last night. Don't see any for sale this morning."

"What the hell you talking about lady, we've never had any . . . Damn." He stops and looks hard. "Old guy, dark green suit jacket, khaki pants and red wooly socks?"

"Lacks fashion sense but yes, that's Tom. He stayed in the Amy Tan room."

"Ah crap. We keep trying to flush him out, every other year, but he keeps coming back. Like locusts, always hanging around."

"What to you mean, every other year! How long has he been coming here?" Jane sighs deeply as shivers range down her back with his answer.

"Since the forties. I'm told."

"What? That's impossi. . . Him and his wife Cynthia stayed in the Amy Tan Room last night."

"Lady, no one stayed in that room last night."

"No. You're lying." Jane throws down her luggage and storms up the stairs. The door to the room is open and bed neatly made. "How?" Shelley, the cat, meows, lifting her head from the middle of the bed where the sunlight is streaming in and glints off dust specks swirling in the air.

In the hallway no ceramic suns hang. She runs quickly up the stairs to the third-floor library. None hang there either.

Jane weakly staggers back down the stairs. In the dining room a lady is cleaning up the cups and setting more coffee for the morning breakfast. "Do you work here?" The older lady nods back. "Sorry, stupid question time. But have you seen any of the sun-catchers for sale?"

The matronly lady blinks several times. "No, we don't sell such things."

Jane walks numbly away and waits as the porter finishes with another guest at the front desk. She pays quietly as the older lady comes down the stairs and pulls the porter aside. "Did she?"

"Yeah, in the Tan room this time."

The lady glances over at her. "Sorry, you're probably wondering what the hell is going on. I'm the owner here since the eighties and James here is correct. Legend has it that one of the earliest writers put a sun-catcher up in the library. I've heard people say they've seen them around over the years. I haven't, but then I guess I never needed one. Not bad things, they seem to give people hope and life before they leave. Is the old man Tom with a wife named Cynthia who hangs out at the Irish pub?"

"Yes?"

"Cynthia is his dog's name. He used to go for walks with her out on the beach. I was told he died in the early forties. Sorry. Nice guy everyone says, but then all of them are here. Good day." She walks back up the stairs.

Jane stands stunned. He seemed so real. She touched him, even.

"You okay?" the porter asks, as another guest arrives to check out behind her.

"Yeah." Jane breathes in deeply several times to ground herself, "Chakra breath! Chakra breath!" and looks down counting three to herself. "I'm good." She grabs her luggage and walks out into the morning sun, as it casts its warm blanket over her. "Too bad really, if he kept talking and prying me with more wine, he might have got a homerun out of it. Then I can appreciate a true gentleman." She laughs and stares at the beach one last time.

An old man with his back to her stands studying the lighthouse on the cove next to them. His white dog runs madly about trying to catch the seagulls. She watches the gulls squawking away tormenting the frustrated canine as he tries to desperately catch them. "He'd probably say something silly right now like, old Cynthia, thank God she doesn't have any wings otherwise she'd end up in Japan chasing dragons. Well small ones anyways, before they grew little Bic lighters in their throats. Crap! His humor is rubbing off on me. Oh, I hope this doesn't mean I'm going to cut off one of my ears and begin writing like mad. I actually hate canned soup." She laughs out loud. "See you Tom and thanks for that butt-kicking. You were right, I sure needed it."

The line of surf angels thunders its reply and the old man in the distance lifts his arm waving offhandedly over his shoulder as if over the ocean's drone he heard her.

Overhead the hotel's sign creaks on rusted hinges. The smell of hibiscus and roses from the small garden fills her nostrils. "Looks like it's going to be a beautiful day after all."

Welcome To The 21st Century, Mr. Claus

His contorted face will haunt the rest of my life, they all do, as his blood splatters adorned the wall in a macabre painting adding to the festive colors of the yuletide season. Making sure my contract was fulfilled I pumped two more silenced bullets into his body. The mob didn't hire amateurs to take out those they needed to have disposed of, and with a six-figure contract I wasn't about to make a mistake. I'd done this enough times to know not to take chances.

The Christmas tree ornaments rattle as he slumps to the ground behind it in a red smear. I swing the long barrel of the revolver around as a noise behind startles me.

"Santa?"

In the dimness of the hallway a young innocent girl, long tresses of blonde curls and large doe-shaped eyes, stands clutching her stuffed Teddy and stuffs her thumb back into her mouth. I push the revolver into my dark sweater, the heat of the nozzle burning my skin, and pull the black ski mask from my face. My heart catches in my chest. *The job is to finish him, not a young child. Damnit. There was supposed to be no one here, just him. My intelligence has lied to me.*

"You're not Santa. I left him cookies and milk. Who are you?" *She may have heard the thump of the bullets, but hadn't seen anything else, that much was obvious. I had to get her out of here pronto.*

"I, I'm ah, one of Santa's elves." I stumble trying to think, keeping a polite smile on my face and moved towards her blocking the view of the room. She looks so innocent staring at me, sucking away on her thumb. The contract forbade any witnesses. *But I can't, I can't off her.*

"You don't look like an elf. No pointy ears." She squinted, her eyes peering at my ears.

"Yeah, not all elves have pointy ears like on TV." *What am I going to do? I can't do this. Killing despicable dirtballs was one thing, but a little child?* "Um, undercover, I'm from the, ah, SBI. Santa's Bureau of Investigation. We check out any threats, possible pranksters. Can't have anyone interfering or harming Santa on his big day. We had reports of, um, poisoned cookies in the area, and stale milk. Gotta check it out. Can't have Santa sick on Christmas Eve, now could we? Anyone else home young lady?"

"Just Daddy and me. My mom got sick and she dropped me off early as a surprise for Daddy. I was supposed to be here tomorrow."

Well, that explained that. The revolver's heat licks at me. *NO. I can't, I wouldn't be able to live with myself. But, no witnesses. It meant my life. My shitty life. What am I going to do? Take a chance? I had never left any traces at an assassination before. Always covering up my tracks and any possible clues. That's why I was one of the mob's top enforcers.*

"Good, but, ah, let's go off to bed now. I gotta check out next door. We're not sure where the compliant came from. We have to make sure everything's safe for the big guy. He should be by any minute now and you don't want to be caught snooping. He won't leave any gifts or treats for you." I give her a big grin. "Now behave and toddle off to bed."

"Santa's swat team, how cool. Is Dad okay?"

"Yeah, he's sleeping, I tucked him in for the night." *And the rest of his life.* "Now off to bed. Santa will be here shortly. Your dad did tell me to make sure you were sleeping before I left."

She walked up the stairs. "Never heard of the SBI but if there's anything bad, in this neighbourhood I'd check out Jimmy from next door. He's a nasty boy, probably the one you got the report on. He's always trying to do yucky things, like kiss me. Ew."

"Yeah, that sounds bad. I'll pay him a quick look. Thanks for the tip." I close the door to the front room. *What am I going to do? If she lives and they find out, I'm done. Or worse they'll hire someone else to finish her and that wouldn't be pretty. No, all of this madness had to end tonight.* She tucks herself into bed. *That face of sheer sweetness will haunt every waking moment of my life, just like the faces of all of those I've assassinated. My life; what a joke, I'd wasted it. Had no one and nothing to live for. Nothing like her. I'd always wanted to settle down and relax with a good woman. Get married have a couple of kids. Who am I kidding? The day I quit working for the mob, they'll probably send someone out to silence me. I know because I'd done that before.*

I stare at that face of sincere innocence. *How is it possible I was once like her so many lifetimes ago? I couldn't do this anymore. I couldn't take her. Unless?*

"Put Teddy beside me on the bed. He keeps me safe. Daddy says there's a lot of bad men in the world."

Shit. Like me and her old man. If she knew the crap her dad had pulled off. Drug running, prostitution and worst of all, confiding with the police about the mob. That's what had ordered this contract. Our unwritten rule, no one talks to the law, and lives.

I spy the glass full of juice on her nightstand. *Yes, that's the answer.* I pull the emergency back-up pills from my pocket I carried with me if I was ever caught.

"Take this pill. It will make you sleep very well."

I fight to keep the tears back as she swallows. "You're a nice elf. Goodnight."

No, I was worse than worthless. "I'll take one as well. So I can rest in peace when Santa gets here. Don't want to disturb him, very busy guy." Tears stream down my face for what I had just done. I already knew I was going to hell many years ago. I knew having a conscious was a bad thing among trained killers. But at some point, being human catches up with all of us. I know if I could have redeemed myself with doing something good, I'd have given this all up in a heartbeat. Now, all I could think of was ending my own heart and hoped someone up there smiled down on me. Like that would ever happen.

The drug acts quickly as she falls unconscious. That face would haunt me forever. *I can't do this* and barely stagger down the stairs, the effects taking hold of me collapsing beside the tree, lights twinkling away like stars from heaven. Lightbulbs explode and glittering decorations tumble away as I fall into the tree.

It was a shitty life anyways.

Moments later the crunch of snow on the roof under a heavy black leather boot. The large bearded man sniffed the cold air and scratched at his white beard. "Ho, ho, ho. Somethings definitely not right here. As one of Agatha Christie's old novels read, 'Murder Most Foul'. Too bad she's not around anymore, could use one of her books to read tomorrow night, when all of this craziness is all over and I can kick back with a couple of Eggnogs." He glanced at his iphone. "Time's a wasting, only two hundred and twenty million more to visit. Glad I got the easy contract this year."

Clicking his fingers, he slid down the chimney frowning at the tray set up for him. "Damn chocolate-chip again. Didn't anyone tell the kids these days that I prefer Butterscotch." He sniffed at the milk. "And skim milk. I gotta change the contract. I'll be looking like a supermodel if I inhale that stuff all night long."

Santa glanced at the fallen tree and the two bodies. He touched both. "Yup, dead and cooling."

Snapping his fingers again, three surly looking elves appeared out of the thin air. They had blacked-out faces topped with red and white furry caps, black SAS-type fatigues with the acronym SCUT embroidered on their backs in fancy gold lettering. "Blinky, Marty, and Elvis. Good all present and correct for work. Like your new gear?"

"Oh Boss. Why we gotta have SCUT written on us? Sounds like we're a bunch of eejits," whined Blinky scratching at his long pointy ears.

"It stands for 'Santa's Clean Up Team'. SCUT is the acronym, which is quite apt because in the urban dictionary it means 'routine and often menial labour'. You guys are perfect." Santa roared with laughter while his workforce glared, not happy in the least to be the butt of it.

"Okay Blinky, you snack on the goodies, make it look like I enjoyed the healthy crap stuff. While you, Marty and Elvis undo the damage wrought here. I need bodies in the sled in double-lined body bags. Can't have anyone else's Christmas wrecked by blood contamination or decomposing bodies under such a nice tree. I'll check on the kid; hopefully she's still alive."

Blurs filled the room as the three whizzed about, lightbulbs reformed, blood splatters were whisked away, elf spit filled the bullet holes and reformed into a smooth plaster finish with matching paint. The two bodies were being thrust into bags by the time the big man thudded up the stairs.

"Hope, I'm not too late. I told the Mrs. I ain't taking crap like this anymore on the eve." He entered the little girl's room, squinting in concern as he touched her forehead.

"Thank God. Still breathing." He bent over and inhaled deeply above her lips, pulling the partly digested pill from her. He held it up under the light. "Carfentanil. Enough to kill three elephants and a rhino in heat. The world is just getting to be a nastier and nastier place." He stared hard at the pill a moment. "Pretty sure I got enough left to trace the maker." Santa sniffed deep, "Yeah got it. I believe my SCUT's will have a follow up visit to perform on Boxing Day. I'll supply the gloves and make sure he never manufactures any more of this foul crap, ever again." He stuffed it into his pocket. Yes, gifts are great, giving is even better. He cracked his knuckles. "Okay kid, you get to live. Can't say that for Dad and the gunman downstairs. Death is way out of my league. But at least you'll wake up on Christmas morning."

He grabbed his cellphone. "Blinky, I'll text you this girl's moms address. Make sure she gets here fast. Don't give me the 'I haven't got time' BS. That's why I hired you. Just drop the damn cookies and get on with it. If you eat all of those tonight and in the other bazillion households we still have to go to I won't be able to fit you into my sleigh next year. What? I don't know. Make up a story. Tell her you're a concerned neighbour. Saw her drop the girl off and dad took off, hasn't come back. The girl is here all home alone. Alright, tell her you're a nosey neighbour. Anything, just do the job. Have Marty and Elvis put the DOA's into cars and make everything look like a big fiery accident. I've a spare jerry can of fuel in the sled. Make sure there's nothing left but ash. Got that? Okay, gotta run, I've only got a few more million households to do tonight. I'm running late on this one and the union don't pay overtime."

Confident he could leave the elves to finish up he dialled North Pole Mission Control. "How's the European team doing? England finished and off to France? Great. Always hated doing France, full of rude Frenchmen. How about North America? What? Santa fifteen's sleigh is broken down? Damn! Knew I shouldn't have subcontracted the engines to the Asian market. Never had this happen before, so much for free trade. Okay, get the backup rocket-powered sled up and running to take over. Tell Mrs. Claus the night just got complicated and not to wait up for me." He hung up the phone as the girl opened one eye.

"At least I get some action and fun, no more old boring-fat-man-in-a-sleigh gig."

"Santa?"

He nearly dropped his phone. "Crap! I mean, Ho-Ho-Ho. This isn't in the script, ah, you're supposed to be asleep. You know nosey kids don't get any presents, only coal wrapped in old MacDonald wrappers. Damn. I've got lots to do in one night that would take anyone else a decade to accomplish. Oh, and thanks for the cookies and milk," he lied, as he waved his hand over her face and she fell back into a deep slumber. "Ah, remember this. Butterscotch-chip cookies and whole milk next year. I'll get you an extra pressie for under the tree." He waited a few seconds to make sure she was under his sleeping spell.

Santa vanished to the roof as his three elves came running back. Two cars went up in a large fireball. "Thanks boys, great job on setting up the car accident. On Boxing day we'll visit the dirt bag who sold the drugs and do some gift giving of our own."

He got in the sled. "I knew starting this new gig would pay off, at least she'll live. Not sure about the dealer, since my nice-guy gig don't stretch to scumbags." Elvis smiled evilly as he cracked his knuckles.

"Perhaps you'll get to try out those knuckle busters I gave you for Christmas last year after all." Santa grinned.

He hit the remote start on his key-fob and the V10 squirrel-nut-fuel powered engine roared to life. "Three thousand horsepower running off Enviro safe fuel, gotta love it. Okay Dancer and Prancer, and you, Glisten, with the lipstick in the third row, let's be off. And quit winking at the other guy beside you, I knew agreeing to the LGBTQ clause would give me grief. Gotta be fair to everyone apparently. Didn't know we even had gay reindeer, but I guess it's time they came out of the closet, er forest. The times they are a-changing, that's why I had the big dudes up there rewrite my contract. Hang on boys, seat belts on. Don't want to get busted for no seat belt use and all cellphones off." He clicked off his cellphone and put it in his pocket. "Last thing I need is one of you steering us into the side of a mountain while texting." He cracked his whip. "We're running late and I've got another seventy distress calls coming in. Oh yeah! Living the dream. Merry Christmas to all and to all a good night."

Yuletide Calling

Beyond the cracked sidewalk, and the telephone pole with layers of flyers in a rainbow of colors, and the patch of dry brown grass there stood a ten-foot-high concrete block wall, caked with dozens of coats of paint. There was a small shrine at the foot of it, with burnt out candles and dead flowers and a few soggy teddy bears. One word of graffiti filled the wall, red letters on a gold background: Rejoice!

Cindy, or Rainbow as she called herself on the streets, sank to her knees pulling the needle from her arm. The world blurred as somewhere beyond the metallic sounds of hard rock music blaring from her cellphone, voices echoed back as the drugs took hold yet again.

"Rejoice all you sinners. Repent your sins." Her dad's voice thundering down from the pulpit, like it had done on so many Sunday mornings before he died and her seven-year-old angelic world collapsed.

Her mother remarried but John wasn't like her father. He'd like to hold her on his lap. When they were alone he touched in places that made her feel good and that was the beginning. Cindy ran away from home after he molested her at nine. Even the drugs didn't take away the sight of him naked before her.

Angelic voices sang behind the harsh guitar riffs. She closed her eyes, succumbing to the hell dancing inside her as opposed to the hell around her.

There were times the drugs flushed all the pain away. This wasn't one.

And worse, she knew if she didn't arrive at some kind of peaceful resolve inside, her life would come to a quick sad end. He would win and have his way with her in hell. Once again.

A giggle from the darkness stunned her as a small, long-eared figure emerged from the dark. "What? Who are you?"

"I'm Yules, your guardian elf. You called me here."

"I called you?"

"Don't you remember? You were five."

Visions swam before her in the haze of drugs. Her opening a Christmas package, and a felt-covered elf sprang free. The ears reminded her of Spock in some weird way. "I love him. Thanks Mom and Dad."

"You whispered to me that night and so many after, 'You're my elf, Yules. That will always be here to protect me. My guardian.'"

Cindy closed her eyes clawing back the memory, as the angels hummed and electrifying guitars sizzled in.

"I'm in training, until I do something good for someone, I can't become a fully-fledged Santa elf. Now we must go. You can't stay here. There's danger."

Only it was too late, as three punks spewed into the alley where Rainbow lay sprawled. Yules twinkled his nose and disappeared, knowing he was under oath not to be seen by others, except her.

She fell into a slump. "Go where, I'm already flying."

"Oh, look a strung-out broad, and she looks very yummy. I think we are going to have some fun with her." They tossed her into the car, spilling pizza boxes onto the floor.

When the ride ended, she was lifted again. The kid slid her body onto a soft pile of clothing among the boxes in the garage. He pulled an old coat over the top, creating a cave that emanated the sweetness of old ladies who frequently powdered themselves—a light rose motif that played ironically well in the deep recesses of Rainbow's ancestral brain. The pizza kid lifted her head to help her lap water from a hubcap. He broke bits of pepperoni and crust into bite-sized pieces and left them where her tongue could reach them. Much later, she heard him practicing his orations like songs. Like monks chanting in the distance, they were a comfort.

In her drug-filled haze Rainbow wasn't sure what was real and what wasn't, only that she was unable to defend herself from those that were no different than her step-dad.

One of the lads began to unzip his pants. "Yeah, you feed her pizza. I've got something I'm going to feed her."

The others laughed as he pulled down his shorts.

"I can't let this continue. This will bar me from ever being an elf, but my oath is to protect her." Yules materialized before them.

"What?" One stuttered.

"Who the eff are you?" The boy with his pants down yelled, his manhood shrinking.

"I am the end of you. Hii Yaa." Yules struck a pose like he'd seen Bruce Lee adopt in his many karate movies.

The three of them stared a moment, before laughing. "A frigging elf! Are you kidding me? Man, that's some good drugs we bought."

Knowing the brilliance of the unexpected, Yules sprang into action like Yoda. A whirling dervish, in one, two, three chops, he'd felled the trio with chops to the chest and between their legs.

Cries rang out as they moaned on the ground. "Now go, before I really lose my temper. Now!!"

The three stumbled into the darkness, the leader struggling to pull up his pants.

Yules picked Cindy up. He stroked her hair, skin cold. Lips blue. "I have little time to save you. Only one choice."

He breathed in as he kissed her lips inhaling her poisons.

The words from a famous song pulled at Cindy's depths. "I have kissed haunted lips." Her heart thumped as the haze of drugs left her. Cindy stared at the funny looking Christmas Elf, struggling to stay conscious. "**Yules?**" His pointy ears holding the green and red cap in place.

She comforted him as returning visions of hugging Yules at night after **HE** came into her life. How many nights had she prayed for help before running away?

The crunch of feet announced the return of her three attackers.

"I'm not done with you yet, bitch and the freak looks out of action." The skinny one, obviously drugged up, came from behind and backhanded her. "Now I intend to get the pleasure that you owe me, and I think my buds want a little of that action as well." He kicked the elf several times in the guts. Yules cried out in pain unable to respond. "Never gutted an elf before," the punk sneered and as he pulled his knife free a white snowy haze blew in behind them.

From the foggy mists boots thumped echoing as a heavy-set, white-bearded man in a red suit emerged. "Unhand her! And my Elf."

The one punk stared wildly at the fat man. "Are you crazy old man? This is one freaky night. Now beat it, before I mess you up as well."

The click of hooves thundered in the air as several reindeer came into view behind the rotund old man. The reindeer lowered their heads, antlers thrust forward. "I brought back-up."

Knives clanked on concrete as the punks ran down the alley.

Yules struggled to stand, but couldn't, drugs pounding away in his head. "Nobody messes with one of my main elves." Santa picked him up and placed him gently amongst the luxurious furs lining his sleigh. "You fulfilled your mission, Yules and risked your life doing it."

Santa stared back at Cindy. "He has absorbed all of the drugs' effects, including the withdrawal symptoms. Yules won't be here to help you again. You are clean now, but this is a one-time deal; got it young lady? Pull this crap again and you are on your own." He pulled a wad of money from his pocket. "Here. Use it wisely. Get yourself cleaned up."

"Thank you, Santa." She ran her hands through her hair feeling her scalp, and the scabs on it from years of abuse. She needed a bath.

Cindy glanced down at Yules. "And thank you. I don't know why you came back to save me, but I'm very glad you did." She kissed his sweating forehead, and I know it won't be easy, but I will change my life now that I have a hero on my side.

"Now, on Prancer, on Blitzen. We've an elf to take to detox and he isn't going to be a pleasant sight in the next couple of days before we begin his training." With that he let out a loud, "Ho, Ho, Ho," and disappeared into the night sky.

Creative Non-Fiction

When Buzzards Are Circling Your RV

It's fifty-four degrees in the shade on Arizona's Interstate 40. You're hoping to see the Grand Canyon before sundown (a note to those of us laughing in the background that have been on that tarmac; there is no shade).

A nervous eye keeps glancing at the temperature needle on the dash as it begins to flicker, edging ever closer to that dreaded capital H, which you know that if the needle reaches it doesn't mean you're in actually in hell, but you could see it from here.

Your A/C is struggling to keep three out of four fingers clutching the steering wheel cool. The rest of you, and a very miserable wife, are perspiring most unromantically.

Buzzards have begun circling overhead smacking their lips at another overheated RV dinner (Okay. Point of fact here for those pedantic ones, buzzards don't actually have lips but beaks, and they can't smack them either). So, buzzards clacking their beaks circle, as ten-year-old radiator hoses begin to expand and contract like bellows of an accordion at two AM of an all-nighter German Oktoberfest.

A shudder rings through your engine as the thermostat clanks shut, the pistons in your engine begin to glow like your wife did after last year's holiday in Acapulco. You still haven't let her forget her famous words "I don't think that SPF stuff really works, do you?" For the next week she became addicted to having her body smeared all over with Aloe Vera lotion, which could have led in other circumstances to nights of pleasure, except you didn't have any hearing aids to stop her screams every time you touched those areas of cherry redness covering 98 percent of her body.

The water pump turns to plasticene, the radiator implodes and your rubber hoses expand miraculously to eight times their size (a note to scientific persons here, rubber only expands about double in size, no matter what Goodyear or Trojan claims) releasing that dreaded mushroom cloud of steam that means the next several hours are going to be of you hiking across the desert, while tumbleweeds rattle by and coyotes howl to the moon, knowing getting lucky with the missus means being allowed to sleep indoors in the car seat and not under the RV for the next week with scorpions and rattlesnakes using you as a blanket and that's if you do find any water.

Facts are that over seventy percent of all highway breakdowns are cooling system related. Most manufacturers claim cooling hoses have a lifespan of seven years, 140,000 K's. So have them pressure tested and replaced every seven years.

Everything these days regarding vehicles seems to be getting more and more complex. Coolant systems and antifreeze included.

Where once we had simple green colored ethylene glycol antifreeze, we now have extended life, super dooper extended life, forever after into the next generation extended life antifreeze which can be used in embalming procedures to keep that smug smile (or scowl) on your face knowing your grandkids will never get a nickel out of your estate since you had the walls of your coffin lined in the new plastic hundreds thanks to the Canadian Mint.

We've used antifreeze in automobiles for many decades, because they not only lower the freezing point of your coolant but more importantly raise the boiling point. The original choice of green as a color has a rather interesting beginning. It was rumored that antifreeze was invented in Ireland when a Shamus McGintee had a batch of homemade beer go green. He left it on his porch in the middle of a cold winter night and discovered the next morning that it hadn't frozen due to the alcohol content. He had the great idea of putting it into his frosted over radiator and proceeded to blow himself, and his car, into a million bits after it heated up.

"Funny stuff that alcohol," was reported to be said at his sixteen-day-long wake after.

Years later a company read the article and decided to use methyl alcohol based antifreeze, still used in windshield washer systems, to produce the first antifreeze. In memory of poor old Shamus they decided to color it green.

Truth is, it's colored that way to distinguish it from other sources of leaks. Red for transmission fluid, brown or black (we'll talk about regular oil changes in future articles) for engine oil. Although now there are several colors of antifreeze out there. So chances are, if it's bright green it's safe, and if it's gold colored there's been an inebriated Leprechaun urinating in your radiator. Ever wonder where he hid his pot of gold?

Have your antifreeze tested for PH content. This will determine if it is acidic or alkaline. Using pure straight antifreeze is not recommended, unless of course you're living in Nunavut. In which case you've already got whale blood in your veins or hooked on watching the Northern Lights while high on mushrooms.

Nowadays there are newer types of antifreeze, like Dexcool, which are based on OAT technology, (no this is not something you devour in the morning with toast). Organic Acid Technology (good to five years 250,000 k's), has a longer lifespan than glycol (typically two years 50,000 k's), but the two don't mix well. Kinda like drinking beer all night and ending it with a triple Vodka Amaratto shooter called "Singing on the great white telephone." Which is exactly what you'll be doing at three AM and this has nothing to do with opera or anything remotely musical.

Even newer are HOAT (Hybrid Organic Acid Technology) antifreezes put out by some manufacturers which also claim to give five-year 250,000 k life spans. But HOAT substances will mix with all other types of antifreeze.

However, these newer antifreezes are considered environmentally hazardous, so coming soon will be the new SOAT based antifreezes, which are totally environmentally friendly (soybean based) substances. When they hit their 'best by' date they turn into a jelly tofu type substance that can be cut, browned, and seasoned with flavor enhancers to taste, smell and look like garlic toast. (Note to lawyer types, several grain companies have already begun a class action lawsuit to stop delivery of this product, claiming reduced lucrative summer garlic breads sales will plummet causing hardships in the bread industry).

But you don't care because you'll be yelling "Should'a had her flushed out and the hoses changed" while watching from the safety of your campfire as buzzards clack away at some other distressed RVer whose old hoses gave up doing the watuzzi with an old sludge filled radiator.

PS: I also hear that these new SOAT antifreezes have a 24SPF and with other smell enhancers (lavender, sandalwood), mildly heat up when applied on bodies for those sexy oh-la-la evenings. Will the wonders of science never cease!!!

"Where's the Dipstick?"

You'll be shocked to open the hood on many vehicles these days and discover that you can't find the dipstick tube for your automatic transmission. Because there isn't one. Or sometimes there's a tube but only a cap on the end. Reminds me of the old lady from the Wendy's ads in the eighties, staring at the large bun with a miniscule black lump in the centre hollering, "Where's The Beef?"

So far many RV companies haven't gone that route but don't be surprised if you buy your next RV or car and remark "Where's the dipstick?"

In fact we owe the birth of the automatic transmission in 1940 to a fellow named Ransom Eli Olds from Lansing, Michigan. Ransom was a well-known inventor who created the world's first assembly line. It was good old Henry Ford who went one further by making his assembly line movable, when his foreman, Two Cheese Burger McGinty, discovered his workers were too lazy after their lunch break to move to the next car in line. "Bugger that, I'll have the car come to them."

This did increase production by 1.2 cars per month, setting a sales record for black cars. Oh yeah, he also got a deal on black paint, hence the sales pitch, "looks great in jet black, coal black or midnight black." Actually, he was color blind and thought he'd bought three vats of dark blue, red and brown for his cars.

Unfortunately, Ransom's foreman, Two Thumbs McTavish, liked to smoke and one day butted his cigarette into a tub of gasoline and burned down the entire plant. Otherwise, he'd given his boss the distinction of the world's first assembly line. Olds later got bought out by GM and the rivalry between the two continued.

Back to good old Ransom. His chauffer, old Gimpy Left Leg McIntosh, who used to stall his Olds Limo around town. "Heck of a time with this clutch pedal. Sorry sir." Ransom had false teeth and in those days they didn't sell PolyGrip yet. He got tired of looking for his teeth under the car seats every time his chauffer jerked the car too hard, although he was known for finding more money under the back seats than any other executive in the company's history.

Ransom had enough one day after finding his false teeth chipped yet again and decided to make the world's first automatic transmission car as a novelty for himself. That is until the King of England came over for a visit, and from his back seat remarked, "By Jove, strange country America. No decent tea to be had anywhere, but I haven't lost my false teeth once. I do believe, old chap, you will have to make one of these automagic-geared cars for my own chauffer, Too Bleeding Stiff Upper Lip McIlroy." Of course, once others saw what the King rode in, and the fact his teeth were in such excellent condition, they all wanted an automagic-geared vehicle as well.

For many years you could only buy Type A (oddly enough A meant Automatic) Fluid. Then somewhere along the way the McTavish's relatives at General Motors got wind of the Olds assembly line debacle and they never forgave the McGintys for crowing 'we built it first at Henry's plant'. They came up with Dexron, which after three beers they knew the McGintys could never pronounce. Ford, ignoring the dig and knowing they had to outdo the McTavishs, brought out Type F (weirdly enough this stands for Ford-O-Matic).

The basic difference between the two is the friction modifiers. If you had a GM vehicle that was beginning to develop a tranny slip in the old days throw in a can of Type F and get nice crisp shifts again. Well, until the tranny blew into a thousand pieces.

An aside note here. Honda used engine oil in many of their earlier automatic transmissions and never had a removable filter or pan. (Sorry, I won't even think of making any funny jokes about anyone that eats raw fish and knows karate and judo).

Up until the seventies ATF contained whale oil as friction modifier until GreenPeace came along and put a stop to that. As vehicles got environmentally conscious things, the world of automatic transmissions went crazy. At Ford, Henry's cousins the McGintys decided the feud was on and brought out Mercon (very similar to Dexron), M2C138-CJ, Mercon LV, Mercon V and Mercon SP. To name a few.

Not to be out done at GM the McTavish's grandkids brought out Dexron II, IIC, IID, and lately Dexron VI. Everyone thought the gentlemen at Chrysler were nonplussed about what was going on until one of the cousins to the McGintys began working there after he got his science badge and they brought out ATF+3, and ATF+4.

I've lost count now as to how many different types of tranny oils there are out there and like fashion statements it seems every manufacturer has a few new kinds every year or so. So it is not only critical to now to make sure you get your tranny fluid flushed or changed as per schedule, but to make sure the right type of fluid is put in. Many are not only incompatible, but don't mix backwards with older fluid types. Which is like remembering what the eighties were like, until you look at some old photos and go, "I really wore those clothes?" Not to mention the big hair!

According to the ATRA (Automatic Transmission Rebuilders Association), 90% of all transmission breakdowns are due to overheating, while according to the AA (Alcoholics' Anonymous) the biggest cause of breakdown is putting the vehicle into R for race and storming through a brick wall, several other cars and a waiting taxicab.

Almost all tranny fluids are a nice red in color in order to distinguish them from other fluids. Once your fluid has begun to change to a darker color or, heaven forbid, brown, then it's time to have the fluid flushed. If it's turned gold, you've parked your RV at the end of the rainbow or lephrecauns have been relieving themselves under your hood.

Also, if you're into smelling things, like flowers or this week's laundry for that fresh as a daisy scent, take a whiff of the dipstick. If the fluid has darkened and begun to stink of overdone burnt pizza crust (I could murder a ham and pineapple pizza smothered in mozza right about now) that's a sign your tranny is getting overheated.

Remember the hotter the temp of your transmission the more often you need to change the fluid. An average transmission should run around 175 degrees F at which range normal service intervals will suffice; usually every 120,000 kilometres. Raise that by twenty degrees and you can count on halving the life of the transmission fluid and another half for every twenty or so after that. Many transmissions are constantly run around 200-230 degrees. Reach anything approaching 250 and real trouble begins. Seals go hard, clutches begin to burn up and next thing you know you've got a box of neutrals, and you're staring at a huge tow bill to the nearest garage.

Most car transmissions run at 200 plus degrees, and RVs more than that, hence the need for regular service intervals - 60,000k's for cars but only 40,000 k's on most RVs. Having, and watching, your tranny oil temp gauge is very important in prolonging the life of your automatic transmission, especially when you've decided to push your twenty ton RV up the sheer mountain passes where the mountain goats will squint at you with you-gotta-to-be-kidding looks, or through the Mojave desert where snakes sip on coolers and use SPF80.

Regular transmission oil coolers in vehicles usually involve running hot tranny fluid into a section of the radiator where it is cooled by about twenty to thirty degrees and then ran back to the transmission. Adding an aftermarket cooler is very wise and can drop fluid temps from seventy to 120 degrees. Newer models of coolers also have internal temp controls that don't allow flow until a set temp is reached, allowing the transmission to come up to operating range faster.

Synthetic trans fluids offer greater protection, but make sure the brand you're using is compatible with the original fluid. As a word of advice I would usually have the tranny filters changed on every second visit along with a complete flush every time.

Some new vehicles now have to be put on a hoist to have the tranny fluid checked, via fill and drain points. Others require the purchase of a dipstick (I'm not kidding you), some need to have computer scanners to unlock certain components and weird tubby affairs inserted anally into a plug in the tranny pan. Small wonder you get a $60 bill just to check the tranny fluid and you might wonder 'what, really, are those quick lube type shops putting into your transmission?' If anything.

Which brings me back to the original point. When you open the hood and remark, "Where's the Bleeding Dipstick?" give us a call at Gerry's Ok Tire North Abbotsford 1-604-826-0519 for further advice, service intervals or fluid types. After all, we're an easy-going bunch here, especially if you bring a dozen donuts and drive a standard.

See ya next time.

Jed Clampett had no idea what he started when he struck Texas Tea, did he?

Good ol' Jed Clampett went hunting to feed his family and ended up striking Texas Tea Black Gold and moved to Beverly Hills. Or so goes the story in the Beverly Hillbillies. Back then oil was oil and as long as it wasn't black as tar everything was good. But as technology advanced, engines began to run hotter, with higher compressions and computers. Then the green movement slowly changed everything.

This reminds me; what happened to the good old days when you knew the best stuff out there was a gold plated whatever? Now there's platinum, titanium, and what next? Superdoopermanium? Wait until they start changing the Olympic medals and gold is the measly runner-up award.

It was back in the sixties when we starting growing our hair, getting stoned and environmentally conscious that some scientists, as they sat out in their backyard talking to little animals, said, "Hey! They quit making dinosaurs a long time ago. This is a problem."

So they decided to start looking at alternatives, like synthetic oils. Much of this research began even further back in the thirties with a German scientist named Dr. Hermann Zorn. He searched for lubricants like natural oils but ones that didn't gel or turn to gum under gasoline engine environments. His work led to the invention of over 3500 esters, including diesters, polyolesters and banana oil (chimpanzees and apes declined testing the banana oil synthetics, although baboons weren't so smart. One look at their rear ends you'll know what happened there). Not good, not good at all.

Just a sidenote; this led to the testing by other Monkees in the sixties and this explains why they ran around so fast on their TV show always looking for washrooms.

Poor Dr. Zorn. Unfortunately, he thought he was working for his company on a synthetic beer/bratwurst combination, which would have made him immensely rich, famous at Octoberfest and a national hero. "Beer and bratwurst in the same glass without any gaseous side effects." Years later they found him wandering incoherently in Berlin's skid-row muttering, "Deichsel und mit getriebenen unterscheiden vermoche nach dem sie darstellen staubwolken au wirhelten."

Which literally translated means, "I was robbed." Especially after the war, when most German scientists defected to North America.

If you're wondering, synthetic oils weren't made by some mad scientist between Frankenstein's monster, stem cell research and inventing a cure for cancer and PMS - much to his depressive haranguing wife's disgust. Which of course made him wish he'd been single like Einstein yelling, "Eureka $E=mc2$." Which wasn't his original solution to the Theory of Relativity, but to the perfect milkshake recipe. The milkshake idea fizzled out after he took out his backyard and half of Detroit in 1948.

Synthetic oils are ester-based substances, along with other additives, which far outclass any ordinary oils. Yes, I know, the first pantyhose were polyester-based and, oddly enough, the first polyester sweaters (the clue is in the name). Scientists soon realized that if you get pantyhose turning fast and hot enough (?), it turns into a rubbery mass called a fan belt. Hence was born the expression, "Get on yer bikes, girls."

This led eventually to SynLube in Vancouver in 1969. The only market at that time was selling their synthetic oils to the Lunokhod 1 Moon Rover and the US Moon Rovers. They soon realized that wasn't a very profitable, or large, market. Okay they did sell four quarts to the Americans for $3,000,000,000 dollars US each, but after six trips to the moon the Apollo program was cancelled.

A small note to history buffs here, they also sold two quarts to the Russians, who at the time didn't make it to the moon and couldn't afford to pay in rubles, but ended up paying with 2,000, bottles of Vodka. "It'll be a delirious three months until we sober up and the Vodka runs out," said one SynLube official. "Three months?" the Irish spokesman replied, "what do you take me for, a tee-totaler?"

Although it does seems funny that with all those potatoes around the Irish never invented Vodka.

So, you ask, are synthetics really better? Here are some facts on synthetic oils to dispel the old Ford Model T tales your grandparents would have you believe.

1. Synthetics will void your warranty. Wrong. They meet and exceed industry API and ILSAC standards (we'll talk more later about those silly acronyms and what scientists get up to on their national conventions).

2. Once you switch to synthetic you can't switch back to conventional oil. Wrong. They are fully compatible and provide superior engine protection.

3. Synthetics are good only in new cars. Wrong again. They're grr—e—e—at (as Tony the Tiger would say) in older cars. It's that superior protection thing again.

4. Synthetics need a break-in period first before switching your vehicle over. Oh buddy, we've fooled you again. Here comes the cattle prod for four wrong answers in a row. With modern engine designs, break-in periods are no longer required.

Any disadvantages to using synthetic oils? Yes. This, believe it or not, is straight out of Wikipedia; Potential stress cracking of polyoxymethylene plastics when mixed with polyalphaolefin particles (just a word to the wise here, no matter how many times you spell this out, the red underlining is all over the place from Word's

SpellCheck, no wonder Bill Gates is going broke). And the rational thought to most of us intelligent, reality watching TV public is "WHAT THE BLEEP?" (that went over my head faster than a 747 at the national cheerleading competition). Actually, what that means is, don't use synthetic oil as car wax, dishwashing liquid or, unless you want to look like Phyllis Diller, Kojak, or Ilea (from the first Star Trek Movie), a shampoo.

Oh, and synthetic oils are not recommended in rotary engines. Here's a little bit of trivia. Did anyone out there know that GM (Generally MadCorp) had built a four-cylinder rotary engine that was going to go into their Corvette advertised as "It sounded like a sewing machine, but out dragged a Mustang? (car, not the horse)." Mazda also bombed with their first R100 car with the rotary (Wankel in some parts of the world, wanker in many others) engine.

So why buy synthetics for $9-$19 per bottle, you ask, when "I can get a great buy on a case of twelve jugs of oil at my local grocery store for $2.99".

Not likely, you get what you pay for. Ever look closely at a container of oil? They all seem to have this funny starburst type stamp on them. Oil is rated by weight and by compositions needed to meet operating standards in various years of vehicles. Multi-grade oils were originally called All-Season oils. When you look at the can and read 5W30, that means in the winter the oil will pour out at the thickness of a five weight rated oil and in the summer with the thickness of a thirty weight rated oil. For many decades we had a few specific rated oils, mainly 5W30, 10W30, 20W50. Lately, with engine tolerances getting tighter and emission standards being raised, we've seen the advent of oils as radical as 0W60. Next year they'll be bringing out 000W120 which will pour out like water when sitting overnight on the surface of Pluto and glug out like maple syrup when orbiting the sun for a week (I guess they're still trying to sell a quart of oil to NASA at $4 trillion. "Hey I just gotta sell them one bottle and I can retire like granddad", said Ned Clampett).

Compositions were first rated, and for decades later, by the API (American Petroleum Institute). Every once in awhile the people there get together to have one of their swanky week-long soirees. Now, being scientists, they do mad scientisty things like put lamp shades on their heads (still a gut buster with that crowd) and decide to establish new oil standards for cars and RVs (wow! Riveting stuff of legends in the cutting-edge hydrocarbon field). The current standard is SN - good for cars from 2011. The last standard was SM established in 2004. The one before was SL, for vehicles from 2001. So, if that can you're holding says something like SD, it's good for pre-1971 vehicles. In other words, nearly pure oil and not much else. Yup, you definitely get what you pay for.

But don't get fooled by just the API ratings, there are others out there now. The newest ILSAC (International Standardization and Approval Committee) ratings are GF5 for 2010 vehicles and older. These are those scientists that weren't invited to the API annual conventions and you'd think these folks with the wow-knock-their-socks-off name should pretty well have the market sewn up on oil ratings. Nope, here's where it started to get crazy. Along comes the ACEA (European Automotive Manufacturers Association). Yeah? How does that make ACEA? I asked as well. The Europeans, still upset about the whole synthetic beer/bratwurst thing, and the Americans absconding with their scientists, decided to establish their own ratings.

Then VW came along establishing their own ratings for their vehicles. The current benchmark is 504.00 for gasoline and 507.00 for diesels. Yes, they are really mad about the beer/bratwurst issue, don't find lampshade jokes very funny and are trying to confuse the heck out of us.

Mercedes-Benz then joined the fray with their own ratings MB 229.1 to MB 229.51. Way too confusing to explain in less than 4000 words as these are Very Sophisticated Scientists, who won't even admit to being coolly upset by the beer/bratwurst issue. Last time I tried to talk about the hilarity of the lampshade stunt they hung up on me. And I'm not even going to mention JASO (Japanese Automotive Operating Standards Agency) or the other automobile companies joining the bandwagon en-masse. (PS no funny jokes about these guys at JASO, they know Karate!)

So if you own an RV, or towing any other vehicles with your RV, it would be wise to check with a certified shop to make sure the oil they use is meeting the various spec's required by your vehicle. If you're unsure, check your owner's manual (that's if you've still got it and not, like me, used it for toilet paper when stuck in the back country for four weeks). As for the supermarket oil that's a steal at $2.99 for a twenty-litre pail? When you consider the cost of your average engine job - between $4,000 and $8,000 - that works out to about $20-$40 dollars for that cheap basically crude oil in a can. Not a bargain after all.

For more information give us a call at Gerry's OK Tire, North Abbotsford (yes, I know, cheap unsolicited plug here) 1-604-826-0519 for quotes on engine rates, towing and oil specs. Next article? Transmission fluids. And if oil had your head spinning, this will give you vertigo! So, until next time, (and as Jed would say) y'all come back now, y'hear?

Trust Me, I Didn't Make This Sh*t Up!

"You may be seated. We are conducting proceedings here today in the form of a Court of Law. This is, of course, not a true Court Case. No person or body of persons is actually 'on trial' to be found guilty or not guilty, the purpose of this 'trial' is to reach a verdict upon the most likely course of history given all the facts presented.

I, Judge Noah Cant, will be presiding over this, the case of The Established Egyptian Historical Society versus The Society of Refuted Archeological Facts. The Established Egyptian Historical Society is 'prosecuting', i.e. challenging, The Society of Refuted Archeological Facts to defend its version of events, which is that Khufu did not build the Great Pyramid in Giza. The 'Jury' has been selected at random, but from a group made up of engineers, archeologists, and historians, as it is felt that this would lead to a more precise 'verdict'. Counsel for the Prosecution, please prevent your evidence."

"Thank you, Your Honor. Members of the Jury; we will prove to you here today that indeed Khufu *did* build the Great Pyramid Giza. In1837 Howard Vyse, an English archeologist, found a cartouche in Campbell's Chamber, which is situated above the King's Chamber. Now known as the Khufu Cartouche, it is part of a short inscription that reads Ḥwfw śmrw ꜥpr ('the gang, Companions of Khufu'), i.e. one of the gangs of workmen that constructed the chamber. A second cartouche, with this same gang name, was discovered on the south ceiling towards the west end of Campbell's Chamber. This is surely evidence of it being built by him. A recently discovered logbook, the Diary of Merer, tells the life of a middle-ranking official with the title inspector, and is thought to date to the twenty-sixth year of the reign of Pharaoh Khufu. It describes several months of work with the transportation of limestone from Tura to Giza during the 4th Dynasty. Tipped as one of the most important finds of the twenty-first century, most experts agree that it reveals how Pharaoh Khufu's Great Pyramid of Giza was built over a twenty-year period.

The mortar found in between the granite blocks of the Great Pyramid has been carbon tested and has been shown to be 4,600 years old proving that, indeed, this mortar is from Khufu's time.

I don't fully understand what everything in the diary means, but I've spent a while looking at the meaning of the words and what the diary says is that Merer was going to Tura, quarrying stone, putting it on a boat and taking it to a place called Akhet Khufu. From there, he went to another place called Ro-She Khufu, where they were building a dyke for water. This, the transportation of the raw materials, and the carbon-dating of the mortar used in the building of the Great Pyramid, surely proves that it was therefore built for one of the most-loved Pharaohs of ancient Egypt.

The Prosecution rests."

"Thank you. Counsel for the Defense, your evidence, if you will."

"Thank you Your Honour. Firstly, let us present to the Court some known facts. The Great Pyramid is sitting on thirteen acres of land, which have been levelled to within a quarter of an inch. It contains two and a half million blocks of rock estimated to average twenty tons, with some weighing perhaps six hundred tons. A weight of this magnitude is unfathomable, but if you consider it is heavier than *all* of the cathedrals, churches and chapels built in England since the beginning of Christianity, this will give some greater understanding. These stones were cut from an Aswan quarry *six hundred* miles away. So our first question is; exactly how were these rocks cut? The Prosecution makes no mention of this point, and transported by boat? How big would the boats have to be so as not to sink under such weights? And where was the labor force sourced? Not from slaves. There were no slaves known to be in the Old Kingdom under Khufu, so you'd have to pay, house and feed these workers. And how many workers would this have required?

Back then it was estimated that there were maybe only somewhere around 500,000 people living in all of Egypt at that time. It is claimed by The Established Egyptian Historical Society that this structure was completed in twenty years. To just build this structure in twenty years as claimed, you would have to cut and fit into the pyramid fourteen blocks every hour, day and night, seven days a week, or roughly one every three minutes, and that doesn't include all the efforts to cut them and ship them from Aswan to the site. I have submitted as Exhibit One the formula we have created to prove this fact.

How is it therefore possible that the pyramid was also conceived, designed, materials procured, and the structure built during Khufu's reign of twenty years?"

"Objection, Your Honor. Newer evidence uncovered by us indicates that Khufu reigned longer than twenty years, maybe for thirty-five years."

"Sustained and noted. Defense Counsel, do you wish to respond to this at this time?"

"Yes, Your Honor. We have been made aware of the 'new evidence' and have prepared a formula for that too, which has been submitted as Exhibit Two. It would still mean that you would have to put in place one block every eight-and-a-half minutes, day and night, for thirty-five years, again straight from day one of his reign with, again, no time for the conception, design and procurement of materials. I have yet to provide the most astonishing evidence on the sheer complexity of the design details, which I will relate to the Court later.

Now, as regards the actual construction of the pyramid. Firstly, and strangely, apart from the Diary of Mere, there have been no recordings of the cutting and moving of the stone blocks, nor the assembly of the Great Pyramid, or any other pyramid, come to that. Historians for the Prosecution claim that these structures were erected using an earthen ramp circling the pyramid. Modern engineering experts have said it is not possible to construct this to such precise dimensions in this manner, especially as some of these blocks weighed as much as six hundred tons. Calculations show that it would take about six hundred men to move a sixty-ton block alone. Also, the ramp suggested by the Prosecution would not be shallow enough to allow the huge blocks to be dragged up by people. A ramp of a shallow enough gradient to allow this would have to have been 4,800 feet long - that's more than three times the length of the pyramid itself. And how could an earthen ramp stay in place under the weight of those blocks and be stable enough for the structure to be built so precisely? The ramp itself would need to be built out of stone, and if the ramp were made of stone, where are the remains today?"

"Objection! The Defense has wandered into the realm of supposition and not facts."

"Your Honor, if I may. Most of the evidence provided by the Prosecution is also supposition."

"Quite right. Overruled. Please continue."

"Thank you. Now, as I mentioned, the Egyptians lacked astronomical, geological and mathematical expertise, so here is where things begin to get not only improbable, but perhaps impossible, without some form of higher knowledge involved. I have submitted a sheaf of facts marked Exhibit Three which I believe will prove this point and I shall run through them with you now.

The total weight of the Great Pyramid is estimated to be 5,955,000 tons which, when multiplied by one trillion, is the estimated scientific weight of the Earth.

Take the longest lines of latitude and longitude and run them in straight lines and at the center are the pyramids of Giza.

If you take the height of the pyramid and multiply it by 43,200 you get the radius of the Earth. If you take the base perimeter of the pyramid and multiply that by 43,200 you get the equatorial circumference of the Earth. The number 43,200 is important because it is derived from the key motion of the Earth called the precision of the Earth's axis. Our planet wobbles on its axis one degree every seventy-two years and 72 x 600 = 43,200.

There's more. The square base of the Great Pyramid divided by twice the height equals Pi, 3.1416.

Now, the precise nature of the pyramid is amazing. The difference in length of any of its sides is eight inches and it is actually eight-sided, not four, with slight dents in each side. The twenty-two-inch thick plane it sits on is within one inch of dead-level over thirteen acres. Gaps between the casing stones measure just a fiftieth of an inch and the apex of the pyramid is located directly over the center with no deviance. The lower passageway is 350 feet long. It's straight to one fiftieth of an inch through the blocks they've laid, and through 200 feet of solid bedrock. There are two supposed airshafts going upwards from the King's Chamber pointing to the stars of Orion's belt and Alpha Draconis. That would be near impossible to do even with today's laser equipment, let alone with only copper tools and chisels.

Talking of Orion, the alignment of the pyramids is the same as the three stars of Orion's belt as they appeared from Earth in 10,500 BC, matching not only their position, but the size of each pyramid corresponds to the magnitude of their respective star. This is a very important time in Egyptian history. They called it Zep Tepi, or 'the first time'. The literal translation is 'the golden age when men lived in communication with the gods'.

Now things begin to get very interesting. The Meridian Building of the Greenwich Observatory in London was built to align with true north and even it is out by nine-sixtieths of a degree. The main pyramid is aligned to true north within one-twelfth of a degree. It sits exactly on thirty north parallel, that's an imaginary line one third the distance between the equator and the North Pole.

If a line is drawn through the apex of all three pyramids and another through the left shoulder and headdress of the sphinx then the entire Giza complex becomes a Golden Mean Spiral based on the Fibonacci spiral of numbers, which is a sacred set of numbers that govern all patterns and growth in nature. And to add to the credibility of my statements, the speed of light is calculated at 299792458 m/s. Guess what the GPS coordinate of the Great Pyramid of Giza is? Yes, 29.97924529°58′45″N 31°08′03″.

My final Exhibit is that marked number Four. This is carved in one of the oldest temples in Egypt, the temple of Dendara. The first seems to depict a number of 'flying machines', and the second, what appears to be some kind of device similar to today's lightbulb. Granted it is rather on the large size, but it is clearly wired and there is a suggestion of a filament inside what appears to be a glass casing. Make of this what you will, but it would seem to support the notion that the Egyptians were somehow aided by inventions way beyond their technical expertise, and just perhaps, there were other such devices that could have assisted in constructing the pyramids long before Khufu's existence.

Our esteemed Khufu was indeed a sincere Pharoah as the only sculpture ever found of him is a seven-point-five centimeter high, for those Americans present, about three inches in the Cairo museum. I find that rather perplexing for a man that spent at an estimated cost today of five billion dollars erecting something to remember him forever and oddly with no inscriptions nor cartouches made inside the great pyramid until two were found by Howard Vyse after he drilled into Campbell's chamber above the kings chamber.

It is now known that the first cartouche is a fake; Khufu is introduced by his Horus name first, perhaps the closest we have today is a surname, not by his birth name of Khufu, as it was common to do so at this time. It mentions the goddess Isis, but all records show that she did not exist for another generation, the 5th Dynasty, whereas Khufu existed in the 4th Dynasty. To top it all off, the spelling of Khufu that Vyse first found is incorrect, it today would actually read as Raufu and not Khufu. The most damning evidence that this is a fake is that it is painted, not carved and painted, and it is written in cursive rather than hieroglyphics. It is believed by some that Vyse himself painted these cartouches.

Further, there's a structure called The Inventory Stele, located in front of the Sphinx. This is now covered but a locked inside a container to 'quote' protect it from vandals and the elements 'unquote'.

Inscribed into the Inventory Stele's frame on the lowest panel are a few lines of hieroglyphic text which have stirred controversy, because they explicitly contradict the nowadays mainstream theory that Khufu's son Khafre constructed the Great Sphinx. The text has been independently translated by James Henry Breasted in 1906, by Georges Daressy in 1991 and Christiane Zivie-Coche in 1991. It is a detailed historical account of Khufu discovering and rebuilding an old temple, restoring its divine temple statues, and repairing a worn and damaged Great Sphinx, and implies that the Sphinx predates the

Giza pyramids. The mortar found in between the granite blocks of the Great Pyramid has indeed been carbon dated to be 4,600 years old proving that, indeed, this mortar is from Khufu's time. However, as the Stele indicates that Khufu had restored a great temple, it is likely that this was the Great Pyramid which, if you will, been repointed.

Consequently, the current 'Khafre-Sphinx Theory', that his son Khafre built the Sphinx, and the story told on the Inventory Stele, cannot both be true, as Khufu could not be repairing the Sphinx that had not yet been built by Khafre. Hence, probably, why it is under lock and key.

Which brings me to this very final damning bit of evidence. We now know that around 8,000 BC this part of Egypt was a lush, forested area and it was then that the lands began to dry up until we have the climate in the area that we have today. Erosion marks on the Sphinx, which is the largest limestone structure in the world, shows that it was subjected to water erosion for thousands of years. Seashell growth on the Sphinx and great pyramid along with saltwater crystals on the great pyramid when it was opened up, back in the 1200's, have recently been carbon dated and shown to be 12,000 years old. If these structures have been coated in 12,000-year-old salt and seashells, pray tell how it is possible for a man that lived only a mere 4,200 years ago to have built them?

Your Honor, the Defense rests."

"Thank you, Counsel. The Jury will now retire to consider its verdict."

- - - - - - - - - -

"Your Honor, the Jury are returning."

"Thank you, Clerk.

The Foreman of the Jury, please stand. Have you reached a verdict on which you all agree?"

"Yes, Your Honor."

"How do you find?"

"We find that owing to the reams of evidence supplied by the Defense it is highly likely that Khufu was *not* the architect nor builder of the Great Pyramid."

"I agree entirely. Case closed!"

Novel Teasers

The Ainsworth Chronicles
Book One: The Joining
Prologue

Somewhere in the darkness the coarse flax fibers of the Hangman's noose sing,
Its hollow voice swinging to the hangman's beckoning.
Waiting for the answers buried into the gurgle of time and the finality of voices ending.
From the stillness comes a subtle calling. Echoing reminders of what remains, Disturbed and unsettled.
~Frank Talaber~

Chapter One

F

ront deskman Samuel Desmond's eyes opened in horror as the wet, naked man thumped towards him bearing only a bath towel, a watch and the look of a man stepping into a warzone. The splodge of soapy footsteps echoed behind him as he thumped down the ornate front staircase of Victoria's Fairmont Empress Hotel.

"Sir, do you realize you are naked in our lobby, dripping soap and water all over our new and *very* expensive Isfahan rugs?"

The man thumped his hand on the counter. Water splattered. "I'm wet, pissed, cold and locked out of my room. Jake Holden, Blanshard suite."

Samuel looked down, bowing to the sheer anger seething in Jake's eyes, and clacked away on his booking computer. He hesitated a moment, pressed the button for the day manager and, summoning up his courage, turned back to Jake while water continued dripping onto the counter.

"It would appear you are not a registered guest. I would need ID to let you back into any suite."

Jake stepped back and opened his towel. "Does it look like I've got any ID on me?"

Samuel's eyes widened in shock. "But I'm not allowed to let anyone in without ID."

Jake re-wrapped the towel, leaned over and grabbed the clerk by the scruff of his neck, effortlessly pulling him over the counter, until all Samuel could see was the man's watch. Mickey Mouse's left hand stood at ten, his right at two.

"The only ID I got are these fingerprints and if you don't let me back in
    my room your face is about to become an ink blotter. *Kapish?*"

Her private cellphone rang as Carol Ainsworth, ostensibly Day Manager, actually undercover cop on assignment, was about to bolt from her office in response to Samuel's panic button. She wasn't sure what she'd expected to find but a naked six-foot giant of a man yelling into Samuel's face and half dragging him across the counter wasn't on her list of possibilities, not in a world-class hotel.

Forgot to turn off my phone. Carol glanced at the text from her sister and the first word was

Urgent. She paused, her sister wasn't a person to send idle chat.
"Urgent! Nathan has vanished."

As she quickly texted back Samuel struggled to reach the buzzer.

"Will call ASAP."

Carol turned off her phone and quickly marched over to the front desk. Her and her sister, Barbara, didn't talk much but Barb was never one to overreact. Whatever happened to her nephew must be serious.

So much for a quiet first day on the job. Okay, calm down. One thing at a time.

"Yes, sir, how may I help you?" She dropped her hand to gain comfort in the holster she didn't have on this assignment. *Damn it! Shouldn't have listened to the morons telling me not to carry!* Her cop instinct took over, mentally noting every detail of any possible importance. *White Caucasian, six two, light tan, light brown hair, Mickey Mouse watch on left wrist, ripped to the max. Probable weightlifter strung out on steroids. Jeez, I might as well be back on the skid rows of Vancouver! What the hell would a real hotel manager be doing right now?*

She tried to think of something, anything, she'd learned in the week of intense hotel management training they'd put her through in preparation for this assignment that might be of any possible use to her in this situation. As a street cop she'd just chop him across the back of the knees and slap the cuffs on him as he fell. Somehow that didn't seem like the way to treat a guest of this grand establishment. *Plan B's definitely lock him up and then ask questions, though.*

"I asked for the hotel manager," he growled.

Carol glanced around the newly refurbished lobby, with its gold balustrades and pastel shaded panels. Fortunately, no other guests were milling around this time of the afternoon so hopefully this wouldn't turn into a full-blown media fiasco. That was the *last* thing she needed, considering the guests who'd be arriving in the next little while.

"What seems to be the problem here?" She folded her arms in front of her.

"I said I asked for the—"

"And I, sir, *am* the hotel manager, and before I discuss anything with you, you will let go of my desk clerk." She caught the nearly imperceptible rise of his eyebrows. "And gently. The Fairmont Victoria Empress Hotel does not take kindly to hotel guests strolling naked in public areas, nor do we care to have them accosting our front desk staff." His eyebrow raised higher as he glared at her.

Carol had certainly handled bigger men. She stood her ground and glared back. If she hadn't been on assignment, she'd have told him to drop the desk clerk before she shoved his eyebrows so far up his ass it'd take a laser scope to get them out, but since she was, she didn't.

The glare-down continued as Samuel's face turned redder. Finally, Jake broke eye-contact and glanced down at her name tag. Carol had established control. She allowed herself to breathe.

Time to press her advantage home.
"I *said* Let. Him. Go. And I'm not telling you a third time."

Jake lowered Samuel to the ground. "Sorry, didn't expect a skirt. I mean a female manager." And he certainly hadn't expected a gorgeous brunette. She even looked good in her standard designed-for-all-shapes and-sizes corporate uniform. She wasn't intimidated in the least, not by his size or his state of undress. In fact, she was absolutely in control of the situation. Something very sexy in that. He liked his women assertive. Her eyes, though. Something in her eyes grabbed him right in the gut. Too much knowledge of the world and how bad it could be, that was it. He'd learned long ago to read people's faces in his career, it'd saved his life many times when undercover.

Something about this woman he knew almost nothing about stirred his blood and wearing just a bath towel probably wasn't such a good idea. Especially in light of what he *did* know about her. She was undoubtedly Canadian undercover detective on duty Carol Ainsworth. *Our file reports don't do her justice.*

"Jake Holden, and you have my apology. I've been overstressed at work recently and decided to take a relaxing trip here." He extended his hand. It was partly the truth, he'd taken this assignment to get away from LA, a place where you always had to watch your back and no man was a friend. *Especially the crazy ones strung out on drugs.*

She made sure Samuel was breathing well on his own before she shook hands. The touch sent an erotic jolt through him. He glanced down and smiled. *No ring. Possibilities.*

"Apology accepted. Carol Moore, Day Manager of the Fairmount Empress Hotel." Carol studied Jake. She liked what she saw. And then again, she didn't. Those dark eyes of his — they reminded her of places she hadn't been and feelings she hadn't felt in a long time. Not since Alan, her fiancé, with the same dark, dangerous eyes she fell in love with was shot dead on duty six years ago. *It's been too long. Too damn long. So get a grip, get over it, and get on with it.*

I've got possibly even more urgent matters to deal with my nephew.

"So why don't you tell me the problems leading up to this little *au naturel* trip into my lobby, Jake Holden?"

"Two things. One, I was taking a — quote — luxurious bubble bath — unquote — as stated in your hotel's brochure and after using over half the bottle found it didn't even make enough suds to coat the tub. Two, seeing as how my bubble bath was a no-go, I stupidly stepped out to grab some ice for my whiskey, leaving my key inside and locked myself out of my room. And since I didn't think the hotel would appreciate me breaking the door down, I came downstairs so someone could let me back in. That's when this employee of yours informed me while I'm standing here cold, wet and naked, he's not going to let me back in my room without proper ID."

"I can verify that indeed he does not possess any identification." Samuel straightened his tie and blushed. Of course, he took the precaution of backing as far away from the counter as possible. "Sir, the hotel's policy is quite clear on allowing the use of an extra key. We must have ID. We have high profile clients attending and high security standards at this hotel. However, I was about to call the manager when you put my neck in a vice, rendering me unable."

Carol caught Jake twitch one hand and decided to take over before Samuel got himself killed. "Okay, Samuel. I've got this." Carol turned to Jake. "I'll take you up and you can show me your ID then, is that acceptable?"

"Yes. And what about the bubble bath?"

"Well, I can assure you if the hotel's brochure states we provide luxurious bubble baths, we'll provide you with a luxurious bubble bath and I personally will make sure this matter is handled." She passed him a business card, even though he had no place to put it. He glanced at the card and handed it back.

"Good. I'm starting to get just a tad cold, standing here in nothing but my birthday suit. Things are beginning to shrivel up into my throat."

Jake stepped backwards. A cool rush of air reminded him he was naked except for the undersized bath towel and his proximity to Carol was making continued coverage by that undersized bath towel precarious. The scar below his left ear twinged in response to the memory of what happened the last time he'd responded to a woman. *Crazy bitch. And she was better left forgotten.*

Jake maintained as much dignity as possible as he walked toward the elevator. He had to admit the situation was totally ludicrous. He hoped to hell there weren't any witnesses and no videos of the past ten minutes captured on any unseen guest's phone. He could read the local headlines now. *Naked Man Roams Lobby of Five Star Hotel.* So much for being discreet in this assignment.

One thing he knew. By the time he'd gotten what he'd come here for, he'd also know a lot more about Carol than her name. *Maybe one hell of a long, cold shower is more in order than a hot soapy bath.*

Sandy tied the rubber tube around her arm and flicked at her skin a couple of times. The stink of the sewers they were in, didn't seem to effect either. "Oh man, everybody says this

White Lady skank is good shit."

"Yeah, Wildflower said it was the best, like mixed with enough fentanyl to put you away. I saw angels, girlfriend. Lights, the light. You, like, brought me back from the light."

"Cool. Yo-yoing is so freaking trippy." Cindy sat on her haunches, unable to stand. Coming back from the dead had that effect on a girl. She held the free government Naloxone needle with both hands because she shook all over. Her skinny frame was pocked with jab wounds and scabs where she'd scratched herself over and over, something she did every time she came down.

Sandy found a vein undamaged enough to take the needle and plunged it into her own arm. "You know the deal. After I go limp, count to ten and bring me back. Don't get any better high than flat-lining and coming back." Her needle-scarred arm shook, and she slumped backwards.

Her eyes rolled into the heavens. The needle clinked to the concrete floor.

Cindy raised the needle. "One, two..."

Blue light flooded the chamber, coming up from the sewer tunnels leading in and out of the room.

"Three, four... *what the fuc—*"
Blue flames tore up through her, the Naloxone vial exploded.
"Sandy's gonna die without the ..."

She screamed as flames tore through her, taking her over until she became the flames and the flames became her.

You and she shall join us instead. Another mass of blue flames descended on the drugged-up woman on the ground and lifted her body up, then slammed it to the ground. Cinders sparked upward before Cindy's eyes exploded in embers and her body burned from the inside out. A haze of blue sparks skittered over the ground.

Both blue flame elementals stared at the two piles of ashes left behind and at the countless needles stuck into the Chambers wall, some leaking their contents onto the cold cement floor.

Neither was the one we seek.
He is coming.
Yes, he disturbs us, the undead and those seeking deliverance.
We are restless and the one we dread is coming with a vengeance.

They scratched at each other with long angry fingers. Flames and sparks exploded. They swept down the cold tunnels and left the chamber, needle tubes clinking in the dark.

He comes.

In the blue glow a pair of eyes stared waiting before he moved to get up watching the blue sparks slowly going out one after another.

Carol followed Jake into the elevator, tapping the plastic key on her other hand as the elevator rose, catching the scents of the fragrant bubble bath and his natural sweat. *Gotta admit, if a naked man had to roam around in the lobby, at least it was a good-looking one.* That was the problem, he reminded her a lot of Alan, muscular and hard. *You could bend chisels on those biceps. Crap, focus on work lady, I've got other serious matters to attend to.*

Jake reached down to snug the towel tighter. "You know, it's the hotel manager's job to keep the guests happy. If you wanted to help make all this up to me, you could have dinner with me. You're not married, are you? I don't see a ring."

"No. I was engaged but my fiancé passed away a few years ago."

"Sorry to hear that. A few years ago? Dating anyone seriously now or are you open to dinner? I was joking about it being part of your job description and really, I'd like to say thank you for the way you handled things back there."

Man, so much for being sincerely remorseful. He doesn't take long to dive in when the opportunity presents itself. "I'm afraid not."

"Meaning no you're not going out with anyone or meaning no you won't go out for dinner?" He glanced her over.

Christ, the way he's looking I think he just peeled my clothes off with his eyes, son of a bitch. God, I hate men like him. Sometimes. "Why don't we do this? You leave me a message on my cell phone. It's on my card. I don't discuss personal business while on duty."

"The one I handed back to you since I didn't have anywhere to put it?"

"I'll give it back to you when we get to your room. I might consider going out for dinner later." Carol wasn't an idiot. Both of them liked what they saw in the other, but she had more important things to deal with first. She was working and her first group of Mafia were about to arrive. That took top priority.

The doors opened, and they trundled down the carpeted corridor. Carol gave the key reader a quick swipe and pushed the door open.

"Here you go. And as promised, here's my card again."

"I'm free tomorrow at eight. Like seafood? Heard of a place that has great reviews just down the street, Nautical Nellies."

"I'll think about it. But only if you wear more than a towel. I don't think the fish would blush, but the women might get flustered."

Jake walked over to his jacket and pulled out his wallet, handing her his ID. "Lady, I think the scallops would turn red seeing you naked. And I think I might just too." He grinned as Carol took the proffered document, ignoring his blatant come-on as she glanced at his driver's license.

American.

"Seeing me naked isn't going to happen and I'd watch your tongue and manners in this establishment. Any other reports of rude, vulgar or disrespectful behaviour to guests or staff and

I will have you evicted."
He scowled at her. "My apologies."

"Now, this appears to be in order. I apologize for the confusion." She committed his driver's license number to memory. For some reason alarm bells were going off in her head.

He escorted Carol to the doorway, admiring her rear view.
"And what makes you think you're going to see me naked?"
"A guy can always hope, can't he?"
"I think blood's rushing to the wrong part of your body."
"I don't suppose you'd care to stick around for a drink or three?"

"Don't push your luck, Mr. Holden, I haven't even agreed to have dinner with you yet. In public. Let alone have drinks with you alone in your room. That goes beyond our employee guidelines, even for management."

Oh, yes. She was definitely his type. Guts, fire and willpower. "My apologies for being rude and presumptuous, and thanks again for letting me into my room. Please apologize to your clerk for me. I'm known for my short-fuse back home."

"I will, but I really think you should apologize to him yourself too, if your ego can take it. I'll let you know about dinner." Carol walked out before he could respond. The entire episode had certainly given her a new respect for hotel staff. *Do they really have to deal with things like this?* And her naked guest was American. A fluke, or was he there because of the expected guests? Dinner was definitely on the cards because she seriously needed to check this guy out, and not just for his physique, although it helped, he was easy on the eyes. Something didn't smell right. One background check coming up, but first things first, she rounded the corner at the far end of the hotel and rang her sister.

"Carol, thank God you called. Nathan's missing. I found his window open and he's gone." The voice of her sister trembled. Carol knew how much she loved her son and her two daughters.

They were her whole world. "Wow! Okay I'll be there tonight." "Tonight?" Barb's voice shook.

"I'm in Victoria. So I'll head over when I can, but I really can't leave my post right away.

Understand? I'll explain more when I get there. Later in late afternoon."

She could hear Barb begin to sob on the phone. "You're here? In Victoria?"

"Yes, can't say anything more, working undercover. I'll be over as soon as I can. Where did you see him last?"

"I woke up in this morning and... he wasn't there." She stopped, allowing herself to think about what Carol had just asked. "The bedroom, I tucked him in. He's gone, and his bedroom window was open."

"Okay, I know this is hard, but you got to hold it together, for him, for yourself and for me. I'll be over and you show me what you know. Now have you called the police?"

"Yes. They left a couple of hours ago."

"Good. I'm really sorry I can't leave right now but you're in good hands."

"Thanks Carol. I wouldn't know what to do if you weren't
in my life."
"We'll find him."
"But what if he's ...'"

"He ain't. You gotta trust yourself and think positive. I *will* find him no matter what."

"Yes, yes, think positive. See you tonight."
The phone went dead cutting off the sound of Barb bawling freely.

Not having children Carol couldn't really feel the depths of Barb's anguish. But she knew
Nathan, he was a good kid, raised by a loving, caring mother. *And here I thought I'd have a couple weeks of a somewhat sedate undercover operation babysitting pretentious rich people and the mob in stuffy Victoria. Not the pinkies extended and pass the tea and crumpets day she expected.*

A six-year-old boy stands on the corner of Shelbourne Street and Hillside Avenue and stares at the sky as his hands tingle. The blue begins to splinter into shades of purple and orange, even though it's only midday. Houses vanish, concrete dissipates. His skateboard melts beneath him until his feet touched gravel road, not asphalt.

"Mommy?"
Only fields of waving grass answer his plea.

Behind him an older woman emerges from the swirl of dust, stepping out of the past into the present. She stares at the boy and gestures for him to approach. She holds two chocolate bars in her hands. She seems nice enough as she offers him one. He reaches up to take it but hesitates.

"My mom said don't talk to strangers."

"Of course not. But I'm just a sweet old lady, what do you have to fear from me? I think you'd make a wonderful playmate for my son."

He takes the chocolate bar and begins to unwrap it.
"Come with me, I'll introduce you to him."

The boy follows. His skateboard reforms in his hands. Concrete coalesces back into reality, replacing gravel with asphalt, and houses grow anew. The chocolate wrapper lies crumpled on the deserted sidewalk.

Carol closed her office door behind her and dialed Big Dan McKinney, her superior. A bulky six-foot two that didn't take shit from anyone. Carol had the greatest respect for the man that some called tough as nails. Others, but never to his face, called him an outright asshole. One thing he was, was honest and up front. "What's up, lady. Didn't expect to be hearing from you already. Have the mob arrived yet?

"No sir. I've got a problem. Just got a text from my sister, who lives in Victoria. Her son, my only nephew, appears to have been abducted. I want

—"

"That ain't happening. We just put you on the case and slammed you through intense upper hotel management." He hesitated. "Is your sister's last name Pendray?"

"What? No? Why ask?"

"Have you read the morning papers yet like I told you to, so that you keep up to the latest in town?"

"No, I just dealt with a crazy naked man in the lobby and was about to call the IT guys when

I got a text from my sister. She asked for my help."

"Look at the damn first page of the paper."

Carol grabbed the daily paper that was on her desk and read the newspaper's lead story.

Pendray Heir Missing! The young son of one of Victoria's elite families is missing. The pioneer Pendray family discovered their six-year-old son Robert was not in his bedroom this morning. Police believe he was abducted from his second storey bedroom during the night and are asking for any information.

"Shit. That's not her, his name is Nathan."

"Crap. Okay, I get that this is important to you, but I need you to stay on this case. I'll make some calls and try to get someone to step in or sub as much as possible. I'll contact Victoria, appraise them of the situation, get hold of their files and tell them we want you to join in that investigation as well. I'm double dutying you, so don't let me down. Once the journos hear of this the shit is going to be spread all over the place. So, low profile, but the focus is on the mob, got it?"

"Yes, sir, and thank you."

"You owe me a favor, I'll get hell for this, but I get it, its family. Hope none of this is linked to the mob showing up, but I don't believe in coincidences or Chinese lucky draws. If there's a connection here. Find it." He was about to hang up. "Oh, I've just been informed the Americans have an operative there in the hotel as well."

"Are we supposed to be working together on this case then?"

"They haven't said as much, but that's the Americans. What I hear you'll hear." "I think I may have already met him." She told him of Jake in the hallway.

"So much for keeping a very low profile. Could be the guy, call IT and check him out. I'll pull some strings. Damn Americans. Thought they were our friendly next-door neighbors."

"Not after that crack Trump made about us burning down the White House."

"Well, we did, way back in history, and kicked their butts twice in a war, otherwise we'd be singing the Star-Spangled Banner and drinking that watered-down piss water they call beer.

Keep me abreast of either case." Dan hung up the phone.

Yup, never a man to mince his words.

Carol called the Crime Lab's best IT guy, Louie Degraff next. She pulled up her secure email as she waited for an answer. "Hey, Louie, can you run a check on a Jake Holden for me? I'm e-mailing his fingerprints right now."

"No problem, that's why I'm here. You use the business card trick?"

"Yeah, that thing comes in handy. Got a still of him off the lobby security camera as well, so you can run a facial recognition search and see who we see who we really come up with."

"*Ahh,* you did that just for little old me? You spoil me. 'Kay, I'll get back to you *ASAP.*"

"Don't suppose yesterday's a possibility?"

"Not unless somebody invented time travel and didn't tell me. Patience is a virtue. Hit you back soon as I can."

"Thanks. Text me on my private line, I've got other business to attend to."

Carol leaned back in her chair. She couldn't wait to hear back from Louie. Her gut told her Jake Holden was either mob or American law enforcement who might, or might not, be on or off duty. And if he was on duty, he'd be butting into her operation. But whoever he was and whatever his reason for being here, one thing she was sure of. With those looks he was definitely trouble of one kind or another.

She called her sister on her private line. "See you later today, I've joined the case will talk more when I get there."

She checked incoming emails, but nothing on Barb's file had arrived yet.

The Ainsworth Chronicles
Book Two: The Mystery of Ms. Teak

"I have sometimes wondered if it were possible that unrecognized forces of the past,
or present,
or even the future,
work through the thoughts and actions of living men."
December 14, 1933
Robert E. Howard

"The only thing necessary for the triumph of evil
is for good men to do nothing."
Edmund Burke

"I stand before the doorway between all that is and all that was.
Each breath takes away from those left remaining.
Wondering where is the truth in all that truly matters.
Or does anything ever truly matter?"
Agnes Van Lunt

Prelude

Bass drums thunder into the roiling madness of hell torn asunder
While screams coalesce into whispers of wants.
Angels shimmy seduction on stilettos and guitars shriek like sirens in heat,
Yet on the edge of darkness, I linger patiently.
As the devil snaps his fingers
In time to the chaotic symphony of his creation
I lurk in the shadows, along with those unlucky enough to venture within.
Sweating, I inhale nicotine's deep addictive essence.
And sit,
Waiting.
Flicking discarded ashes about me like spent lives.
Knowing my time will come again.
As the band plays on.

Chapter One

Victoria, British Columbia, 1862

"Agnes I'm going to fricking kill you," Carol blurted under her breath as her high, black leather boots with lace inserts sank into the thick slop of Government Street in downtown Victoria, "when I get out of this."

A chestnut-colored draft horse whinnied as it approached pulling the open carriage, the smell of manure ripe in the warm summer air. She glanced at the front page of the Victoria Colonist newspaper in a nearby stand. "What? 1862? I'm supposed to be in October 1929."

As the carriage passed by, a stinking mixture of manure and mud flung up from the oversized wheels to land on the high pleated hem of the lacy ankle-length dress Carol was trying to keep clean.

"Bastard!" She stepped onto the wooden sidewalk and swiped at the fabric with her dainty gloves. "It's going to take hours to hand wash this."

Taking a seat on the cast iron bench next to her, she clutched her shawl around her as tears threatened.

If I ever get out of this and get back.

****

One Week Ago, Present Day.

"There are two heat signatures in water." Dimitri glanced at the navigation screen of his darkened luxury cruiser, disguised in the black waters of Victoria's Inner Harbour. "Swing back. Eject clean-up crew. No one to be knowing what happened here tonight, da?" he spat at Ivan, his second in command and the other men in the control room.

My bosses back in Moscow not going to be liking this one bit.

He reached for his wireless mic. "Starboard ninety degrees. Preparing units one to five. Silent Run."

A rumble rolled through the ship as the visor door in the side of the hull raised into the night sky. From above, Dimitri eyed the five shadowy Sea-Doos, armed by men in scuba gear, as they sped towards the fire still blazing from the exploded cruise ship. Sirens screamed in the gloom. The Victoria Fire and Naval Rescue would be here in minutes.

"*Blyat*," Dimitri swore as several blips winked on his radar screen. "What the hell is that, Ivan?"

Through his earpiece, Ivan strained to identify the sounds the boat picked up via its external mic. "Call them back, *seychas.*"

Dimitri studied his screen. "Why?"

"Distant motors off the port side. Moving extremely fast. *Da.*" He glared up at Dimitri next to him.

"*Po Hooy*, take them all out. There must be no witnesses." He watched the burning drug ship they had boarded and taken down only an hour before, as instructed by his Mafioso contracts. They were supposed to invade it and appropriate the vessel's drugs, not sink the damn thing.

"They came from this ship here." Ivan jabbed at the screen.

"What ship? *Lisus Khristos*! Where that be coming from?"

"Like us, they're using jamming equipment. I'm getting typical American signatures."

"Fucking *Pindos*. Okay, da. Call men back! We not tangle with American authorities in Canadian waters. Mob not paying enough."

Ivan straightened up in apparent shock. "Too late. Units one and two are gone. I hear rapid gunfire." He held his hands over his ears, trying to focus on his wireless.

A substantial *blub* erupted from the middle harbour as the bombed ship dipped below the surface of the inky tide. Slicks of oil and flame rippled over the broiling waters as Dimitri watched from his viewing window on the command bridge.

More machine-gun fire roared into the night. "I think we lost another, and Canadian signature vessels are heading our way." Pulling open a cover, Ivan flicked three switches, and three bright lights erupted in the Inner Harbour's pitch dark waters. There wouldn't be enough equipment or body parts remaining to identify. Dimitri's undercover men would make sure of it.

"The last two are returning. No pursuit in sight. The Yankee bastards must also not want to be found out." Ivan cursed as he caressed the unshaven stubble of his face.

"Good. Back us up, and be keeping main guns and missiles trained on vessel's signature. They approach? Engage," Dimitri ordered as he turned from the captain's window, running his hand over grey hair, which suddenly felt greyer.

"The ship these men came from is an American ship. Only one of that size is registered in this harbour, *The Sea Horsey*. The structure of its jamming would indicate American, possible FBI Ops," Ivan spat out.

"Damn! In briefing, they said Americans interested in Mafia being here, but said no expecting armed naval presence, especially with advanced weapons they maybe have on board, da?" Dimitri thought quickly. "But how they knowing about drug shipment? We release drone to follow ship."

"Would appear everyone is heading back to *The Sea Horsey*, including the two earlier heat sources that jumped from the boat moments before it exploded. They were picked up by the operatives that came from it." Ivan grimaced as the three comrades flicked switches, allowing the survivors on board.

"Ivan, have undercover backup units be calling all hospitals and emergency clinics, and get our men to hack into nearest hospital and access records too. If anyone be checking in within next two hours—for water inhalation or any wounds or hypothermic shock—I wanting them to be tracked down and dealt with, da?

"As for us, make for the San Juan strait. Keep in Canadian waters until we be finding out what the hell going on here. No one must follow us. Be hitting Americans with full-on jamming signal. Now," Dimitri ordered and closed his eyes as, at nearly full throttle, the dimed luxury cruiser lurched for the open waters of the Salish Sea.

"*Pizdets.*" A glimpse at their radar screen told him they weren't being followed.

His bosses were going to be out a lot of money from the shipment going down, and he knew whose head would roll. "*Blyad*, why I giving up smoking before voyage? Have Victor bring another bottle vodka to my quarters."

****

Present Day

"Hello. What can I do for you, young lady?" The female constable addressed the strange-looking young girl from behind the protection of her plexiglass shield.

Agnes brought a hand up the flannel nightdress to pull at the high neck, which threatened to choke her. Clutching the counter, she blinked to bring the officer into focus. "Sorry. I got the zorros and felt dizzy. I just got here," Agnes said as she shook her head.

Where did Jeanie go?

She looked around the police station and noticed there was no dial phone on the desk. She caught her reflection in the large mirror. For the first time, she was as solid as her surroundings, but Jeanie wasn't to be seen.

This doesn't look like 1952, so I must be in the future again. But at least I'm not in those grody sewers this time.

Her gaze flicked back to the woman behind the shield, to the cell phone in the officer's pocket and the tiny camera on her chest, before settling on her badge. 'Constable Travis, Victoria Police,' it read.

So I am in the future, and there's only one person I need to talk to. Why I know this, I have no idea, but I do. A memory from my past that I haven't lived yet. Golly, this time-travel stuff is confusing. I'm sure my Jeanie would be giggling about these phantasmagoric contradictions.

"Just got here? From where, miss?"

"Don't know actually. Got yanked from where I was," she lied. "This is Victoria, 2019, isn't it?" she said for effect as she stared around.

"Give me a second." The female officer raised an eyebrow as she pressed a button below her counter for help. She retreated a couple of steps and spoke softly over her internal mic. "Young female, bearing emo or steampunk retro clothing. Looks out of it. Ten or eleven, possibly smacked out."

She returned to the young girl before her. "You are correct on both. You okay? Been taking any drugs? Mushrooms?" She studied Agnes, waiting for the expected answer. "I will ask again. Who are you, and have you any ID? I'll need to contact your parents."

The dark-haired girl patted her pockets.

Parents? Don't have any here. Long dead.

"I don't have any ID, and my parents aren't here. Say, I'm looking for a detective named Carol Ainsworth. I need to speak to her." She held her hand to her head trying to stay conscious as a wave of nausea washed over her.

Popping up here does take its toll on one's stamina. She patted her pockets. *Oh yeah, way too young to be packing my flask of bourbon. Darn.*

"Sweetie, I don't know what's happened to you or why you're dressed in that…Victorian garb, if you're part of a school play or are lost, but I do know there's no officer Ainsworth in this detachment. Now, come inside." She pressed the button to open the door to the precinct as two male officers arrived. "Let us get you some water and contact your parents. I'm sure they must be worried about you."

"No. As I said, they are not here. Probably been dead for a long time. Carol isn't an officer, she is a detective, and I *need* to talk to her."

Constable Travis looked more puzzled than ever as the two men escorted the girl into a holding area. "I'm afraid you're mistaken, young lady. That is quite the story. How, may I ask, did you think of this crazy story and a make-believe police officer?"

The girl looked up at her, eyes blazing. "Not 'officer.' Detective. Undercover at the Empress. She'll want to speak to me. Tell her I'm Agnes."

Travis stared at Agnes as she sat before her in the interview room. One of the male officers looked her over and whispered back to Travis, "No wonder you called. Why's a young girl wandering the streets in only a nightdress and lace-up black leather boots? I agree, she should be drug tested, or we at least wait to see if she comes down off her high. Might be able to get some sense out of her then."

"Agreed," Travis replied. "Only I don't get why she's telling such a bizarre tale." She turned back to Agnes. "Now, sweetie, who did you say you are?"

"I am Agnes. Agnes Van Lunt."

Ainsworth Chronicles
Book Three: Into The Dark Side
Prelude

In the thick undergrowth the thump of padded feet echo
to a full bloated moon as it cries out to the dark.
Whisps of cold misting breath disturbs the stillness.
On I prowl, alone.
Not caring, unendingly alone.
The moon cries out my echoing voice as it appears from behind a
disguising cloud,
like the crack that stares back at you from the ceiling as you stare up at
it.
Widening, slowly, almost unnoticeable, except for the flickering
trembles in my mind.
Knowing, fearing, it will collapse, raining all that you feared outside to
the world.
All that you knew you were capable of but never admitted to.
Except to the little uglies inside that keep calling forth in your
subconscious.
The ones you were told that were alright, to accept and like,
but kept clawing at the little truths, slaying them one at a time.
The crack widens imperceptibly every morning.
CRACK.
Every time you aren't paying attention.

C R

A
C

K

Chapter One

Beware of the man who does not talk and the dog who does not bark.

Native prophecy.

"Come out with your hands up! We have the trailer surrounded!" Carol's voice bellowed from the megaphone. SWAT team members in helmets and black flak jackets lowered their visors and took position. A dozen guns clicked at the ready.

"We've got him." Carol's heavy breathing broke the silence as the SWAT team closed in further on the trailer home. "This time."

"Come out! If you don't, we're coming in!" Big Dan, her boss, bellowed through his megaphone.

I will never surrender. He dropped the drug dealer's bloody body with a thump, his guts spewing free from where Woden had sliced him open. *Fair repayment for your fentanyl-laced drugs that had just killed three users. There are so many evil ones living in this time and making money from other people's misery.*

Hate burned in his eyes, searing into that gaping hole in his heart.

"Last chance!" shouted Carol.

"He's too dangerous. Cover all possible exits and pump in two smoke bombs," Big Dan commanded.

What seemed like a long silence ensued, but it was probably only a few seconds. Then, a muted, tinny voice whispered outside the mobile home, just within his hearing range, Carol's voice, on the walkie-talkie.

"Everyone ready? On three." She waited a few seconds then began to count down via the hand signal. First three fingers... then two...

Woden visualized in his inner mind the line-up of heavily armed police, the one holding the smoke bombs, the hush of fingers rubbing along triggers. *They were police, good souls. I must not kill them. Unless I have to.*

This time.

On the sign to advance, two officers ran silently up to the trailer window: one smashed it in with a metal baton, another heaved in the two smoke grenades. Two thumps and smoke poured out of the shattered glass as two more burst their way in through the metal-framed door with a battering ram.

Woden slammed open the upper sunroof in a crash of plastic, ran along the roof and, shouldering aside the advancing officer with immense speed and strength, leapt across to the field.

"Open fire!"

In response to Big Dan's command, a thud of bullets sprayed though the air into the woods in a futile attempt to down their prey and end this craziness.

Carol hung back. The scene brought to mind all the Star Wars films, the myriad of scenes that depicted the Stormtroopers blasting away to their heart's content, but not one of the fiery beams found its target.

"Get him!" Big Dan ordered, and four took off after him at a considerable speed, considering the weight of suit and gear.

Carol shook her head, knowing the phenomenal, almost superhuman, speed Woden could utilize meant they had no chance of catching him. She knew he was already long gone. The third time in the last two weeks.

At least it wasn't as bad as the las time. Memories of a biker gang flooded her head - six, maybe seven - it was hard to make out how many bodies when so many of their parts were strewn around the room in a horrible mess. Two young girls, one dead from the drugs, the other half crying, half screaming at the carnage she witnessed before they arrived. One thing Carol knew; unless she also dealt in the drugs, he'd not hurt her. At least the innocent ones were safe.

She knew what he was after and in some ways she had a hard time justifying capturing someone that was actually doing some good, albeit in a macabre fashion, in our drug-laden society; killing those that were making money from killing their customers. Killing their customers! Where was the sense in that?

Minutes later, Big Dan walked out of the trailer holding the hanky over his nose. "Damn! Reeks of puke and guts in there."

Carol rested her elbow on the roof of the police car, finishing her smoke. Dan didn't show up at many crime scenes these days, and rarely on anything like this case, especially here in Victoria, BC. She knew he hated anything to with 'woo-woo shit,' as he called it, and left this up to Carol to deal with, her being what he called his newly elected officer in spiritual, ghostly matters. Or, as he was so fond of telling her, 'my woo-woo detective bitch'. Big Dan was a hard nut, had to be in his position, that's how he made it to the top of Vancouver's Police Department as Chief. He also admired Carol, as she was known to be smarter and tougher than most of the men in the line of Vancouver's detective work.

He snorted into the cloth and stuffed it into his pocket as he strode over to Carol. "I need to see you and Agnes. Your car, five minutes. Just need to take care of this scene first," he ordered in his deep voice, that some said reminded them of Darth Vader on tranquilizers.

"Why?"

"You're my paranormal detective. That's all you need to know. Like I said, right now!" He stormed away.

The others stared at her in shock. "Think we've done something wrong?"

Carol butted out her smoke. "Well, it's not the first time I've been reamed out, and it definitely won't be the last."

One Week Earlier

Water flooded Carol's eardrums drowning out the crash of raging water as it swept her along like a dying salmon returning to its creator along the Englishman River. Fighting to stay conscious in the sweeping water's torrent, Carol tried to block out the terrifying sound of the foaming waters cascading over the edge and disappearing into fine rainbow mist, knowing that very soon she would be joining it.

A low branch came through the spray, her last chance for salvation before careening over the waterfall and being smashed on the rocks below. She reached up and missed.

Carol gasped, struggling to keep her head above water and fighting to stay conscious as she was flung along in the violent rapids, trying to find purchase on something - anything - as she was swept along the stony shore.

From nowhere a voice: "Grab it, my drowning puppy."

A stick. No, a cane!

Carol grabbed at the offered lifeline and allowed whoever was at the end of it to pull her from the waters, her certain death only meters away.

"Man, I thought you could swim." A familiar voice, one she never expected to hear. At least not here.

Carol sputtered, coughing water from her lungs, trying to catch her breath. A more annoying voice, coming from someone she hated and loved nearly more than her boyfriend Brad, laughed at her. A hand thumped her on the back, and she puked up what was left of dinner and the river water. Carol took several gasping breaths. "I... What the... fuck... are *you* doing here?"

"Apparently, saving your sorry ass. And I think the words should be, 'thank you so very much for saving my worthless life." Charlie smiled his all-knowing cheeky smile, leaning on his ever-present orca-headed cane.

Carol gasped. She could barely hold on to consciousness, let alone talk. Another deep cough spewed spittle from within. "I ..., apologize. I'm... very grateful and do, ... do, thank you very much, Charlie." She felt the back of her head where she'd been whacked by one of the drug dealers. Blood still seeped out of the gash.

"Ah, I always thought you had great manners. You're welcome, my drowning mutt of a friend."

Carol hacked some more, spitting onto the shore. "Again, thanks Charlie, I... owe you my life. But what are you doing here?"

"You know, bored. Thought I'd stop by to visit you for some fancy-shmancy tea at this swanky hotel you've been hanging out in. You know one can only play so many games of poker with the raccoons and squirrels. Their chatting gets on my nerves and they cleaned me out of my winter nut stash. They told me you'd gone to the Englishman River and I had a twinge there might be some bother. So, here I am. And here you are. In some bother. As usual."

He smiled as she shivered from the cold, water dripping from her face and blood oozing out of her hair. "So, the spirits were right yet again." Carol hacked up more water unable to reply. "Let's get you seen to and feed you some of those lovely scones and hot tea. Or whisky. Whatever works for you." She nodded yes, and they made their way back to the trail that followed the raging rapids. "Then you can tell me what got you here and then we'll visit these not-so-friendly gents that did this to you, shall we?"

Checking her holster, Carol realised her gun was long gone. Great! Another expense. Big Dan's bellowing was already echoing in her head.

"So good to see you, Mother. You look well today," Davis Bhullar said as he entered her Vancouver nursing home room.

"I've brought another gift for you, my darling mature princess."

She smiled adoringly. But not at him. At the graduation photo of his sister Janice. Although he'd made something of his life and enjoyed a lucrative career as a vet, she was always her favourite. No expense had been spared on the haute couture purple gown and professional photographer, who had posed her perched on a low red velvet chair, the sea of purple arranged around her clashing marvellously with the bouquet of scarlet roses cradled in her arms. She was *her* princess. He detested his mother, despite calling her his princess, he did it because he knew it reminder her of his sister and brought grief to her heart.

There was only ever one picture of him displayed on the dresser and that was the hurriedly shot school graduation photo. He had been taken a little unawares and his mouth was slightly open, like some half-wit. It had been pushed right to the back of the dresser display and never made it here to the care center. "No room," she told him.

His mother had cried every day for weeks when Janice had disappeared, taking much of her grief out on him. She had yet to be declared dead, but that time would come, and if it didn't before mother passed away? Well, even more grief to her beleaguered soul.

He smiled at the thought.

The weak, simple son she had called him, and much worse, often getting slapped in the face for nearly anything when their traveling salesman dad was not at home. So many times he wanted to scream out in rage, squeeze her neck in his hands, stare into her eyes and watch her soul leave her. Only he hadn't and now, in a way, he was glad of that. This was so much better. A slower form of torture, after all those years of agony she had inflicted on him. The agony of not knowing whether Janice was alive or dead. He smiled again inside as, staring longingly at the beauty in purple, tears streamed down his mother's face. He made a half-hearted attempt to hide his gleeful grimace, but he needn't have bothered. He was invisible now, she saw only Janice.

He bent down to place the pretty jade green bracelet around her wrist, the wrist that belonged to the hand that beaten him so many times. The hand that held the stiff leather belt used to whip his tender bare skin. Sometimes his sister watched, smiling at him. So many times. The do-no-wrong sister, who merely got just the occasional scolding. No beating for her; no sir!

"So shall we go for a nice picnic down by the lake today?"

She nodded and he helped her into the wheelchair.

Yes, and maybe we'll talk more about the sister that could do no wrong in your eyes. Well, she could smile no longer and do no right or wrong now; not from six feet under.

Afterword
And Above All Else

To my wife Jenny; who does all of my corrections, grammar and proper punctuation before the rest of the world, and any editor, gets to see it, along with putting up with all of my sh*t. This novel and all of my others wouldn't be possible without all of her hard work.

PS. And she still loves me unconditionally (also she just edited this over my shoulder!).

If you really enjoyed this novel,
please feel free to leave a review.

The author will highly appreciate it

And it will help boost the rankings on the book-selling sites.

Thank You!

Stillwaters Runs Deep
Book One: Raven's Lament

Set in Haida Gwaii and based on a true incident.

A rare tree is felled in an ironic protest against logging, releasing an age-old god who decides he now has a vendetta.

Who is he targeting and why? And how do you set about defeating such

Stillwaters Runs Deep Book Two: The Lure

(Set in Vancouver, BC

Ever go out drinking and don't remember what you did?

What if there was a bar where spirits can take over your body and do whatever they please until you sober up?

Stillwaters Runs Deep

Book Three: The Awakening

A deranged shaman breaks his way into jail to stop all hell from breaking free while a mystical being seeks revenge for injustices against her family.

The Ainsworth Chronicles, Book One: The Joining

Welcome to the most haunted city in North America; Victoria, BC, and to Detective Carol Ainsworth's first day undercover at the five-star Fairmont Empress Hotel. Babysitting two Mafia families celebrating their union through marriage seemed straightforward, only she did not bargain on ghosts, a hot FBI agent, a hotter Mafioso, or the ancient curses. Add a mysterious psychic lady claiming to have been invited and Carol finds her first undercover assignment way more challenging than she ever could have imagined.

The Ainsworth Chronicles

Book Two: The Mystery of Ms. Teak

In order to save a young boy's life, Agnes, our esteemed psychic, has to alter timelines and agree to bring someone long-dead into the present.

Meanwhile, Carol has her hands full with pissed-off Russians, born-again ghosts, and a young girl claiming to be our aforementioned psychic.

The Ainsworth Chronicles

Book Three: Into The Dark Side

This dark and gritty psychological thriller explores the depths of human despair as Carol Ainsworth dives deeply into darkness as she tracks a cunning serial killer disguising murders as drug overdoses.

Cover Pending

Seeds Of Ascension

Book One: Spirits Awakening

Roger is thrust onto a path he never dreamed his life would take as one of the chosen few to attain something that philosophers and spiritualists have discussed for centuries; the ascension of humanity

Seeds Of Ascension

Book Two: Gateways

Roger discovers his guardian angel is not only real, but an alien that needs his help in order for humanity to reach ascension with the rest of the universe.

He first needs to discover the true essence of what he is to become by learning about the spiritual chakras

Short Story Anthology, Volume One: What I'd Say To Buddha If I Met Him In The Pub

What would you do it a holidaying alien popped into your head? Ever think what might happen if you're elected to tear down an old church and find a living person inside? Your mom brings home a sad-looking pooch; it changes your life and becomes your best friend. Clearing out old trinkets, you discover wartime field glasses with an embroidered heart encased inside a silver locket. Would it be a good thing if humanity discovered the serum to live forever?

And many more...

Short Story Anthology Volume Two: What I'd say to Einstein If I Met Him On The Dance Floor

Why is Frank Talaber called Canada's Foremost Off-Beat Author? Read on...

Two stories of being bewitched by a mystical witch and figuring out how to out-trick her (you hope!). Secrets your mother didn't ever want to reveal, until you found the photograph. Hitchhiking west coast shaman-style. What if you worked in the post office and began to read enticing postcards? Memories of a love so great, it still haunts you.

And many more bizarre stories to make you realize how does this guy sleep at night.

Short Story Anthology Volume Three: What I'd Say To Agatha Christie If I Met Her In The Knitting Circle

More off-the-wall stories, including:

Meeting your first wolf; or is he!

Late nights in a truck stop and the strange people that show up.

What if NASA used a person with multiple personality disorder to go to Mars?

Ever dream of being on a popular TV Series?

Also includes some of my non-fiction stories submitted to an RV magazine, and the short story which will form the basis for the upcoming Trust Me, I

Autumn's Summer

What if you were given up for adoption NOT because your mother didn't want you, but because she was trying to protect you from a curse? Autumn embarks on a voyage of discovery with the spiritualist, Summer, to find new meaning to her life. Learning that in Celtic traditions they are Anam Caras; soulmates through multiple lifetimes and

Shuttered Seductions

Julia-Rae only wanted to shut him out of her heart like every other man that ever got close, *not* to fall in love with him. He only wanted to seduce her and convince her to sell her company to him.

Only what do you do when you fall in madly in love with the enemy and the enemy with you? Will the dark secrets they hold tear them apart or bring them closer together?

What's a Lady Got to Do to Fulfil Her Life

Leanne Benson is a successful real estate agent in LA who abruptly loses everyone she loves on the same day. Reeling from these losses and drawn to the memory of her late mother, who gave up her ambition to be an artist to raise a family, Leanne embarks on a journey of discovery that will take her up to the Oregon Coast, into the enchanting Banff National Park in Canada, and ultimately to a better understanding of who she is and who

Other Novels by Frank Talaber
Stillwaters Runs Deep Series

Book One: Raven's Lament
(based on a true incident)

A madman cuts down a rare tree in protest of logging, releasing something he didn't intend to. Reporter Brooke Grant investigates the story, finds the love of his life, only to lose her to said being. Enlisting the aid of a deranged shaman he has to save his love and stop the world from being changed forever.

Reviews

WHISTLER INDEPENDENT BOOK AWARDS Fiction
Evaluation 2023

Easy to follow and immerse oneself into this well-told story.
The pace unfolds so naturally, I forgot that I was reading - which
is essential to achieving this result. Loved the narrative voice that
brought Characters to life through vivid descriptions and unforced
dialogue. Time and place are masterfully captured through poetic
and beautiful imagery. The writing style is wonderful, a celebration
of words, both visual and imaginative. This story has depth, the
themes are heartfelt and lingered long after I finished reading it. The
pulse of energy - otherworldly, Raven's Lament is a classic in waiting
with dream-like narration. I loved every inch of it.

**[Thanks Frank & good luck!] Molly Harrison WiBA
Coordination**

I was touched when I sensed the author's profound reverence for
trees; especially when I read his descriptions of the 'sobbing trees' as
they were axed down. This novel has the ring of an epic "Lord of the
Rings" journey -this is one journey that I'll always remember!

This is one of these books that you don't want to lay down until
it's finished. Great stuff!

Stephanie A. Bridgeman

"After being stranded twenty kilometers from the nearest road
at the tip of Rose Spit, Haida Gwaii, and having to push Frank's
spanking new SUV a few kilometers along the beach before the tide
came in and we ran out of booze, my first reaction on being asked to
write a back cover blurb was, "over my dead body." Some people will
do anything to get an endorsement."

Susan Musgrave/Cargo of Orchids/Given
Raven's Lament

264

Damn! I've been reading this book for three hours, can't put it down, and I have to get up for work in the morning. Your writing flows so well, I'm drawn completely into your novels while time goes by effortlessly reading them.

Barry Harris

What If a Book Could Make You Question Reality? That's exactly what Raven's Lament (Stillwaters Runs Deep Book One) by Frank Talaber does. This captivating book takes you on a thrilling journey where ancient secrets, environmental concerns, and supernatural forces collide in the most unexpected ways.

This book is an impressive read that left me completely hooked from start to finish.

Rakhi Verma

Stillwater Runs Deep
Book Two: The Lure

Ever go out drinking and don't remember what you did? What if there was a bar where spirits use your body for whatever they want until you sober up? What if the city's mayor has been murdered, his family missing, no clues and a witch has been released from her centuries old imprisonment? A deranged shaman shows up leaving clues and vanishes. So begins police detective, Carol Ainsworth's first big detective case.

Reviews

A refreshing change from the usual and all too familiar cast of deities and spirits. Talaber pulls his characters from the vast and untapped riches of aboriginal myth and legend, bringing to life their intricate stories largely unfamiliar to wider audiences. He intertwines their ancient tales with the dark, gritty and dangerous under belly of contemporary urban life. The whole makes for an interesting and compelling read with an ending that's impossible to predict.

Robert Winslow

Damn Frank—this writing is as tactile as a 1955 T-Bird. Very nice descriptions, good dialogue, a thinking man's book but one that can be read entirely for pleasure. Good work.

Michael Arkin/Judicial Indiscretion

Paranormal fantasy, mystery thriller rolled into one. The Lure is a well-crafted story that builds suspense through flowing narrative, life-like characters, and believable dialogue. If you're a fan of any of the above mentioned genres, or if you're just looking for a page turner to get lost in, The Lure will not disappoint.

Cris Pasqueralle/Destiny Revealed

A gritty book flavored with primitive urges and mysticism. As I followed Carol's foray into the realm of shamanism, I realized that it took a special touch to pull off a complicated plot the way you did. Your prose was concise, powerfully descriptive, the dialogue lively, and your photographic mastery of the fixtures and streets in Vancouver's hub, in clear evidence.

Kenneth Edward Lim/The North Korean

Carol, the head detective, has to solve several murder cases: with many twists and turns. There's Shamans, Animal Spirits, and "The Lure" thrown in for good measure. No wonder, Carol wanted to resign! Yes, this novel is a roller-coaster ride, with the author cleverly hinting along the way, ending with a roller coaster ride! Read this book. It is different. It's as if Elmore Leonard has risen as a shaman, to guide others to write about Indian lore.

Nancy Bridgeman

Your book was a rollercoaster ride thorough my emotions which, when I got off, left me stunned and breathless.

Your portrayal of sociopaths and the criminal mind in the pursuit of the sexually willing was so disturbing I had nightmares and had to set the novel aside for days. But the writing was so compelling I had to finish it, and I'm glad I persevered.

I literally cheered "go get them!" when Charlie used his protectors to deal rather uniquely with the antagonists.

I was enlightened to the Native spiritual culture which pleased me for which I now have a greater understanding and respect.

Carol G.

I want the author to take me to their world. I love the adrenaline rush I get from reading a book that scares the crap out of me. You know, the ones that have you screaming to the characters in your head or out loud. It tells me that the author did his or her job by getting me emotionally involved. I give up on books if I don't feel something. This book isn't one of those.

April Wolfgong

Stillwater Runs Deep,
Book Three: The Awakening

Its Ghostbusters teamed up with a female Mickey Spillane who has a Native Shaman sidekick nuttier than a squirrels winter stash as a side kick.

Agatha Christie, roll over in your grave, new sleuths on the prowl. A deranged shaman breaks his way into jail to stop all hell from breaking free while police detective Carol Ainsworth has to bring justice to a forest being's murdered mother.

How angry would a mythical god be if he found himself beginning to awake inside a mortal after centuries? The duo are determined to find out who killed the previous native elder before all lightning and thunder breaks loose. They encounter deranged inmates, mystical beings, ancient serpents, wood sprites and someone who should have been dead long ago.

Not your usual crime/mystery!

Not your usual criminal investigators!

You thought Jack Nicholson was mad in The Shining...

Wait until you meet Charlie Stillwaters in the Sweat lodge.

Reviews

There are many aspects true to First Nation's beliefs. For example; the transformation of animals and anomalies within our realm. Frank Talaber's writing is clear and concise, leaving no grey areas. But his true talent as a writer is not only a sense of time, history and capturing First Nation's humor, but going from the real to the surreal and the supernatural. A gift he plies very well.

Tom Patterson Nuu-Cha-Nulth Artist and Master Carver

I've read and reread his previous series, Stillwaters Run Deep, several times. Frank's writing is original and compelling. You run into characters and situations totally unexpected. Keeps you on the edge of your seat and your heart.

Greta Olsson

Just when I was beginning to wonder where the next great Canadian story teller would emerge from, Frank Talaber has written a modern crime mystery with a twist. In "The Awakening" Talaber weaves the richness of Canada's west coast aboriginal spirituality into the science of modern forensics. CSI comes to Haida Gwaii as the shaman and the detective conduct an investigation that will take them and the reader on a journey to a place where murder, redemption and ancient mysticism intersect.

Michael G. de Jong, QC, Minister of Finance, Government House Leader,
Province of British Columbia

I just finished The Awakening and laughed out loud several times. Charlie is an incredible character. Looking forward to reading more of your novels.

Love your books and stories!! You are fabulous!!!-—Great story weaver and a mechanic. What could be better? A big fan.

Ingrid S. :)

The Ainsworth Chronicles, Book One: The Joining

Welcome to Victoria in Beautiful British Columbia, the most haunted city in North America, and to Detective Carol Ainsworth's first day undercover at the very grand old lady, The Fairmont Empress Hotel. Ready to deal with the two Italian families flying in for a wedding to unite them, she did not bargain for the ghosts, the FBI agent or the ancient curses that come along too. Add to that the very wonderful and mysterious psychic lady claiming you've invited her, the young boys disappearing, and the weird things happening to the unfortunates looking for their next fix trapped alongside spirits in the sewers, Carol found her first undercover assignment way more challenging than she could have imagined.

The one saving grace was the great Empress High Tea that Agnes introduced her to and the fabulous scones that are to die for. Literally.

Reviews

I hate you! My wife, who is off on medical leave, won't get out of the bathroom. Can't put your book down. LOL.

Bruce W.

The ghosts of Victoria, BC are restless. The Joining is a riveting read for crime fiction lovers and those fascinated by tales of hauntings. Talaber expertly draws you into a multi-leveled world of local history, crime, and the supernatural, where a blue fairy, comprised of two sorrowful creatures, is more powerful than it knows. A perfect read for those foggy West Coast nights.

Melanie Cossey, A Peculiar Curiosity

I bought four of his novels, all right up my alley, urban Fantasy and Paranormal thrillers. But as we were leaving my girlfriend opened up the copy of The Joining, I had purchased and said, "Stop! You gotta go back I have to buy this book." Frank had hooked her in the first three pages. Well Done.

Joyce Nicholls

I've read and reread his previous series, Stillwaters Run Deep, several times. Frank's writing is original and compelling. You run into characters and situations totally unexpected. Keeps you on the edge of your seat and your heart.

Greta Olsson

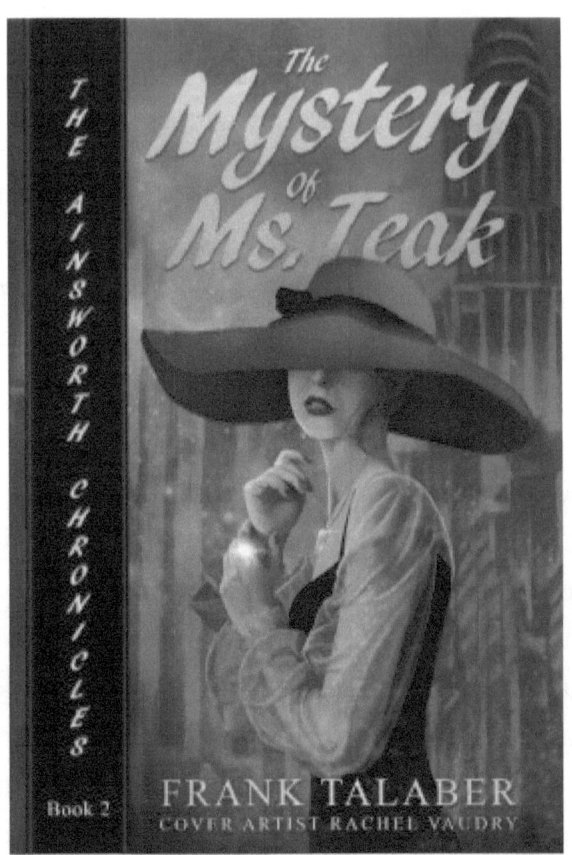

The Ainsworth Chronicles, Book Two: The Mystery of Ms. Teak

Agnes at her craziest best. Only what secret does she have to hide from herself and the one she thought dead? How does one psychic stop another from hunting her down, especially when the other hires the services of a mystical being long thought perished! As for Carol, she has her hands full with pissed-off Russians, the reborn builder of much of Victorian Victoria (yes, *the* Sir Francis Rattenbury), a young girl claiming to be our aforementioned psychic, and, to top it all off, there's something very wrong with Nathan, her nephew that they saved from death. But in traditional English fashion High Tea is *of course* still being served.

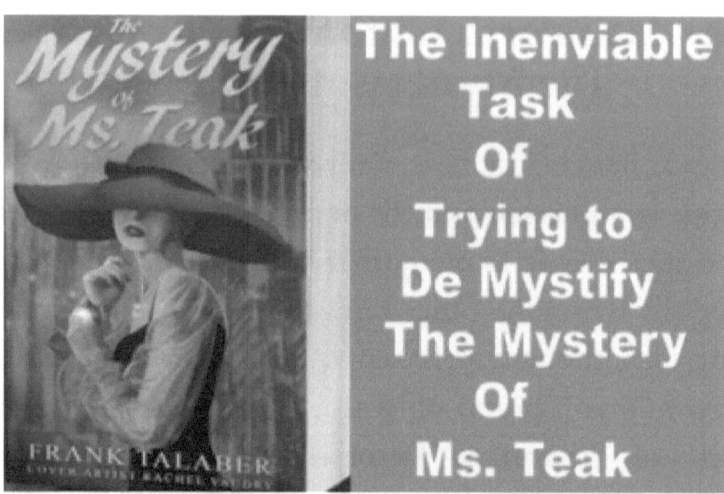

If you are into Videos, check out my Youtube video.
Trying To De Mystify The Mystery of Ms. Teak

https://youtu.be/TQKXOrJlpgw

On my YouTube Channel
Let's Be Frank, Canada's Foremost Off-Beat Author

Reviews

Do not read this book! Seriously, do not read this book - unless you are prepared to deal with a rift on your personal timeline. You will find that this book causes you to postpone activities that you would otherwise be doing.

You will be transported into a world of history and mystery, crime and grime, Spirits and other worldly time travel, with the delectable Detective Carol Ainsworth.

An amazing tale, which I thoroughly enjoyed.

Paddy Kopieczek

Fasten your seatbelt as Frank Talaber takes you on a multi-dimensional trek through time where history comes alive to reveal buried secrets and tortured souls. From the stately tea salons of old Victoria to the haunting desolation of British Columbia's rugged West coast waters, The Mystery of Ms. Teak will both entertain and invite you to confront the demons that live within us all.

Michael DeJong

I hate you, I can't put this book down. Every page gets more interesting, suspicious, wondering what is going to happen next. I sit down to only read one more chapter but end up having to read two more, because I need to know what happened in the past. Each chapter keeps you wanting more and now I hate it even more since I can't get to it before Long weekend coming up. I just read the last six chapters, clinging to every word, every sentence thinking I know what is going to happen next. Oh no, you take me in a completely different direction. Great book.

Sandy Strebe

As a weaver of books you're beyond compare.

Greta Olsson

The Ainsworth Chronicles, Book Three: Into The Dark Side

(cover pending)

This dark and gritty psychological thriller explores the depths of human despair as Carol Ainsworth dives deeply into darkness as she tracks a cunning serial killer disguising murders as drug overdoses. Alongside her shaman ally Charlie Stillwaters and psychic Ms. Teak, face off once more with the enigmatic Raven, the team must confront a disturbed vigilante targeting drug dealers and the supernatural forces watching from the shadows.

Review

"In the thick undergrowth the thump of padded feet echo to a full bloated moon as it cries out to the dark. Whisps of cold misting breath disturbs the stillness."

And with these few lines, Frank Talaber has me hooked again. All my favourite characters are back. Carol Ainsworth, Big Dan, Charlie Stillwaters, and Ms. Teak. Together, they must solve a mystery of who is killing women and making it look like drug overdoses. The old enemies are back as well, Woden and Raven. The reading is so easy and riveting. I had to read it twice to make sure I didn't miss anything. The characters all grow throughout the book, in different ways. I had to keep reading just to find out how the mystery gets solved. And George? I can't wait to see more of George in the future. Oh, and Robin Hood???

Damn you, you're still a bastard, Frank!

Barry Harris

Seeds Of Ascension Book One: Spirits Awakening

In a normal relationship a man gets married and has the time of his life on a memorable honeymoon in Hawaii. A small dilemma begins for Roger Harrison when normality ceases existing with the discovery of metallic alien metal planted in his body.

Roger is thrust onto a path he never dreamed his life would ever take as one of the chosen few to start something that philosophers and spiritualists have discussed for centuries; the Ascension of humanity.

Only this isn't how the human race's next level of evolution was supposed to happen, and nor did Roger think he was the guy that would pull it off.

Toss in a guardian angel, alien hunters and Roger soon begins to realize his life's perfection ends with the understanding that memories are the illusion to which reality is draped and all is rarely as it seems in the journeys of a soul's growth. Especially when he doesn't even know how to spell chakra, let alone deal with having to master the seven levels in order to attain ascension.

Nor can time, as he knows it, be measured in heartbeats or lifespans and a heavy price must be exacted in order to stand in the gateway between memory and knowing, reality and illusion.

Especially when that effort means stopping those who would doom humanity's next phase of evolution.

Review

Have read one third of Ascension Book One. As always, I am amazed at the word choice and ideas. Laughed out loud twice, (cringed many times). No doubt I love your amazing way of making a new thought world. Cheers. Always a fan. Looking forward to the rest of the book!

Ingrid Siltala-Mort

What if a book could change your perspective on the universe and humanity? Sometimes, we stumble upon a story that doesn't just entertain but transforms the way we perceive the world.

This book is one such masterpiece. It beautifully weaves together themes of cosmic mysteries, self-discovery, and the resilience of the human spirit. The narrative feels alive, pulling you into a world where reality and the extraordinary blend seamlessly.

This book is a gripping read. What I loved most is how the author's creativity shines through, making every page feel fresh and unexpected. The storyline is unique and filled with moments that stay with you, long after you've turned the last page.

The writing is remarkable poetic, thought provoking, and immersive.

It's a book for anyone who loves stories that make them think and feel deeply. I found this book to be a mesmerizing journey, one that I'll revisit to uncover layers I may have missed the first time.

The author has a way of painting vivid imagery and infusing life into each scene. Their ability to craft a story that feels both personal and universal is truly impressive. I can't wait to explore more of his work.

International Books

Seeds Of Ascension Book Two: Gateways

Roger discovers his guardian angel is not only real, but an alien that needs his help, in order for humanity to reach ascension with the rest of the universe. This thrusts him into unlocking the portals needed to reach this goal. That and him discovering the true essence of what he is to become, by learning about the spiritual chakras within him and having to pass these tests.

Review

Love your amazing imagination. You take what I see on History Channel to the next impossibly believable level and make me believe! Sometimes you make me laugh out loud and other times when I'm reading, I close my eyes and visualize the scene unfolding before me. Your writing flows that effortlessly.

Ingrid Siltala-Mort

Short Story Anthology Volume One:
What I'd Say To Buddha If I Met Him In The Pub

(Includes Sylvia's Sun-catchers, voted #1 by the readers in Rejected Manuscripts Anthology)

Enter the literary world of Frank Talaber, Canada's Foremost Off-Beat Author

Literature written beyond the realms of genre he is known to grab readers; kicking, screaming, laughing or crying, and drag them into his novels.

Don't believe me? Check out these short stories.

What if a holidaying alien popped into your head? Literally? Ever think what might happen if you're elected to tear down an old church and find a living person inside? Your mom brings home a sad-looking pooch; it changes your life and becomes your best friend. A new girlfriend takes you to a bar where spirits are waiting for you to get drunk enough to allow them to take over your body. Clearing out old trinkets, you discover wartime field glasses with an embroidered heart encased inside a silver locket. What if humanity discovered the serum to live forever? Would that be a good thing?

And many more bizarre stories to make you realize, how does this guy sleep at night?

Short Story Anthology Volume Two:

What I'd Say To Einstein If I met Him On The Dance Floor

(Includes Sylvia's Sun-catchers, voted #1 by the readers in Rejected Manuscripts Anthology)

Why is Frank Talaber called Canada's Foremost Off Beat Author? Read on...

Two stories of being bewitched by a mystical witch and figuring out how to out-trick her. You hope. Another about secrets your mother didn't ever want to reveal, until you found the photograph. Hitchhiking west coast shaman style. Say what? What if you worked in the post office and began to read enticing postcards? Memories of a love so great, it still haunts you. How about a man who takes drug-addled lives and works to save them in his own non-woke way? What if you climbed Mount Everest and ran into a Yeti?

...and so many more to entice you into the bizarre creative mind of Frank Talaber. Enjoy.

Short Story Anthology Volume Two:

What I'd Say To Agatha Christie If I Met Her In The Knitting Circle

More off-the-wall stories, including: Meeting your first wolf; or is he!

Late nights in a truck stop and the strange people that show up.

What if NASA used a person with multiple personality disorder to go to Mars?

Ever dream of being on a popular TV Series?

Also includes some of my non-fiction stories submitted to an RV magazine, and the short story which will form the basis for the upcoming Trust Me, I Didn't Make This Sh*t Up.

Shuttered Seductions Romance Novel

Written under Pseudonym, Felicity Talisman

*She only wanted Not to fall in love with him.
He only wanted to steal her company. Roy only wanted to
seduce Julia-Rae and convince her to sell him her company.
Julia-Rae wanted to shut him out of her heart like
every other man that ever got close. Only what do you do
when you fall in madly in love with the enemy
and the enemy with you. Will the dark secrets they hold
tear them apart or bring them closer together?*

Autumn's Summer

Written under Pseudonym, Felicity Talisman

Great loves come and go,
profound ones mark your soul,
in ways that take the rest of your lifetime to comprehend.

What if you were given up for adoption NOT because your mother didn't want you, but because she was trying to protect you from a curse?

A mysterious package is delivered by Richard's solicitors one year after his wife Autumn's death. What he expected to find, he didn't know, but he would never have guessed in a million years what was about to unfold.

A beautiful leather-bound diary written in his wife's hand contains many secrets; that his lonely empty-nester wife's life changed profoundly after a purely-by-chance meeting in, of all places, a normal, mundane, corner grocery store. She embarks on a voyage of discovery with the spiritualist, Summer, to find new meaning to her life, that, once commenced, transports her to realms and dimensions she never knew existed.

He also learns of a heart-breaking secret and love affair she kept from him until after her death.

Review

I thought I'd have a quick peek at Autumn's Summer and then finish the book I was currently reading! I was entranced and spellbound from that moment, my current read neglected! Couldn't put it down, read it in one day. Yes, the love scenes were intense, passion blossoms in many forms! I enjoyed this immensely! *Shelley Walsh*

What's a *Lady* Got to Do to *Fulfill* Her Life

Felicity Talisman

What's a Lady Got to Do to Fulfill Her Life

Written under Pseudonym, Felicity Talisman

Leanne Benson is a successful real estate agent in LA who abruptly loses everyone she loves on the same day. Reeling from these losses and drawn to the memory of her late mother, who gave up her ambition to be a painter to raise a family, Leanne embarks on a journey of discovery that will take her up to the Oregon Coast, into the enchanting Banff National Park in Canada, and ultimately to a better understanding of who she is and who she is capable of being.

Review

Talisman here shows genuine descriptive prowess, making Leanne's journey memorable with cleverly wrought scenes filled with humor and, yes, steamy encounters with a variety of lovers—all handled with aplomb and the sure hand of a talented writer. If you are looking for an erotic, ultimately inspiring trip into the majesty that is nature and human experience, this is the one for you.

Frank's Bio

Born on the wild Canadian prairies but tired of the winter months in Edmonton, Frank immigrated to the more temperate cedar forests of coastal British Columbia. Yes, they get snow in Chilliwack during the winter months, and on that odd occasion Frank is forced to search out the snow shovel, dust off the cobwebs and have a go. At the snow, not the cobwebs.

His run-of-the-mill day job of auto technician/service advisor seems at odds with being an inspired, off-the-wall, author, but his zest for life, the environment, and the little muses that won't let his pencil stay still, spring from his mother's Hungarian ancestry. It's the Gypsy blood, he says, which pounds through his veins with wild abandon, driving him to the realms of fantasy.

This is the muse inside, the essence of Frank Talaber.

People who have read Frank's books describe him as a natural storyteller who writes like his soul is on fire and his pencil is his voice screaming. They go further to say that they find his books grabbingly intense and hilarious at times, screaming everyday life from such a realistic viewpoint you're drawn into his world, hook, line and plum bob, unable to stop; almost cursing that they can't set the book down, page after page. Frank takes great pride in the realism of his work, painstakingly visiting most of the locations, (obviously, only the "real-life" ones!) and he is so thorough that many readers have remarked that they can hear, taste, visualize, smell and feel the essence of the place. "It really is like being there" one remarked. There isn't a greater compliment to be made.

His tagline is Canada's Foremost Off-beat Author (also the name of his YouTube channel; check it out for his witty and informative videos) who writes in urban fantasy, science fiction, crime, spiritual, romance, erotica and comedy genres. Well, anything that comes to him, basically! Except westerns. Although he does like to ride Gangnam style; does that count?

Literature written almost beyond genres, whose compelling thoughts are freed from the depths of the heart and subconscious before being poured onto the page. Or, as he often says, "you don't have to be mad to be a writer, but it sure helps".

Visit Frank Talaber's Published Author page on Facebook at: https://www.facebook.com/FrankTalaber/

(If you want to join his fans' newsletter to hear about his latest ventures, go to the above page and scroll down on the column on the left).

Website:
https://franktalaberpublishedauthor.wordpress.com/

Facebook Short Stories Page:
https://www.facebook.com/
franktalaberpublishedauthor/

Twitter:
@FrankTalaber https://about.me/ftalaber

Linkedin:
https://www.linkedin.com/feed/

308

www.ingramcontent.com/pod-product-compliance
Lightning Source LLC
Chambersburg PA
CBHW020431030726
47495CB00006B/1757